"You're so beautiful." Michael spoke as if he were in the midst of a revelation.

Laura's breath caught, and something deep inside her unfurled and went all soft and malleable. A pulse of pleasure, pure and unadulterated, the strength of which she hadn't experienced in years, radiated slowly outward from her center. It left her feeling hot and definitely bothered as they both continued to stand there awkwardly, neither seeming to know what to do or say.

Don't, Laura wanted to cry. *Don't look at me that way. Because if you do, I won't be able to...*

To what? Do her job? Handle it? Resist him? Walk away?

Dear Reader,

It's always cause for celebration when Sharon Sala writes a new book, so prepare to cheer for *The Way to Yesterday*. How many times have you wished for a chance to go back in time and get a second chance at something? Heroine Mary O'Rourke gets that chance, and you'll find yourself caught up in her story as she tries to make things right with the only man she'll ever love.

ROMANCING THE CROWN continues with Lyn Stone's *A Royal Murder*. The suspense—and passion—never flag in this exciting continuity series. Catherine Mann has only just begun her Intimate Moments career, but already she's created a page-turning military miniseries in WINGMEN WARRIORS. *Grayson's Surrender* is the first of three "don't miss" books. Look for the next, *Taking Cover*, in November.

The rest of the month unites two talented veterans—Beverly Bird, with *All the Way*, and Shelley Cooper, with *Laura and the Lawman*—with exciting newcomer Cindy Dees, who debuts with *Behind Enemy Lines*. Enjoy them all—and join us again next month, when we once again bring you an irresistible mix of excitement and romance in six new titles by the best authors in the business.

Leslie J. Wainger
Executive Senior Editor

Please address questions and book requests to:
Silhouette Reader Service
U.S.: 3010 Walden Ave., P.O. Box 1325, Buffalo, NY 14269
Canadian: P.O. Box 609, Fort Erie, Ont. L2A 5X3

Laura and the Lawman

SHELLEY COOPER

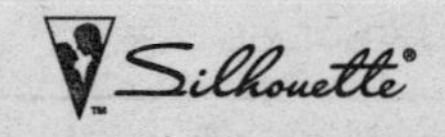

INTIMATE MOMENTS™

Published by Silhouette Books

America's Publisher of Contemporary Romance

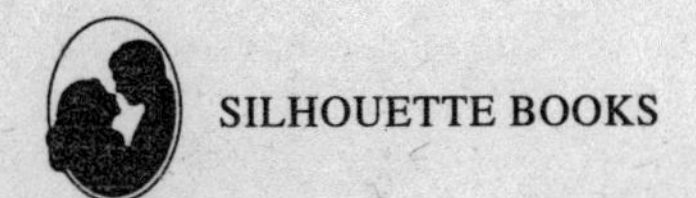

ISBN 0-373-27244-8

LAURA AND THE LAWMAN

This edition published by arrangement with Harlequin Books S.A.

Visit Silhouette at www.eHarlequin.com

Printed in U.S.A.

Books by Shelley Cooper

Silhouette Intimate Moments

Major Dad #876
Guardian Groom #942
Dad in Blue #1044
Promises, Promises #1109
Laura and the Lawman #1174

SHELLEY COOPER

first experienced the power of words when she was in the eighth grade and wrote a paragraph about the circus for a class assignment. Her teacher returned it with an A and seven pluses scrawled across the top of the paper, along with a note thanking her for rekindling so vividly some cherished childhood memories. Since Shelley had never been to the circus and had relied solely on her imagination to compose the paragraph, the teacher's remarks were a revelation. Since then, Shelley has relied on her imagination to help her sell dozens of short stories and to write her first novel, *Major Dad,* a 1997 Romance Writers of America Golden Heart finalist in Best Long Contemporary, as well as many more. She hopes her books will be as moving to her readers as her circus paragraph was to that long-ago English teacher.

To my grandmother, Martha Belle Varner,
for the Easter egg hunts, sleepovers, countless games
of canasta and, most important, the laughter.

And in loving memory of Leonard Varner, who had
muscles to rival Popeye's, could ride a bike backward
and always praised me by saying, "You done good, kid."

Prologue

The two men met in the parking lot of a busy truck stop located off of Interstate 80 in western Pennsylvania. It was nearing midnight, and they had each traveled in excess of sixty miles to make the assignation.

Together they entered a brightly lit diner and sat down in a small booth in the rear. From that vantage point they could keep an eye on all comings and goings.

As the sole liaison between undercover cops and the department they all served, the men were used to meeting in out-of-the-way places. Places where they were unlikely to be seen by those they didn't want to see them, and even less likely to be overheard.

Neither spoke until two frosty mugs of root beer, along with two huge plates of food, each loaded with enough fat and cholesterol to guarantee a heart attack, had been placed on the table.

"When's he going in?" Erik Hitchcock asked after taking a hearty swallow of his drink.

"Two weeks," Gregory Phelps replied, spearing his sixteen-ounce Delmonico steak with a knife and fork. ''Have you told her yet?''

''No.''

''Why not?''

''Word came down they don't want her to know. They think it'll be safer for them both. If she doesn't know, she won't make a mistake.''

Erik paused to take another sip of root beer, then gave a loud belch for which he didn't apologize. ''What about your guy?'' he asked, wiping the back of his hand across his mouth before slathering butter and sour cream on a baked potato. ''Have you told him we already have someone inside?''

''No. I got the same word you did.''

Both men ate in silence.

''Know what I think?'' Erik finally asked.

''What?''

''My girl's from New York, right? And your guy is from Pittsburgh. He's a hometown boy. I think the chief wants Pittsburgh to get the credit for this, not New York. That's why he's sending your guy in.''

''Even though NYPD's commissioner is his brother-in-law?''

''*Because* NYPD's commissioner is his brother-in-law.''

''Why didn't we send my guy in first, then?'' Gregory asked.

Erik grabbed the dessert menu and studied it for a minute. ''He didn't fit the bill for the job opening. No one in Pittsburgh did.''

''So they had to bring someone in from the outside.''

''Exactly. This case is extremely delicate. We send someone in, she has to be an expert.''

''Or he,'' Gregory interjected.

''Or he,'' Erik acknowledged with a nod. ''Anyway, when we knew we didn't have anyone for the job, that's when the chief went begging to his brother-in-law.''

''And it's been sticking in his craw ever since?''

''Like the ham sandwich Vinnie Turco choked to death on.

That's why, when *this* opening unexpectedly arose, and we had someone who did fit the bill, the chief decided to send your guy in."

"Two pairs of eyes and ears are better than one, eh?"

"Especially if *our* pair of eyes and ears pulls off the job." Erik looked rueful. "I have to be honest with you. I'm pulling for my girl. She's smart, she's good, and she's got a great pair of legs."

"She's also going back to New York when this is over," Gregory said, "and we have to stay here with the chief."

"Good point. She's making progress, though. She's been inside a month now. It'll be six weeks by the time your guy goes in. It might be too late for him. Hell, it might even be all over. Rumor has it a big shipment will be arriving shortly."

"Has she found out how it will be coming in, and how it will go out?"

"Not yet."

"Then my guy still has a chance. Who knows? If things go well, when this job is done maybe the chief'll be in such a good mood we'll all get promotions."

Erik emptied his mug and replaced it on the table with a thump. "For that to happen, your guy would have to be something else."

"He is."

"Maybe," Erik allowed. "But can he work miracles? And can he work them before my girl does?"

Gregory shrugged. "Only time will tell."

Chapter 1

Antonio Garibaldi scanned the 4,000-square-foot auction floor and felt his stomach plunge like an elevator whose cable had snapped. He had never been so nervous in his life.

It was only to be expected, he told himself. After all, he lived and worked in a world where murder, violence and treachery were commonplace. A cop couldn't work undercover for any length of time and not carry on an intimate relationship with fear.

In general, fear was a good thing. It kept a man alert. Without it, he'd lose his edge, and probably his life. Truth was, though Antonio had a reputation for being a daredevil—some even said he took unnecessary risks—he was always nervous before starting a new job.

But the way he felt this morning was different. He'd never been *this* shaky before, and that threw him.

Maybe it was because the man he was replacing, a man who had presumably stumbled by accident across what Antonio was deliberately trying to discover, had disappeared without a trace.

Maybe it was because the recommendation that had allowed him to secure the position of head auctioneer for the Merrill Auction Gallery had claimed an expertise Antonio didn't possess. Though he'd regularly attended auctions since he was a child, and though he knew more about antique furniture than most dealers, the only auction he'd ever conducted had been during his recent, intensive two-week training session with one of the country's foremost auctioneers. Though he'd received high marks, that auction had been roughly a quarter the size of the one he'd be in charge of today.

Maybe it was because it had been months since he'd been with a woman, and his hormones were in overdrive.

Or maybe—and this seemed most logical to him—it was because he'd been looking forward to this job too much. A lot was riding on its outcome. Joseph Merrill was a suspected drug kingpin who controlled a large portion of the drug traffic in the tristate area encompassing western Pennsylvania. Many lives would be lost if he wasn't stopped. Working as an auctioneer for the man would be one of the most dangerous and demanding jobs Antonio had ever undertaken.

But it was more than that. He had a personal stake in the outcome of this case. He was counting on it to revitalize his interest in police work.

Family duty and a sense of adventure were the driving forces that had led Antonio to become a cop. Three generations of his family had proudly worn a uniform and badge. His father was a highly decorated officer. Two of his brothers were also cops. Police work was in his blood.

Given his propensity for danger and excitement, it was only natural that he'd gravitated into undercover work. Antonio was a good undercover cop. He did his job well and always got his man. He'd lived on the edge for years now, receiving commendations and advancing in rank. Until recently he'd loved every minute of it.

A few months ago shortly after his thirty-first birthday, a vague, indecipherable restlessness had filled him, and he began feeling less satisfaction in his work. He found himself consumed by a yearning for something more, although what that something more could be remained tantalizingly out of reach.

It was the repetition, he had decided one sleepless night, while he'd tossed and turned in his bed. For two years he'd been doing the same kind of undercover work. He needed something new. Something daring. Something exciting to spice things up.

When the opportunity to pose as head auctioneer for Joseph Merrill's auction gallery arose, Antonio had felt a wave of excitement wash over him. This was the change he'd been waiting for. The bonus was, he would be working full-time in a world he loved, a world he had—for too short a time as a youngster—shared with his mother, who had died of cancer when he was eleven.

The sound of the crowd penetrated his thoughts, and Antonio drew a quick, impatient breath. Now was not the time for a trip down memory lane. If he didn't stay focused on the job at hand, he wouldn't live long enough to bang the opening gavel, let alone nab Joseph Merrill and his cohorts. He might crave danger, but long ago he had decided there was no job worth getting killed over, and no suspect worth dying for.

His name was Michael Corsi, he reminded himself. He had a brand-new social security card, a driver's license and several credit cards in his wallet to attest to that fact. For the next several weeks, a month or two at most, Antonio Garibaldi would cease to exist. For his safety, and for the good of the job, he had to submerge himself in the role he was playing and forget about anything else.

A last glance at the crowd had his stomach fluttering once more. Then he saw her, and the butterflies in his middle stilled.

She was beautiful. There was no other way to describe her. The pink silk suit she wore flattered her trim figure without being overly revealing. It also exposed a generous length of long, slender leg to his appreciative gaze. Her shoulder-length brown hair gleamed in the artificial lighting, framing a face that, in repose, looked like a Madonna: small, heart-shaped, ivory-complected and utterly feminine.

He felt a stab of regret that he couldn't see her eyes because she was half-bent over one of the seated patrons. Then, as if drawn by his regard, she slowly straightened and looked directly at him.

For one endless, unguarded moment, they simply stared at each other. Her eyes were a brilliant emerald green. In their depths, Antonio saw intelligence, vulnerability and a loneliness that pierced his heart. That muscle began thudding unevenly when a new emotion was added. Awareness. Awareness of him as a man. He saw her throat work.

A second later it was as if someone had thrown a switch. Her eyes went blank, and she looked away. Reaching into a jacket pocket, she pulled out a compact and checked her hair and makeup. Snapping the compact shut, she sent him a dazzling smile that held none of the honesty he'd glimpsed a minute earlier. Antonio blinked. What had just happened?

He didn't care, he told himself, returning her smile with one of his own. For the first time that morning, he relaxed fully. Here, at least, might be the answer to his sexual frustration. If she was agreeable, that was, which he fervently hoped was the case. She was precisely the kind of distraction he needed to help him loosen up, and he made a mental note to meet up with her on his first break.

"Beautiful, isn't she?" Joseph Merrill asked softly from behind him.

Antonio nearly jumped out of his skin at the unexpected arrival of his new boss. He didn't question how the older man knew exactly who had captured his attention. Joseph Merrill ran a tight ship. He made it a point to keep his eyes and ears open, and to know what his crew was doing at all times. He would have had to be half-blind to have missed how fixedly Antonio had been staring at the woman.

"Exquisite," he replied, turning his attention to the man at his side. "Who is she?"

"Her name is Ruby O'Toole." Joseph paused briefly before adding, "She's my woman."

The possessive note in Joseph's voice was unmistakable, as was the warning glance he shot Antonio.

"Ruby is a gifted appraiser of artwork. Part of her job involves helping out on auction day. Today she'll be one of your bid spotters."

Antonio had heard of Ruby O'Toole, and her beauty, from his fellow employees. He'd also read about her in the dossier on Joseph Merrill that he'd studied before going undercover. He felt a flicker of disappointment that his planned interlude with her would not come to pass. Getting involved with Joseph Merrill's lover on anything but a platonic basis would be most unwise. It could also prove fatal. Antonio hadn't stayed alive this long by being stupid. He wasn't about to start now.

Philosophically he shrugged his disappointment away. There would be someone else. There always was.

While an intimate relationship with Ruby O'Toole was definitely out, it didn't mean he couldn't befriend her, however. There was more than one way for Antonio to get the information he needed. He could get it from Joseph Merrill himself by earning the older man's trust. Or, if that didn't work, perhaps he could coax what he needed to learn from the woman with whom his boss shared nightly pillow talk. And if, at the end of the job, he found himself slapping handcuffs on her slender wrists, he would do so without a qualm.

"It's almost time to start," Joseph said, surveying the room with a proprietary air. "Nervous?"

Not for the reason you think. "A little."

"What's to worry about?" Joseph gave him a broad smile and clapped him on the back. "So it's your first day on the job. Big deal. It's not like you haven't done this a thousand times before. And it's not like this is the big time. I'm awfully proud of this place, and I do quite well financially. But face it. Sotheby's it ain't."

The rapidly filling room was a hive of activity. Folding chairs, arranged in neat rows, covered the center of the polished hardwood floor. About three-quarters of the chairs had already been claimed, the occupants chatting quietly to one another and fanning themselves with their assigned bid numbers.

No, it wasn't Sotheby's. But a good deal of money would exchange hands that day, and it was up to Antonio—correction, Michael—to see that it moved smoothly.

Antonio glanced at his watch. "Would you like me to start?"

"It's your ball game," Joseph said. "I have complete faith in you. Throw out the first pitch whenever you're ready."

Antonio made a rapid inventory of the items in front of him. Gavel? Check. Sale catalogue? Check. Glass of water? Check. He was prepared. He knew exactly what to do.

Filing away every thought, every impression, every sight and sound, to be carefully detailed in his notes later, he picked up the gavel and banged it solidly against the table. The time for worry, speculation and nervousness was over. It was show time.

"Good morning, ladies and gentlemen," he announced in a strong voice. "Welcome to the Merrill Auction Gallery. Today we have some very special items for your consideration. If everyone is ready, let us begin."

He turned to the large screen at his right, on which was projected a sterling silver tray. To his left, an assistant held up the actual item.

"Our first item up for bid is this beautiful tray. It was designed in the Chippendale style by Henry James Ashworth of Massachusetts. The U.S. Ambassador to Tunis received it as a gift from a visiting dignitary in 1957."

Antonio swept his gaze over the crowd. "Who will give me five hundred dollars for this coveted collectible?"

The hands started going up, and he was on his way.

"Laura! Laura, where are you?"

Laura Langley continued walking through the crowd, her gaze focusing on each bidder as a bid was offered. It took all of her self-control not to react to the woman who was calling her name. She was Ruby O'Toole, she reminded herself. The odds of anyone who knew Laura Langley being in this room were not high.

"There you are." The urgency in the woman's voice changed to fond exasperation. "I can't turn my back on you for a minute, you little minx."

Out of her peripheral vision, Laura saw a woman scoop up a toddler. The tension left her body, and she relaxed.

She was Ruby O'Toole, she reminded herself again. She couldn't afford to forget that.

The image brought to her mind by the name she had been saddled with was of a zaftig, peroxide blonde, something she most definitely was not. At five-six, with stubbornly straight brown hair, and weighing at most 125 pounds soaking wet, not to mention almost as flat-chested and hipless as her brother, she could hardly be called zaftig.

Though the thought amused her, she didn't smile. In her role as Ruby O'Toole she did a lot of smiling. But, left to her own devices, Laura Langley rarely smiled.

There were other differences between Laura and Ruby. Considerable differences. Laura had an IQ of 145 and was a member of Mensa. Ruby had an IQ of 110, which was strictly average. The nickname braniac had haunted Laura throughout her school years. Ruby had never been accused of deep thought. Laura cared nothing about fashion. Ruby was obsessed with clothing and accessories. Laura hadn't looked at a man in a romantic way for four long years. Ruby lived and breathed for male attention. Laura was real. Ruby was purely make-believe.

They did have one thing in common: their knack for appraising art. That knack was the reason why Laura had spent the last part of April and all of May in Pittsburgh, instead of on the streets of New York City, which was her home. It was now the first weekend in June. The way things were going, it looked as if she'd be spending this month here, too.

She had never intended to be a cop. In fact, she'd been teaching art history in a Queens high school when, at the age of twenty-four, fate had stepped in and turned her life upside down.

Four years ago her husband pulled into a gas station with their infant son strapped snugly in his car seat. A drug deal gone sour on the opposite corner led to the exchange of gunfire. When the bullets stopped flying, Laura no longer had a husband or a child. They had become just another statistic, a line item on a police report indicating the NYPD was losing its war on drugs.

After she'd climbed out of her depression, which had taken the better part of a year, she had gotten mad. Raging mad. The way Laura saw it at the time, she had two choices. She could either go insane with anger and grief, or she could do something to make the loss of her husband and son mean more than a senseless waste. For a while it had been iffy which alternative she would select. In the end, though, she had chosen to act.

Thus, an unprepossessing art history teacher had been transformed into first a patrolwoman and later an undercover cop for the New York City Police Department. A highly decorated undercover cop who seemed fearless in the face of danger because she had nothing left to lose.

Unfortunately, the Laura who had arrived in Pittsburgh six weeks earlier was not the same woman who had excelled at the Police Academy. For one thing, she was no longer quite so fearless. The rage that had consumed her for so long now was abating, as was the single-mindedness with which she had allowed her job to swallow up every aspect of her life for three long years. While she still keenly mourned the loss of her husband and son, the memory of that loss no longer filled her every waking moment.

In its place Laura felt an unexpected restlessness. And a powerful yearning she couldn't define. Chalking the emotions up to too much work and too little rest, she had determined to take a much-postponed and much-needed vacation once the Merrill case was brought to a close.

If it was ever brought to a close.

As anxious as she was to take that vacation, now was not the time to think of all that. A glance at her watch told her it was time, however, for her break.

Signaling to her replacement, she grabbed a cup of coffee from the concession stand and propped her feet on an empty chair in a quiet corner of the room. Sighing, she took a sip of coffee and tried to ignore the way her breasts pinched in her push-up bra and her feet pinched in three-inch stiletto heels.

The coffee went a long way toward reestablishing her equilibrium. It was shattered a moment later when she saw Joseph headed purposely toward her. Her break was only ten minutes long, and she'd hoped to be able to use that time to rest her aching feet in peace. She should have known better. When they were out in public, Joseph rarely left her side.

Trailing behind him, predictably, was Matthew Rogers, his right-hand man and bodyguard. Matthew's massive shoulders strained against his suit jacket. His hands were as big as hams. He looked as if he could bench-press three hundred pounds easily, without breaking a sweat. He also looked like the thug that rumor whispered him to be.

"Well, what do you think?" Joseph asked.

He moved to stand directly behind her, while Matthew took up vigil a few feet away, his watchful gaze scouring the crowd. Leaning down, Joseph laced his arms loosely around her shoulders.

Trying not to flinch at the contact, Laura took another sip of coffee. "About what?"

He nodded toward the podium. "My newest employee."

She followed Joseph's gaze to the man who was currently in the middle of a bidding war, two women equally determined to be the proud possessor of a pair of diamond earrings. Already the bidding had surpassed the earrings' assessed value, and was climbing steadily higher, with no end reasonably in sight. Laura couldn't help wondering what the women wanted more: ownership of the earrings, or Michael Corsi's undivided attention.

He was worth vying for. It had been a long time since she'd

seen any man with such striking good looks off the movie screen. But with his olive coloring, dark brown hair, roman nose, determined chin and chocolate-brown eyes that also held a good measure of intelligence, Michael Corsi could give any number of male heartthrobs a run for their money in the fluttering-of-the-female-heart department.

In addition to his good looks, he possessed a charisma that had the crowd eating out of his hand. He was the perfect auctioneer. What galled Laura was that, against her will, *she* found herself wanting to eat out of his hand, too.

Dismay filled her, and her heart thudded unevenly. Before her face could betray her thoughts, she returned her gaze to the cup in her hands.

It wasn't just that everyone in the room believed she belonged to Joseph, although that was a major consideration. What was even more important was that she knew who Michael Corsi was and who he wasn't. And who he wasn't was one of the good guys.

To be attracted to any man seemed a betrayal of both her husband and her son. To be attracted to Michael Corsi was ten times worse. He wasn't fit to shine the shoes Jacob had worn, which still lined the floor of her closet in her home back in Queens, let alone to try and take his place.

When she'd learned Michael Corsi would be working for Joseph, she'd had her contact officer investigate him. The information he'd relayed back to her had been extremely interesting. Michael Corsi had done time for dealing drugs. Was his acting as an auctioneer just a front for his real job, which was helping Joseph in his drug operations?

She didn't know. Not yet, anyway. But she intended to find out.

This time, when her gaze traveled to him, she felt nothing but disdain. The past six weeks spent trying to win Joseph Merrill's confidence had been more stressful than she'd expected. She was exhausted. As a result she'd misread simple appreciation for a handsome, albeit amoral, man as attraction.

It was nothing, she told herself. Just another lapse proving how badly she needed a vacation.

Yet no matter how hard she tried, she couldn't forget the moment she had first gazed into his eyes. For a slice out of time she'd forgotten where she was. She'd even forgotten who she was.

It wasn't Ruby who had returned his piercing regard, but Laura. Laura, who had let her guard down and allowed the emotions of the past four years to shine in her eyes plainly for him to see. For surely *he* would understand.

When she'd realized her folly, she'd done what she could to repair the damage. She'd banished Laura and had Ruby smile her empty, flirtatious smile at him. She hoped he didn't puzzle too long over the seeming contradiction.

"Ruby?" Joseph said, sounding far away. "Ruby, did you hear me? I asked you a question."

"What?" She blinked and shook her head. "I'm sorry. I guess I'm a little preoccupied."

"I was wondering what you thought of my newest employee." There was a trace of impatience in his voice, and Laura knew she'd made a mistake by letting Michael Corsi unnerve her to the point where she'd forgotten the role she was playing.

She pretended to assess Joseph's new auctioneer the way she would a painting she was trying to value. "The crowd is involved, and he's moving things along at a good pace," she said carefully. "He's also getting top dollar for almost every item. Overall, I'd say he's doing an excellent job. I think he'll be a good addition to the team."

"He will, won't he?" Joseph murmured.

"You seem surprised," Laura said.

"Just intrigued."

"About what?"

It was Joseph's turn to seem distracted as he dropped his arms from around her shoulders and straightened to his full height.

"About whether Michael Corsi just might turn out to be far more valuable to me than he ever anticipated," he murmured.

Laura wondered what he meant, but didn't dare ask. Only six weeks had passed since she'd finagled their meeting and talked her way into the job as his art appraiser. She didn't want to appear overly interested in his personal business, didn't want to arouse his suspicions that she was anything more than a woman who did her job well. A woman who preened under male attention and who always kowtowed to a man's acknowledged superiority. Joseph's acknowledged superiority.

If the rumors were true, and she believed they were, Joseph was one of the biggest drug distributors in the eastern United States. He hadn't acquired that status by trusting blindly. As Laura kept reminding her contact officer when she reported in to him, this was nothing like making a buy from a street dealer. If the department was serious about taking out the big guys, then they had to be willing to put in the necessary time.

She would have to earn Joseph's trust. She'd made great strides in that arena, but he had yet to invite her into his inner circle. Laura had every expectation that the invitation was looming ever closer on the horizon. She just had to bide her time and play her part.

In the meantime every penny Joseph paid her, minus applicable expenses, was going straight into police coffers. They weren't losing money on this deal. When it all ended, hopefully many lives would also be saved.

"When I asked what you thought of him," Joseph said, "I wasn't talking about his performance on the podium. I want to know what you think of Michael Corsi as a man. Do you find him attractive?"

Laura stilled. At the time she'd started the job, she'd been prepared to have Joseph direct his attentions her way. In fact, that had been essential if she was to earn his confidence. What she hadn't been prepared for was the revelation that he was gay, that he wanted her to pose as his lover, and that he was willing to pay her a generous stipend, in addition to her regular salary, for her to do so.

His standing in the community was important to him, he'd told her. He didn't want it jeopardized, and he was apprehensive about what might happen if the truth of his sexual orientation were to become common knowledge. If she took the job, he wouldn't expect her to live a celibate lifestyle. She was free to take a lover, so long as she exercised extreme discretion.

Since his request had meant she would be working even more closely with him, and that he was growing to trust her, Laura had readily agreed. Was he toying with her now? she wondered. Testing her loyalty? At times Joseph Merrill was an extremely difficult man to read.

"Is he gay?" she asked.

Joseph leaned over her again. "Checking to see if I'm staking a claim?" he whispered into her ear.

"You are my boss," she replied lightly. "I wouldn't want to overstep my bounds. You pay me too well."

Joseph chuckled his appreciation. "I do like a woman who knows on which side her bread is buttered. Alas, he's not gay, more's the pity. So, what do you think?"

Laura gazed at Michael Corsi and felt a flutter in her midsection. There it was again, that unwelcome awareness of him as a man. A starburst of anticipation radiated outward, leaving a tingling sensation in its wake. She fought it back, searching instead to retrieve her earlier feelings of disdain.

"He is a handsome devil, isn't he?" she said, knowing Joseph would expect Ruby to make such a remark.

"Adorable," Joseph replied. "Too bad they buried your heart with your fiancé."

Rule number one of undercover work was to come up with a good cover story. Before she had known he was gay, she'd wanted Joseph to be attracted to her. But she hadn't wanted their relationship to become intimate. To prevent that eventuality, while hopefully keeping his interest in her heightened, she had concocted the story that Ruby O'Toole's fiancé had been killed in a car accident on the eve of their wedding. The loss was still too fresh, too painful for her to enter into a new relationship.

"Yeah," she agreed, sighing theatrically. "Too bad."

"Yet you still dress and act provocatively around men. You still flirt outrageously with them." There was a speculative gleam in Joseph's eyes that she didn't like and needed to put to rest. Immediately.

"That's because all the men around here know I belong to you. Flirting with them is safe."

Reaching up a hand, she patted her hair. "Besides," she cooed, "a girl needs to know she hasn't lost her technique. I may not allow men to touch right now, but I definitely want them to look. I won't be in mourning forever, you know."

Joseph chuckled. "Spoken like a woman."

"I am a woman, Joseph. I've never made that a secret."

It was an unfortunate choice of words. She realized her mistake when Joseph said, "I wonder what secrets you *are* hiding from me."

Hours of practice in front of a mirror had perfected the guileless look she aimed his way.

"Secrets?" she asked, an air of honest bewilderment in her voice, although her heart was thudding heavily. "I have no secrets."

"Everyone has secrets, my dear. Everyone has something to hide. No one is exactly as he presents himself to others. I can't help wondering what it is you're keeping from me."

Her laughter was light and airy, and pure Ruby. "I'll never tell," she said, batting her eyelashes at him. "That's for me to know and you to find out."

"Oh, I will, my dear, I will," Joseph assured her, and she felt a chill.

His words reminded her of exactly how dangerous he was. The man Michael Corsi had replaced as head auctioneer had disappeared without a trace. He wasn't the first person to suddenly leave Joseph's employ, nor was he the first to drop out of sight, never to be seen again. Of course, without any bodies, and without any evidence whatsoever that Joseph had played a role in those disappearances, no charges could be brought.

The speculation in Joseph's eyes faded and he said, "Have I told you lately how glad I am that I hired you? If not for you, I would have auctioned an extremely valuable painting for what would have amounted to peanuts."

Laura had barely believed it herself when she'd discovered the old master mixed in with a pile of worthless canvases. It was a once-in-a-lifetime find. She'd gone immediately to Joseph with the news, hoping to raise her value in his eyes. She knew he would think that Ruby easily could have arranged for someone to buy it at a pittance, then turned around and sold it for its true value, pocketing the profit for herself. That she hadn't went a long way toward proving her loyalty to him. It was after that discovery that Joseph had asked her to pose as his love interest.

Over the past six weeks she had learned a lot about Joseph Merrill. One of the most important things she'd uncovered was that he wasn't exactly a wizard where the items he auctioned off were concerned. He could barely tell an oak chair from a pine one, let alone discern the difference between a valuable master and a starving-artist watercolor. His success as an auctioneer was due solely to the talents of the people he hired to work for him. Joseph hired only the best. Which indicated to Laura, at least, that his business was a front for something else.

"You may have expressed your gratitude a time or two," she replied in a breathy voice, "but don't let that stop you. A lady never gets tired of having her ego stroked."

Though he had a smile on his face, the eyes Joseph turned her way were cold. "I'll be sure to keep that in mind. I have a favor to ask, my dear. A favor that you are uniquely qualified to grant. Of course, it goes without saying that I'm counting on your discretion. I don't want any tongues wagging, nor do I want you to feel you have to violate your self-imposed vow of celibacy. But it would be nice if you somehow got past our Mr. Corsi's barriers and encouraged his confidence. I would be extremely interested in finding out if he has any secrets I should know."

The words were an order, not a request. So much for his concern about Ruby's love life. Laura should have known better than to believe that Joseph had an altruistic bone in his body, or that he was bothered by Ruby's monastic lifestyle. Everything he did, he did with a what-was-in-it-for-him attitude. She'd be foolish to forget that.

"My break is almost over," she said, swinging her feet off the chair. "If you don't mind, I think I'll go to the ladies' room and put my face back together."

"Not at all. I hope you'll take into consideration what we were just speaking about."

"Of course."

Flashing him a brilliant smile, Laura walked away. Once safely in the ladies' room, she sank back against a stall door and groaned out loud. There was nothing for it. She would have to flirt with Michael Corsi. She would have to find out something about the man to report to Joseph. If she didn't, he would grow suspicious.

Her stomach clenched as a more disturbing thought occurred to her. What if Michael took her flirtation seriously? What if he wanted more than flirting from her? What would she do then? Joseph would surely encourage any such liaison.

She was Joseph Merrill's lover, she reminded herself. At least, that's what everyone believed. Michael Corsi, if he valued his job, would be careful about crossing that line. The thought reassured her.

She had to look at this as an opportunity. An opportunity to win Joseph's confidence. Flirting with Michael Corsi—discreetly, of course—meant she was one step closer to ending the case, one step closer to going home. One step closer to her vacation.

And if, when that time came, she found herself slapping handcuffs on Joseph's newest employee, she would do so gladly.

Chapter 2

She arrived on a gentle cloud of perfume that made his head spin. Antonio didn't have to glance up from the figures he was tallying to know who stood at his side. Only *she* could smell this good.

Patiently she waited for him to acknowledge her presence. When he finally did raise his gaze to her, he saw that, up close and personal, Ruby O'Toole looked even better than she did from a distance. And she smelled heavenly.

Damn. He was going to have a hell of a time maintaining his objectivity around her. Not to mention keeping his hands to himself.

"You did a nice job today," she said. "Joseph is pleased."

Her smile, though warm, didn't quite reach her eyes. Because her face was so enchanting, he doubted most people even noticed. He probably wouldn't have noticed himself, if he hadn't been trained to do so, and if he hadn't already been on guard against her.

On the other hand, her voice was like liquid smoke. It did things to his insides that should have been illegal.

"Thank you." His voice came out raspy, and he cleared his throat. "Need a drink," he lied, quickly raising the glass of water to his mouth.

When he replaced the drained receptacle on the podium, she extended her hand. "I'm Ruby O'Toole."

The fingers she slid into his palm were soft and supple, her nails perfectly manicured and coated by a pale-pink polish the color of her suit. It was obvious that Ruby O'Toole had never toiled in the trenches like other mere mortals.

"I know who you are," he said.

Her eyebrows arched delicately. "You do?"

"Your reputation precedes you."

Again that arch. "My reputation?"

"For beauty. And charm."

She looked pleased. "I thought it was time we met, since we're going to be working closely together."

Despite the recent drink, his mouth went dry. "We are?"

"*Very* closely. You have my word, Mr. Corsi, that before the week is over, you and I will be on exceedingly intimate terms."

Antonio nearly did a double take. He stared at her, not quite ready to believe what his gut, and the uncontrollable pounding of his heart, were telling him. Was she coming on to him?

"What kind of intimate terms are those?" he asked carefully, ignoring the exceedingly intimate visions of entwined limbs and naked body parts dancing across the viewing screen of his mind. He wasn't a man who jumped to conclusions. If time permitted, which sometimes it didn't, he always made sure to weigh the necessary evidence before taking action.

Her eyes widened in mock innocence. "Why, business terms, of course. What other terms could they be? After all, I hardly know you, Mr. Corsi. We haven't even been properly introduced."

The woman was good. Damn good. He would give her that much.

"Call me Michael. After all, we are going to be on intimate business terms."

"Michael," she said slowly, as if savoring the feel of his name on her tongue. "And you must call me Ruby."

"Very well, Ruby. Tell me, what exactly are these business terms we will be sharing so intimately?"

"Assessing the estates Joseph purchases. I valuate all the artwork and jewelry. Joseph plans on using you to valuate the furniture and glassware. We'll be working side by side. I'm looking forward to it. Peter, the man you replaced, could be such a dull boy. I'm counting on you to liven things up."

He glanced over to where Joseph stood, talking into his cell phone. A new thought occurred to him. Had his boss put Ruby up to this? An initial test of his loyalty, perhaps?

Antonio decided it was time to learn what this woman was really up to. And just how far she would go with Joseph standing so close by. Since she was eyeing him as if he was the main course on her menu, he decided he would return the favor.

She didn't flinch. In fact, the longer and the harder he looked, the more she seemed to preen. And the faster his heart thundered.

"See enough?" she finally asked coyly.

"You wanted me to look," he replied, glancing again at his boss, who was still deep in conversation with whomever he was speaking to on the phone.

Ruby had obviously seen him eyeing Joseph, because she said, "If you're worried about him, what he doesn't know won't hurt him. I promise. If you want to look again, at a later time, I won't tell."

Disgust washed through him. He couldn't believe it. Her lover stood not ten feet away, and she'd all but invited Antonio to jump her bones. Was it just hours ago that he'd anticipated such a welcome from her? He didn't need this. Not here. Not now. Not ever. He had more important things to occupy his mind than the unwanted advances of his boss's mistress.

His own relationships might be fleeting. They might never have the altar as their ultimate goal. The nature of his work—erratic hours, multiple disguises and false identities—all but demanded it be that way. Still, he did practice fidelity when he was with a woman, and he expected the same respect from her.

Did Ruby O'Toole have no moral backbone? How had he ever thought he was attracted to her? Right now it was all he could do not to let his feelings show on his face.

He was behaving out of character—Michael Corsi could handle women like Ruby in his sleep—and that had to stop right now. Besides, he should be glad his personal feelings were no longer going to be a problem where she was concerned. He could concentrate solely on the job he was sent here to do, without the bother of unnecessary complications.

It was obvious he hadn't hidden his feelings as well as he'd thought, because she said, "Perhaps, Michael, I've given you the wrong impression. Regardless of what you might be thinking right now about my dubious moral character, I'm not easy. What I am is an incorrigible flirt. Ask anyone, and they'll tell you. Ask Joseph. I don't mean anything by it. And I never follow through, except with the man in my life."

While it didn't surprise him that she had resorted to damage control, especially if Joseph had ordered her actions, it did amaze him that she'd admitted so readily what she was. Despite that, he felt an uncontrollable urge to shake her up a bit. Turnabout was fair play, after all.

"Where I come from, we have another word for what you're doing," he murmured.

"What word is that?"

"Teasing. Didn't anyone ever teach you what happens to teases?"

A defiant light lit her eyes. "No. What happens to them?"

"They often find themselves in sticky situations. The kind where they could easily get hurt."

She gave a nonchalant shrug. "I've survived so far."

He gritted his teeth. "I can see that you have. So tell me, Ruby, why are you an incorrigible flirt?"

"It's simple, really." She gave a delicate shrug. "I like having men look at me, and I like looking back."

Antonio recalled the way her smile hadn't quite reached her eyes. "Really?"

Her gaze grew watchful. "Yes, really. What other reason could there be?"

This time, he was the one who shrugged. "I don't know. Maybe you flirt so blatantly with men because you want to keep them at arm's length. Is there a reason you don't want a man close?"

She looked taken aback. When she spoke, however, her voice was calm.

"You're forgetting one thing. I'm very close to Joseph. And he's very possessive of his belongings."

How close was she, really? Close enough to possess the secrets Antonio needed to learn?

"So I've heard. Never fear, Ruby. You may be on display, but I have no intention of sampling the merchandise."

Before she could comment, Joseph joined them. Behind him, standing at a respectful distance, was his shadow, Matthew Rogers. Antonio wondered if Ruby had to send the man out on made-up errands, just to get some time alone with Joseph. The irreverent thought cheered him.

Clasping Antonio's hand, Joseph gave it an effusive shake. "Nice job, Michael. Very nice job."

"Thank you, sir."

Joseph turned to Ruby. "I just got off the phone with Howard Cabot. We got the Bickham estate."

"That's wonderful, darling," she exclaimed, rushing into his arms. "You've been negotiating with the heirs for months now. All your hard work has finally paid off."

"Yes, it has." Joseph broke the embrace and stood back to survey the two of them. "I'm sure you'll both understand that in this case, time is of the essence. I want the whole place catalogued, valued and auctioned off before the heirs have a chance to change their minds. Pack your bags, you two. You leave first thing Tuesday morning."

A shout from the other side of the room claimed Joseph's

attention, which was a good thing, since it prevented him from seeing the look of dismay that crossed Antonio's face.

"We're having dinner together later?" he asked Ruby when he turned back.

"Of course."

"I'll see you then." He nodded to Antonio. "I'll leave it to the two of you to work out the fine details of the trip. Sorry to run, but as you can see, I'm needed elsewhere."

Antonio stared after Joseph's departing figure. He'd just started his job, and already Joseph was sending him out of town. Was something big going to happen while he was gone? Was that why Joseph was sending him away?

"Where's the Bickham estate?" he asked.

"A tiny town in the extreme southeastern tip of West Virginia," Ruby replied.

"How big is it?"

"In the ten-million-dollar range. Excluding the house and grounds, of course." She sounded as disheartened by the whole thing as he was.

"So it's not something we can value in a day and be home in time for dinner."

"We'll be lucky if we'll be done in three days, and that's working overtime."

Great. Just great. Still, it gave him a chance to prove himself to Joseph, and early on in the game, too. It also gave him a chance to get to know Ruby better. Much as he found her character lacking, it was an opportunity he'd be foolish to ignore.

"What kind of car do you drive?" he asked, turning his attention to her.

"Corvette. A two-seater. Why?"

"I gather you don't pack light." His voice was dry.

"You gather right." She looked amused.

"Then we'd better take my truck. It'll give us more room."

Her look of amusement fled. "Your truck?"

"Yes. That a problem?"

"It's a long drive to the Bickham estate, a lot of it through mountainous terrain. It'll probably take us six hours, not counting rest stops, to get there."

Just his luck to be trapped in a vehicle with her for six hours. At least it wouldn't be a cramped Corvette.

"I assure you, the ride will be quite comfortable. I also have a cap over the bed. You could bring along ten suitcases, and there would still be room. Can't say that about your Corvette, can you?"

"Hardly," she replied.

"You weren't thinking I'd make you ride in the back, were you?" he couldn't help chiding.

Her chin went up. "A gentleman would never do that."

Now was as good a time as any to let her know that he might be more than he presented himself to be. That, if given the right incentive, he might be willing to cross the line from lawfulness into illegality.

"Who said I'm a gentleman?"

"My mistake." Her voice was downright frosty.

"Is 8:00 a.m. okay with you, or do you need more beauty sleep?"

Now she was the one gritting her teeth. He'd obviously struck a nerve. Good. He didn't know why he felt the need to get a rise out of her, he just did.

"Eight o'clock is fine." She turned on her heel and hurried off in the direction Joseph had taken.

"See you then," he called after her.

Watching her retreating figure, Antonio wanted to kick himself. What had happened to his detachment? Why had he made his distaste for her so obvious? Why had he goaded her the way he had?

He had spent hundreds of hours sitting and waiting, watching criminals until just the right moment to strike and take them down. He had dealt with the scum of the earth—street-corner drug dealers who would peddle their wares to anyone, even children—and he hadn't let his true feelings show. On the contrary, he'd done everything in his power to convince them he was one of them.

But in a mere matter of seconds he had let Ruby O'Toole wriggle under his skin. Even worse, he'd let his aversion to her get in the way of the job he had to do.

No matter what his feelings for her, he had to heal the breach between them. He had to make something good come out of their enforced togetherness.

Because auctions were held every Saturday, employees at the Merrill Auction Gallery had Sunday and Monday off. That gave Antonio two days to come up with a plan. Starting first thing Tuesday morning, he would try to get to know Ruby, to gain her trust. She was an important link in the chain comprising Joseph Merrill's business dealings, a link he couldn't afford to overlook.

She had been right about one thing, he thought, as he gathered up his belongings: for at least three days next week they would be working very closely together. Four days, if you included travel time. Four days in Ruby O'Toole's company was bound to test his patience, not to mention his resolve. It might very well drive him mad.

For his sanity's sake, he hoped she left that intoxicating perfume at home.

Even though Ruby was not the type to carry her luggage to the curb, on Tuesday morning Laura made certain she was waiting there a full ten minutes before Michael Corsi's expected arrival. The last thing she wanted was for him to come knocking on her apartment door. Though the sparsely furnished rooms suited Laura just fine, they lacked the frills and finishing touches that would undoubtedly grace any dwelling where Ruby resided.

As a precaution only, Laura thought it best not to raise any further questions in Michael's mind. The man had already proven that he was no slouch when it came to his powers of observation.

Promptly at eight o'clock, a gold, late-model Chevrolet Silverado pulled to the curb. After countless spine-numbing rides in the ancient pickup her brother had owned when they were teenagers, she was pleasantly surprised to find that Michael Corsi's vehicle looked quite comfortable. In fact, if she wasn't mistaken, the engine practically purred. There wasn't a hanging muffler or a worn-out spring in sight.

Laura met his gaze through the windshield. Just the sight of his handsome face made her heart flip-flop. She couldn't even comfort her guilty conscience by arguing that he reminded her of her late husband. Michael Corsi was nothing like Jacob, in either looks or manner. Still, good guy or not, and whether she wanted to or not, something deep inside her couldn't help responding whenever she saw him.

And she was going to be stuck in close quarters with him for the next four days. How would she ever cope?

She wasn't deluded about the real reason Joseph had sent her and Michael away together. Yes, the Bickham estate needed valued, and valued soon. But it also gave Joseph the perfect opportunity to force her to spend time alone with Michael.

It wasn't going to be as easy as Joseph expected. If the expression she'd glimpsed in Michael's eyes on Saturday, and the way he'd deliberately goaded her, were anything to go by, active dislike was the predominant emotion Ruby stirred in him.

Laura was honest enough to admit that her behavior definitely had something to do with that reaction. She *had* gone a bit overboard in her flirtation with him. A bystander might even be compelled to say that she'd come on entirely too strong. It had been a self-defense mechanism, a way to protect herself—exactly what Michael himself had said she was doing. But from what did she need protection? He was certainly no danger to her.

Worse than the way she'd come on to Michael, however, was the manner in which she had done it. She'd hardly been discreet. It had been pure luck that few people had been around at the time, and that no one had seemed to notice, not even Joseph, although she couldn't be sure about Matthew.

She had to find a way to make peace with Michael. The

next few days would be excruciating if they were constantly at each other's throats.

Besides, alienating him the way she had wouldn't get her job done. It wouldn't get her closer to any secrets he might have, such as his real involvement with Joseph. Like it or not, the job had to come first, and her personal feelings last.

To that end, she was determined to be civil to him, no matter how great the provocation. She wouldn't let him get to her the way he had on Saturday. She wouldn't make any more stupid mistakes. She would calmly, coolly and rationally do the work that both Joseph and the police department expected her to do.

A soft click announced the opening of the driver's side door. Seconds later the man who had occupied far too many of her thoughts over the past three days was standing before her.

One foot still in the street, Michael balanced the other on the curb. Leaning forward slightly, he squinted at her in the bright sunlight while he slid his right hand into his pants pocket and draped his left arm negligently across a parking meter.

He really had no business standing that way, Laura decided, as she shielded her eyes from the sun and tried to ignore the way her pulse leaped. It was too provocative by far. The material of his faded blue jeans strained against his muscled thighs in a way that drew her eyes upward to an area they had no business being drawn to.

As if that wasn't bad enough, once she'd torn her gaze away from the danger zone, she found herself entranced by the way his navy-blue T-shirt hugged an impressive chest, muscular biceps and trim waist. The force of Michael Corsi's masculinity practically shimmered like a wave of heat on the air. If it had been a virus, no female over the age of consent would have been immune.

Laura had always reveled in her sexuality while Jacob was alive. Since his death she had submerged that part of her nature. Obviously, in Michael Corsi's presence, it was trying to resurface. Whether she wanted it to or not.

She'd lost her husband and her child. Much as she had wished they would, her feelings and emotions hadn't died along with them. She was a woman, and she possessed all the requisite feminine responses. While she might not be ready to resume that part of her life, she shouldn't beat herself up over a normal, healthy, human reaction.

The way Michael Corsi made her feel was a nuisance, like a nosebleed or the hiccups. The good news was, she knew how to handle such nuisances. If she ignored the unwanted emotions he aroused in her, they'd simply go away.

"You're on time," he drawled, by way of greeting.

His eyes were hooded, hiding his expression from her. The neutral tone of his voice gave nothing away.

"You're on time," she replied. "Why shouldn't I be?"

"No reason, except..."

The way he let his words trail off told her he hadn't been about to pay her a compliment. Here they went again. So much for her effort at civility.

"Except what?" she couldn't help asking.

He shrugged. "You're that kind of woman."

"The habitually late kind?"

"No," he replied evenly. "The high-maintenance kind. In my experience, they're rarely on time."

She had no business being offended. After all, he'd pegged Ruby to a T. Which meant she was doing a bang-up job of being her alter ego. She should be pleased.

"I am a high-maintenance woman," she said stiffly. "I'll be the first to admit it. But I'm also a woman who takes her job seriously. Whether you believe it or not, Michael, I earn every penny Joseph pays me. I might keep a man waiting for a date, but I am *always* on time for work."

He took his foot off the curb and straightened to his full height. "I apologize," he said, then surprised her by smiling ruefully. "You might find this hard to believe, but I didn't set out this morning to antagonize you. Matter of fact, I promised myself I would be on my best behavior.''

His smile and his honesty disarmed her. Laura couldn't help laughing.

''What's so funny?'' he asked.

''We are. We're quite a pair, you and I. I promised myself the same thing.''

His answering chuckle was appreciative. ''Looks like neither of us is very good at keeping promises.''

''Not this one, anyway,'' she agreed. ''I owe you an apology, too. I don't know why I'm so prickly this morning.''

''Forget it,'' he dismissed. ''Want to give it another try?''

''Being civil to each other, you mean?''

He nodded. ''We do have a long drive ahead of us. And, after that, several days of hard work. Things would go a lot smoother if we got along.''

Laura had never had difficulty staying in character before. But somehow, when she wasn't paying attention, she'd lost Ruby. Again. She had to stop doing that. It was imperative. She couldn't afford to arouse Michael's suspicions. For all she knew, he was a plant Joseph had put in place to test her loyalty. She didn't want to flunk that test.

In Michael Corsi's presence, however, Laura Langley actually warred with Ruby O'Toole for equal time. That had to stop, too. As of yesterday.

''For Joseph's sake,'' she said, ''if for nothing else, we really should try. But I have to be honest with you. I don't hold out much hope.''

''Pessimist,'' he teased, his brown eyes gleaming with humor and his lips curling invitingly.

Laura's mouth went dry. Oh, hell. Michael Corsi in aggravating mode was attractive enough. In teasing mode, he was downright adorable.

Forget civility, she decided. An abrasive Michael was far preferable to her peace of mind. And much easier on her conscience.

''Tell me something,'' she said, racking her brain for a way to put his back up again. It shouldn't be too hard, since Ruby's merely drawing breath seemed to irritate him no end. "You're not one of those men who object to a woman driving, are you?"

Ruby O'Toole would gladly relinquish the driver's seat to any male who offered, but Laura Langley would go stir crazy if she had to sit in the passenger seat the entire trip. She needed something to distract her from her awareness of this man. Negotiating the hills and curves of the drive ahead should do the trick easily enough.

"I believe in equal-opportunity driving," he replied.

Michael didn't know it, but he'd just given her the opening she was searching for.

"A man after my own heart," she drawled sweetly. "Why, if Joseph hadn't staked a claim first, I'd probably be putty in your hands."

She felt a surge of triumph at the flare of impatience that flashed in his eyes.

"I should warn you," he said. "If you take a spell behind the wheel, you could break a nail."

Bingo. "I'll risk it."

"Won't it hamper your incorrigible flirting with the men in other cars? I'd hate to have you cramp your style."

"I'll manage."

"I'm sure you will." The words were not a compliment.

Laura suppressed a sigh of relief. The status quo had been recaptured. She was safe, at least for now.

"Damn," Michael muttered, shaking his head. "I did it again, didn't I? That truce lasted all of three seconds."

Which suited her just fine. She glanced pointedly at her watch. "Don't you think we should be going?"

Michael eyed the three suitcases at her feet. To his credit, he really did try. No uncivil comments were forthcoming, although she noticed he did have to bite his lip.

He even kept silent when his gaze ran over her short black skirt, which was cut low at the waistline to expose her belly button, and its matching skintight sleeveless mock turtleneck top. But when he got to her shoes, which consisted solely of a strap across her instep, another strap that buckled around her ankles, and three inch heels, apparently he could keep silent no longer.

"Nice work clothes," he said with a smirk that would have done Elvis proud.

"Thank you," she replied, unable to resist a last longing look at his jeans and T-shirt. She would have killed to be able to wear jeans and a T-shirt. Ruby O'Toole, unfortunately, wouldn't be caught dead in them. Under any circumstances.

More than the impractical clothing, what Laura really hated was having to spend an hour every morning putting herself together. It was such a pain having to keep her nails manicured and perfectly painted, her hair styled and her makeup just so. It was beyond her why women wasted all that time on their outward image.

Laura had always prided herself on being more interested in a person's character than his or her appearance. She preferred substance over style. Unfortunately, had she played herself instead of Ruby, she never would have captured Joseph's attention. Or Michael's.

"You really like my outfit?" she asked. Flashing him Ruby's patented smile, she smoothed her hands down her skirt. While the movement was made to look alluring, in reality it was a disguised attempt at pushing the tight fabric farther down her thighs. Even though she showed more skin in a bathing suit, the outfit still made her feel extremely self-conscious.

"It's a Benton Thomas original," she added, when he didn't reply.

"Sorry," he said. "I'm not up on the current fashion designers. Aren't you afraid of ruining your clothes? The last time I appraised an estate, it involved dank basements and dusty attics."

She waved a hand in dismissal. "That's what they have dry cleaners for."

"There are some miracles even dry cleaners can't perform."

He might disparage the way she was dressed, but he couldn't hide the gleam of appreciation in his eyes at the way the outfit flattered her figure. The gleam would have definitely pleased Ruby. Though she fought it, and despite her avowal of preferring substance over style, it pleased Laura, too.

"In that case," she said airily, "there's always Joseph. He'll replace it if I ask. He takes good care of me."

Michael's lip curled. "And you're a woman who needs a man to take care of her."

So that's what he objected to. She'd have to play that angle up every chance she got.

"Doesn't every woman?"

"Say that to my sister, Kate, and she'll likely scratch your eyes out."

Bravo for Kate. Laura was squarely in her corner.

"I take it your sister's a card-carrying feminist?"

"My sister is a woman who believes she can do anything as well as a man."

Wide-eyed, Laura asked, "Isn't that the same thing?"

He didn't answer. Instead he nodded curtly toward her suitcases. "You want me to put those in the back?"

She gave him an obliging smile that she knew set his teeth on edge. "If you don't mind."

Muttering something she couldn't catch beneath his breath, Michael tugged the suitcases to the back of the truck. She waited patiently by the closed passenger door while he placed them inside. It didn't take him long to get the hint. With a long-suffering sigh, he came around to her side and yanked the door open.

"Thank you," she said.

She realized her mistake the minute she faced the truck. In her zeal to play Ruby to a T, and to push Michael's buttons, she'd forgotten that it was a long way up into the passenger seat. Her skirt was short. And tight. Laura felt Michael's gaze burning along her legs as she climbed into the cab with as much decorum as possible.

Her temper was boiling and her cheeks hot by the time she'd settled herself comfortably.

"Enjoy the view?" The words were Laura's, but they were said in Ruby's teasing manner.

"A gentleman never looks," he replied, deadpan.

"I thought we agreed on Saturday that you're no gentleman."

He allowed himself a smug smile. "We did, didn't we?"

On that infuriating remark, he closed her door. A minute later he was behind the wheel.

"Buckle up."

While she did just that, he picked up a sheaf of papers from the seat.

"What's that?" she asked.

"A map."

"A map?"

He nodded. "I got it off the Internet. It gives us door-to-door directions to our destination."

"I can't believe it," she said.

He studied the page for a second, then, sounding distracted, replied, "What can't you believe?"

"You're a man. Men don't read maps."

"That's a highly sexist remark."

"It's also the truth," she stated.

"No, it's not."

"What is the truth, then?"

"When a man sets off for an unknown destination, he always consults a map. What he doesn't do is ask for directions if he gets lost. Trust me, Ruby, if we lose our way, I promise to drive around for hours until we find it again."

Laura gave her head a rueful shake. She'd wanted things back to the status quo, and back to the status quo they definitely were. Boy were they ever.

At least now the impulse to throw herself into his arms had passed. Unfortunately, it had been replaced by the urge to wrap her hands around his throat.

Chapter 3

Two hours into the drive, Antonio handed the wheel over to Ruby.

As had been the case during his spell as driver, they rode in silence, without even the radio to dispel the tension between them. At some point he would have to ask her about Joseph, but now was too soon. Way too soon. If he tried to pump her, she'd only grow even more closemouthed, if that was possible. Not to mention that his probing would inevitably raise her suspicions.

They were going to be alone together for the next several days. He had to use that time wisely. What he needed to do was engage her in small talk. Small, civil talk. If such a thing was possible between the two of them.

He needed to get her to relax. If she relaxed in his company, maybe then she would let her guard down low enough to reveal something of value. He would just bide his time and wait. He was good at biding his time and waiting for the proper moment.

Still, even to him, two-plus hours of silence was biding

one's time just a tad too long. There was a huge difference between waiting for the proper moment and wasting the time at hand. Especially when, on a job like this, even one wasted second could mean the difference between life and death.

"Well, what do you think?" he finally asked.

She glanced over at him. "About what?"

"My truck. How does it handle?"

She smiled. In that brief, unguarded, upward curl of her lips, he glimpsed the first honest emotion, other than her displeasure with him, that he'd seen on her face since their gazes had first met across the crowded auction floor. If only she would smile like that always, instead of bestowing that forced, brittle tilt of her lips that passed for coyness.

She made quite a picture in her short, tight skirt, and even tighter top. Her long legs seemed to stretch to eternity, and her equally long arms seemed made solely for wrapping themselves around a man's neck. She was, quite easily, the most beautiful woman he had ever seen. Everything inside of him even remotely related to his Y chromosome responded to that beauty.

Then she spoiled it all by speaking.

"How does it handle? Like a man's cheeks after a close shave."

Antonio's awareness of her was swept away on a wave of irritation. And women accused men of being single-minded. Didn't she have at least one thought in her head that didn't relate to sex?

While sex had been the ultimate goal of all of his relationships, the women he'd been involved with had, without exception, expressed an avid interest in something besides themselves. Those varied interests had made for some lively and interesting debates. He'd enjoyed their company, enjoyed spending time with them both in and out of the bedroom.

Ruby O'Toole really had no substance, he realized, wondering at his disappointment.

"It has great power on these hills," she said, then paused. "You're into power, aren't you?"

He felt his brow furrow. "What does that mean?"

"Nothing," she replied with a shrug.

He hated it when women said that, because he knew that their "nothing" definitely meant something. Forget about Ruby relaxing with him. He was beginning to think it would take a strong sedative to get him to relax with her. Either that, or he'd have to get blinding, stinking drunk. At this juncture in their relationship, he wasn't averse to either idea.

"No, really," he said. "I'm curious. What do you mean when you say I'm into power?"

She heaved an audible sigh. "Only that, like most men, you like to be in charge."

"You mean I'm a control freak."

"Don't be offended. The need for power is a man's number-one craving."

"What about sex?"

She didn't take her gaze off the road. "That's number three."

"Number three?"

"Oh, men like to believe that sex is number one, because they spend so much time thinking about it, but it's really number three."

Folding his arms across his middle, he shifted in his seat so he could stare directly at her. "And number two is?"

"Money."

He drew a deep breath. "So what you're saying is that everything a man does, everything *I* do, is a direct result of my craving for power?"

"Exactly." Her voice warmed to her theme. "Men join gangs, they make weapons, they wage war. They buy fancy sports cars or big, monster trucks, preferably with stick shifts in them, to prove how macho they are. They do all this, because they need to feel powerful."

"You'll notice," he said, nodding toward the dashboard, "this truck doesn't have a stick shift." What he didn't bother telling her was that this particular model only came with automatic transmission.

''Doesn't matter,'' she replied blithely. ''It doesn't change the symbolism.''

''The symbolism being,'' he said with exaggerated patience, ''that this truck represents my need for power?''

''Of course.''

Antonio felt the beginnings of a headache. What crazy impulse had deluded him into thinking he could make small talk with her? He had no one to blame but himself. After all, she had been exceedingly ''friendly'' toward him at the beginning. That friendliness was what had gotten him so bent out of shape. And why? Simply because she wasn't the type of person he'd hoped she'd be.

He was the one who had blown it by not bothering to disguise what he really thought of her. Obviously, if her continued prickliness around him, and the way she was goading him this very minute, were anything to go by, Ruby was the type who held grudges.

Even though he knew he was being deliberately taunted, he couldn't let it go. ''How does this truck symbolize my need for power?''

''Take its size, for instance.''

''What about it?''

She waved an arm. ''Extended cab. A body that stands over six feet off the ground. Nobody traveling behind you, except a guy in an eighteen-wheeler, can see over you. Or around you. Face it, Michael, you're making a statement with this vehicle.''

If he kept gritting his teeth this way, his dentist was going to make a fortune. ''I am?''

''Yes. You're saying you want to own the road, and everybody else better get out of your way. Driving this truck makes you feel powerful.''

''What about women?'' he challenged. ''Don't they crave power?''

''It's their number-one craving also. But they have to go about getting it more subtly. This is a male-dominated society, you know.''

"How does a woman go about getting power?"

"Pandering to a man's ego. Dressing nicely for him and maintaining her figure. Letting a man think she's small and helpless. But mainly through sex."

"Is that what you're doing with Joseph?" he asked softly. "Asserting your need for power?"

She didn't blink. "Of course."

The thought of her in Joseph Merrill's arms made him want to smash his fist into something. Preferably Joseph's jaw.

Antonio decided he'd had enough small talk. It certainly wasn't getting him anywhere he wanted to go. Reaching into the glove compartment, he brought out a crossword puzzle book and a mechanical pencil. At least these puzzles he could decipher. They didn't try his patience the way a certain brunette did.

"What are you doing?" she asked.

He pulled a lap board out from under the seat and opened the book to a fresh page. Tapping the pencil against the board, he read the first clue.

"Working a crossword puzzle."

"You like crossword puzzles?"

He filled in the answer before replying. "Yes, I do."

"I don't care too much for puzzles."

He looked over at her. "Why not?"

She shrugged. "Too much work. I'd rather spend my time doing other things."

"Like your hair and your nails, you mean?" he asked snidely.

"Absolutely," she agreed.

Silence settled around them once more.

"You wouldn't happen to know a six-letter word for an igneous rock composed of labradorite and augite, would you?" he asked a few minutes later.

"Gabbro," she replied immediately, seemingly without thinking.

Antonio sat up straight in his seat. When he glanced over at her, her gaze was focused on the winding road. For a woman who professed not to like crossword puzzles, she knew the answer to a fairly obscure clue. Yet another mystery for him to solve.

"Would you mind spelling that?" he asked carefully.

She did. He checked, and the word fit.

"How did you know that?" he asked.

"I must have seen it on a game show." There was a sudden cautiousness in her voice.

"A game show?" He didn't bother to hide his skepticism.

"I just love game shows, don't you?" she gushed. "Especially the ones where you can win a lot of money."

"Ah, yes, man's number-two need," he drawled.

"Exactly."

"You have an interesting take on the human condition."

She looked at him out of the corner of one eye. "What take is that?"

"That every man, and woman for that matter, is solely out for him or herself. Power, money, sex, they're all that matter. If you don't look out for number one, no one else will. Let me know, please, if I'm mistaken."

"No. You've summed it up quite nicely."

"Tell me," he asked. "How did you come by this conclusion?"

"What's it matter to you?"

It mattered because, as far as he was concerned, the way she was wasting her life on a man who shouldn't deserve her was an even bigger crime than the one that very same man was allegedly committing.

"It doesn't, really. I was just curious. Did you pick your theory out of thin air? Or did you formulate it after exhaustive study? Perhaps you wrote your doctoral thesis on the topic."

"Now you're mocking me."

He gazed at her seriously. "How am I mocking you?"

"I didn't go to college."

"How could I know that?" he asked softly, although he was well aware, from reading about her in the dossier on Joseph Merrill, that Ruby O'Toole did not possess a college degree. "All I know about you is that you work for Joseph and that, in your words, you belong to him."

He knew one other thing. She was smarter than she let on. Did part of her strategy for snaring Joseph also include acting dumb?

"If you must know," she told him, "I've earned the right to hold the opinions I do. The right of experience."

"You certainly are experienced," he muttered.

"Did you say something?"

He looked down at the puzzle. "Just talking to myself."

"Can I ask you something, Michael?"

"Sure."

"Why are you so upset? Are you really going to sit there and try to convince me that you and I don't share the same philosophy about the human condition?"

Her words brought him up short. Way short. How could he have been so stupid? So careless? He'd nearly gone and blown it all by getting his underwear in a twist. From now on, he would have to tread extremely carefully while in her presence. Ruby O'Toole could pull him out of character faster than a magician could pull a rabbit out of his hat.

And if she started thinking about the contradictions... He had to change his tune, but fast.

"You're right," he conceded, hoping to sound rueful, like a kid caught with his hand in the cookie jar. "I do share your philosophy. But no man likes to be seen through so easily. It's a blow to his ego. I was annoyed. I suppose I was trying to get a rise out of you."

"That's what I thought," she replied.

"You were wrong about one thing, though," he said.

"What?"

"Power is not my number-one need. Money is. If I have enough money, I can buy all the power I need."

She bestowed a superior smile on him. "If you say so."

He felt the need to have the last word. "Could I offer you a caution?"

"Of course."

"I recommend you not share your philosophy with Joseph."

Her laughter was light and amused. "Trust me, Michael. I would never be so blunt with a man I'm seeing romantically."

No, he thought sourly. She'd just bat those impossibly long eyelashes of hers at him, and he'd dissolve into a puddle of testosterone need.

Just an hour ago he'd been certain he knew all there was to know about Ruby O'Toole. But after her discourse on man's and woman's need for power—and after telling him how much she needed to sublimate all her wants and desires to those of the man who would take care of her—he wasn't certain at all. Then there was her disclaimer about any knowledge of an advanced crossword puzzle clue, followed by her calling him on the carpet for acting out of character.

He wasn't about to go so far as admitting that there might be some depth to her, after all. But he would concede he didn't know everything he thought he did.

Just who are you, Ruby O'Toole? More important, what are you up to? What secrets do you know? And how do I get you to tell them to me?

They stopped for lunch at a diner outside of Beckley, West Virginia. To Antonio's surprise, Ruby ordered a cheeseburger, French fries and a chocolate shake. He watched in silence as she took a bite of her cheeseburger, then closed her eyes. A look of rapture crossed her face, and she chewed lustily.

Even though he didn't like her all that much, Antonio felt the stirring of arousal at the sight. His own food forgotten, he sat back in his chair and watched her. When a rivulet of juice ran down her chin, he had to fight the urge to lean forward and taste it for himself. Did she make love with as much abandon as she ate?

"Napkin?" He plucked one from the receptacle on the table and thrust it toward her.

"Thanks." She took the proffered item from him with a

smile. When her chin was dry, she asked, "Aren't you hungry?"

He blinked. "What?"

She nodded toward his plate. "You haven't eaten anything."

Antonio picked up his club sandwich and took a bite. He didn't taste a thing.

Ruby tossed him a curious glance before returning to her meal.

He didn't know what was worse: the silence between them, during which his arousal continued to grow painfully as he covertly watched her, or the small talk that inevitably ended up in the opposite direction from the one he intended to take.

At least with small talk he'd have something else to concentrate on. If he just sat here, watching her eat, by the time they paid the bill he'd be so aroused he'd be walking funny.

Of course, with all the blood in his body centered in one vital organ, his powers of thought were severely limited at the moment. Still, if he tried hard enough, he should be able to come up with something to say.

"You're really going to eat all that food?" was the brilliant opening he finally led with.

She arched an eyebrow. "Shouldn't I?"

Antonio tried to sound nonchalant. "It's not exactly low in fat. I just assumed, like most women, you spend all your time watching your figure."

Ruby picked up a French fry. Tilting her head back, she opened her mouth. Three clean bites with her incredibly straight teeth, and the French fry disappeared. Antonio was sweating by the time she swallowed.

"Watching my figure is for men to do," she said, picking up another fry.

He welcomed the shaft of irritation that took his arousal down a few degrees. "You keep eating like that, all they're going to watch is you ballooning up in size."

"Hasn't happened yet," she said, dismissingly.

"Bad habits eventually catch up to us all."

She gave him a curious glance. ''So I've been told. Okay, Michael, I'm game. What should I be eating?''

''I don't know.'' He shrugged. ''A salad, maybe?''

''Rabbit food, you mean.'' She wrinkled her nose.

''Yes.''

''I don't find it filling. Besides, depending on what you put on a salad, it could have more fat than this cheeseburger. Were you aware of that?''

''I was just making an observation,'' he said.

''You seem to make a lot of them.'' She took a sip of her milkshake, then added, ''Want to know the real secret of keeping your weight at a manageable level? It's quite simple.''

''Sure.''

''Everything in moderation.''

''Everything in moderation,'' he repeated.

She nodded. ''You can eat foods high in fat, if you balance them out with fruits and vegetables. And exercise, of course.''

''Everything in moderation,'' he murmured again, his gaze on his plate. He looked up. ''Does that go for your love life, too?''

She met his gaze unflinchingly. ''Sex life, you mean.''

''I beg your pardon?''

''What you're really asking about is my sex life.''

Here they were again: due east, when he'd thought they were headed west. He'd expected a typical Ruby comment along the lines of moderation having nothing to do with her love life. Instead she'd turned the tables on him.

Before he could frame an answer to her question, she asked him an even harder one. ''Why are you so interested in my sex life?''

Because I want to be a part of it. Because I'm attracted to you, and I'm disappointed you're not the woman I need you to be in order to allow you to become a part of it.

''I've never met another woman quite like you.'' That, at least, was the truth. ''I guess I'm just trying to understand you. Since you admittedly use sex to get power, I thought it was a fair question.''

To his relief she looked pleased, rather than offended. Finally he'd said something right.

"It might be a fair question," she replied, "but I hope you'll understand if I decline to answer."

"Of course."

"Are you married?" she asked.

Antonio nearly choked on his iced tea. "You're asking me that now? After the way you came on to me Saturday?"

"So far as I remember, we never did establish your marital status," she replied. "Besides, I told you I'm an incorrigible flirt. Marital status isn't the first thought that enters my mind when I meet an attractive man."

He had no business being so pleased that she thought he was attractive. "Since you're already involved with someone, why should you care?"

"I'm just trying to figure you out...like you are with me. So," she asked again, "are you?"

He wondered what she would do if he told her the truth. That, to the endless frustration of his family, the thought of marriage always left him feeling claustrophobic. His life was crowded enough as it was. While the relatives of other undercover cops worried incessantly over their safety, his five brothers and his sister were terrified he'd never settle down. In this case, at least, Antonio's truth was also Michael's truth.

"Do I look like I'm married?"

Her smile grew broader. "Trust me. I know a lot of married men who neither look nor act married."

He'd just bet she did. "I see."

"I'll try one more time. Are you married, Michael?"

He was Michael Corsi, he reminded himself. It was about time he remembered it and acted accordingly.

"Hardly," he said, injecting as much disdain as he could into the word.

She tilted her head and eyed him carefully. "You got something against marriage?"

He spread his arms in a devil-may-care manner. "Nothing, except it would cramp my style."

"What is your style? Love 'em and leave 'em?"

"Some people have said that."

"Interesting," Ruby commented.

"What?"

"Obviously you see nothing wrong in being a love-'em-and-leave-'em kind of guy, but you definitely find something wrong with my being an incorrigible flirt. Does anyone but me see a double standard at work here?"

She had a point, Antonio conceded. However, he could hardly tell her that *he* was the one who objected to her moral code, not Michael. Nor could he tell her that the only reason she knew of his disapproval was because she had managed to pull him out of character at least a thousand times since they met.

"The question is," he heard her say, "why are you a love-'em-and-leave-'em kind of guy?"

He suddenly found himself feeling wary, although he couldn't identify the source of his reluctance. It was probably nothing more than his desire to remain in character and not blow it by saying something stupid. The way he had earlier.

He was Michael Corsi, he reminded himself yet again. He had to handle this question the way Michael would.

"Does there have to be a reason?"

"There's always a reason," Ruby stated. "In your case, my guess is that you have commitment issues."

He felt his eyebrows climb. "Commitment issues?"

She nodded. "You were probably burned by love in the past, and now you don't want to give your heart to any woman. You don't want to risk the pain. Either that or you hate women. But something tells me that isn't the case."

Relief filled him, and his wariness fled. She was so far from both the cover story he'd created for Michael and the truth of his own life he almost laughed out loud.

"I hate to burst your bubble, but I haven't been burned by love. And I don't hate women. I just happen to like things the way they are. Variety is the spice of life, you know."

In truth, he had never been in love. As a youth, he'd been

too busy sowing his wild oats to commit to one relationship. As an adult, the demands of working undercover prevented him from being with a woman long enough to fall in love. Of course, he couldn't tell Ruby that.

"Since we're analyzing each other's supposed issues," he said, "maybe you'll answer the question I asked you on Saturday. Why are you an incorrigible flirt?"

"Are you really interested? Or are you trying to make me squirm, the way you were then?"

He bit back a smile. Leave it to Ruby not to let that one go by unchallenged. "I'm really interested." To his surprise it was true.

"It's not because I want to push people away, like you thought," she said.

"Then why is it?" he countered.

"Because of my past. My father was not a demonstrative man. My need for constant male appreciation stems from that lack."

"I guess I'm not that self-aware," Antonio said.

"Don't knock it till you try it. Who was it who wrote that the unexamined life isn't worth living?"

He stared at her. "You've read Socrates?"

There it was again, the sudden blankness of expression that hid her thoughts from him.

"Who's Socrates?"

"An ancient Greek philosopher," he answered automatically. "I suppose you heard that quote on a game show, right?"

"I suppose so."

Antonio knew he'd get nothing further from her in that regard. "Do incorrigible flirts get married?"

"To the right man," Ruby replied.

"Meaning a man with gobs of money. A man like Joseph."

"Of course. Some women aspire to be homemakers. Others aspire to a career. I aspire to marrying a millionaire."

"What about love?" he asked.

"What about it?" she said. "It doesn't seem to come very high on your list."

"But you're a woman. It's supposed to come high on yours."

She spared him a disgusted look. "That is, quite possibly, the most sexist thing any man has ever said to me. I think I need to make a phone call to your sister."

He grinned triumphantly at her, and understanding bloomed in her eyes.

"You're paying me back for my map remark, aren't you?"

"Perhaps," he acknowledged. "Seriously, though. You really want a man to take care of you?"

"What's wrong with that?"

"What's wrong with being independent, of having a mind of your own? What's wrong with taking care of yourself? You have a good job. You can afford it."

His sister must have rubbed off on him more than he'd realized, Antonio reflected. Kate would be thrilled.

"I've gone as far as I can in my line of work," Ruby said. "I have expensive tastes. I need a man to provide them."

"You'd just be a trophy wife, you know," he felt compelled to point out.

She used her straw to stir her milkshake. "That's one way of looking at it."

"What happens when you grow older and your looks fade? What happens when Joseph, or another man just like him, trades you in on a newer model?"

"They call it a property settlement, Michael."

She really was the most infuriating woman. Didn't she want to better herself? Why was she wasting her potential on Joseph Merrill, and who knew how many other men just like him that she'd been with? Was the reason as simple as the one she'd stated? That her father never gave her the affection she craved?

The waitress brought their bill. After giving it a glance, Antonio placed enough money to cover the charge, plus a generous tip, on the table.

He nodded to Ruby. "Ready?"

"Just a minute." She fished her wallet from her purse and placed several dollar bills on top of the ones he'd already left.

"What are you doing?" he asked.

"Adding to the tip."

He stared at her in exasperation. Did she think he was a tightwad, out to stiff a person who had served them well?

"I already left twenty percent."

"I know. But waitresses are notoriously underpaid. Every little bit extra helps."

"Joseph won't reimburse that."

"I don't care." Standing, she made her way to the front of the diner.

Bemused, Antonio watched her for a long minute before following. By her own admission, she was a woman whose main goal in life was to marry a rich man, yet she'd thrown away her own money on a woman she would never see again. It galled him anew that she had such low expectations for herself.

As they walked to the truck, he decided to give it one last try.

"Not to beat a dead horse, but you're throwing your life away, Ruby. Can't you see that?"

She eyed him curiously. "You're referring to my relationship with Joseph?"

"Yes."

"Even if it is true, why should it bother you?"

Antonio stifled a curse. She'd done it again. She'd made him forget who he was supposed to be. And what he was supposed to be doing.

"Damned if I know," he muttered.

"I guess this means you wouldn't want an invitation to the wedding."

He started. Had things gone that far between her and Joseph?

"Joseph has asked you to marry him?"

"Not yet. But it's coming, I can feel it. Good thing I don't need much lead time. When your brother's a priest, you can be pretty flexible with your plans.''

He paused with his hand on the passenger door handle. ''Your brother's a priest?''

She dimpled. ''Someone has to atone for my sins. Wouldn't you agree?''

She climbed up into the truck, and he closed the door after her. As he buckled himself into the driver's seat, Antonio decided it was time to do the work he'd been sent here to do. His superiors had gone to great pains to make his cover just perfect. Hopefully, the reason Joseph had hired him was as much for his ''past record'' as for his abilities as an auctioneer.

''Maybe your brother could work on my sins,'' he said.

''You mean you're not the mild-mannered auctioneer everyone believes you to be?''

He started the truck and pulled out of the parking lot. ''Is any man what he appears to be?''

''You do have a past, then.''

''You could say that.''

''A murky past,'' she observed, with obvious relish.

''I did some time once, back when I was young and stupid.''

''How much time?''

''My sentence was five years, but I was released after serving thirty months. Good behavior.''

''What were you convicted of?''

If she already knew, she wasn't letting on. ''Possession, with the intent to sell.''

Still no judgment on her face. ''Were you a dealer?''

He had to tread carefully here. If she was, as he suspected, Joseph's eyes and ears on this trip, and if she was going to report back every word he said, he didn't want Joseph to think he was going to try to horn in on his business.

''From time to time I'd sell stuff.''

''Why?''

''For the money, of course.''

''What did your sister think of that?'' she asked.

To make his cover story easier to remember, Antonio had given Michael the same five brothers and one sister that he had. "She hated it. Unlike me, she's pretty much of a straight arrow."

"Like my brother."

"Exactly."

"You said you were young and stupid," Ruby commented. "Does that mean you've reformed your ways?"

He chose his words carefully and for the greatest effect. "I like money, Ruby. Like I said earlier, it's my number-one need. Truth is, I'd do most anything to get it. I just won't be stupid enough to get caught again."

"I see," she said slowly.

"You sound disappointed."

"Why should I be disappointed?"

That's what he wondered.

Chapter 4

"Who lives out in the middle of nowhere like this?" Michael groused as the truck hit a dip in the dirt road and gave an alarming bounce.

"An eccentric millionaire tired of the lights and noise of the city, that's who," Laura replied, holding on to the dashboard for dear life.

They had been driving along the narrow, winding and extremely bumpy road for more than fifteen minutes. On either side of the road stood tall trees that blocked most of the sunlight, tangled bushes—many with nasty-looking thorns—and a profusion of wildflowers. While the wildflowers were beautiful, and despite the No Trespassing signs posted at regular intervals, she still felt like she was in the middle of an overgrown jungle without a guide to see her safely through to the other side. She wouldn't be surprised if, any minute now, they encountered a group of lions and tigers and bears. Oh, my.

A stray branch brushed along the side of the truck, and she saw Michael wince. In all likelihood, it would need a new paint job by the time they returned to Pittsburgh, and probably new shocks, as well. Heaven knew how Joseph was going to get his fleet of moving vans down this road.

"I understand needing to get away," he said, "but did he have to escape *this* far?"

"If he had simply moved to the suburbs," she pointed out, "people wouldn't have labeled him eccentric."

Laura knew the true cause of his distress, and it had little to do with the remoteness of their destination or the pounding his truck was taking, although he could be pretty weird about the vehicle. Two hours earlier he had spied a wriggling canvas bag by the side of the road. When they had stopped to investigate, they'd found two puppies inside.

At the sight, Michael had sworn furiously, then launched into a diatribe directed toward the soulless creatures who had abandoned the puppies along the side of the road, where they would either starve to death or be hit by a car. He had also insisted that he and Laura find the nearest humane society. He didn't care how far out of their way it took them.

It was a side of him Laura hadn't imagined existed, and it fascinated her. It also touched her deeply. She knew she would forever carry a picture around in her head of the way he had laughingly allowed the puppies to climb all over him and lick his face and hands. There was something terribly appealing about a man who got upset over a couple of puppies. An ex-con who loved animals. She supposed it was the gangster equivalent of the hooker with a heart of gold.

"You couldn't keep them, Michael."

He didn't pretend not to understand. "I know."

"You travel too much, work too many hours."

"I know."

"The shelter will find them a good home."

"I *know,* Ruby."

"But it doesn't make you feel better."

"No, it doesn't."

They hit a series of dips, and the truck began bucking like one of the crack addicts she'd wrestled to the ground early in her career with the NYPD. Michael's arm shot out, pinning her securely against the seat. It wasn't until he had brought the truck to an abrupt halt and she looked down that she realized his hand was cupped securely around her right breast.

For one breathless moment, she simply marveled at how smooth the skin of Michael's hand seemed. Yet there was nothing weak or lazy about it. His fingers were long and extremely capable looking; his nails clean and neatly trimmed. She had never realized before how beautifully sculpted a man's knuckles could be.

Then reality dawned, and Laura came to her senses. "Uh, Michael."

"What?" He was staring at the terrain in front of them and sounded distracted.

"Your hand."

"What about it?"

"Would you mind removing it from my…from me?"

An impatient twist of his head brought his gaze to hers. She looked pointedly down. Comprehension filled his eyes, along with an expression akin to horror. Michael snatched his hand from her body as if the contact burned.

"Sorry about that," he mumbled, his cheeks taking on a ruddy hue. "When we hit those bumps… All I can say is, it was an automatic response."

"I know, Michael."

"I just want you to know I didn't mean to…I had no intention of…I would never just…"

She gritted her teeth. Would it have been so awful if he *had* meant to touch her that way? Not that she wanted him to. Not by a long shot.

"I *know,* Michael."

It wasn't the warmth of his hand against her breast that unsettled her so. There had been nothing sexual in the gesture, just as there had been nothing sexual in her response to it. It was the protective nature of his reaching out to her that rattled her far more than if he had simply groped her.

She'd told him that her father had been undemonstrative and cold. But that was the story she had concocted for Ruby, to explain Ruby's behavior. In truth, Laura's father—and her mother—had been warm, caring and open when it came to expressing their love. A freak storm during her freshman year of college, when the roof of the store they were in collapsed, had taken them from her. A few years after that, she'd lost her husband and son. She still had her brother, who, like the mythical brother she had invented for Ruby, was a priest. But Alex, who was assigned to a church in New Mexico, was busy with his parishioners and their needs. Laura tried to impose on him as little as possible.

It troubled her to admit it, but after four years of depending on no one but herself, it had felt gloriously wonderful to have someone be concerned for her welfare. Even if the sign of that caring had come in the form of a hand closed around her breast. And even if that someone was Michael Corsi, a convicted felon who—if she'd understood him correctly, and she was fairly certain she had—was looking for another opportunity to skirt the law.

She covertly studied the man at her side, taking in his strong profile with its prominent Roman nose and determined chin. The muscles of his arms were well-defined. His shoulders were broad. If he wanted to, Michael Corsi could make one formidable protector.

Laura felt her mouth tighten grimly. What was that old cartoon saying? If only he had used his power for good, instead of evil. If only Michael had learned the error of his ways during his incarceration, then maybe… Her brain shied away from the thought.

Without warning he turned in his seat. They stared wordlessly at each other, and a sudden tension filled the cab. The restlessness that had been so much a part of her life of late took hold of Laura and refused to let go. She suddenly found herself wishing that he *had* tried to cop a feel. The outrage that action would have prompted would have left her immune to any unwelcome and inappropriate thoughts. At least, she believed it would. Unfortunately, nothing much had been making sense in her life recently.

Her confusion, and her chagrin about that confusion, put a bite into her voice. "Do me a favor. If we hit another series of bumps like that last set, would you please remember that I'm wearing a seat belt? I don't need anything, or anyone, to hold me in place."

With a savage motion, Michael faced forward, put the truck in gear and stepped on the accelerator. "I told you it was an automatic reflex. I didn't mean anything by it."

She welcomed the opportunity to rile him further. "Are you saying you weren't trying to feel me up?"

He shot her a dark look. "Trust me, Ruby. If I was trying to feel you up, you'd know it."

Laura couldn't suppress the shiver that raced up her spine. Yes, she supposed she would. In every fiber of her being. Damn it. And damn him.

"Don't worry, Michael. You don't have to keep explaining. You told me once on Saturday, and a couple of times already today. I get it. Believe me, I get it. You wouldn't touch me, even if someone paid you to." A fact for which she should be down on her knees giving thanks. Instead, the contrary and uncontrollable part of her nature actually had the audacity to feel just the teensiest bit put-out by the realization.

"Damn it," he swore when they hit another rut. "You would think at least Joseph's precious client would have had this road paved."

"Maybe he was trying to discourage uninvited visitors from dropping in."

"Works for me. How 'bout we turn around and head back to Pittsburgh, before my truck is reduced to a pile of bolts and metal?"

Laura couldn't resist. "We are expected, you know. Besides, I thought this truck could handle anything."

He sighed heavily. "You're enjoying this, aren't you?"

When she could forget the confusing emotions he aroused in her, she supposed she was. She had to admit, riling Michael Corsi was turning out to be a lot more fun than she'd expected it to be. And it helped to pass the time.

"A girl has to take her entertainment where she can find it."

"And you usually find it with men."

Now this was the irritating Michael she knew and preferred. For a while there, he had managed to distract her by actually seeming to care that Ruby might be throwing away her life on Joseph. Then, of course, there had been the puppies. She had come perilously close, perish the thought, to liking him.

"We are in a foul mood, aren't we?" she said, suppressing a smile. "Just be glad it's not the dead of winter. Even a truck that can handle anything would get stranded out here in the middle of a blizzard."

"Forget about winter," Michael retorted. "I'm just praying it won't rain while we're here."

Rain would be as bad as snow, she suddenly realized. The possibility of being stranded out here, alone with Michael, was not one Laura wanted to entertain.

"You sure we're on the right road?" he asked, as a flock of birds took flight at their passing.

"You were the one with the door-to-door directions," she reminded him. "According to this printout, and your odometer, the Bickham estate is another three miles down this road."

"If my odometer is still working," he muttered.

"We'll know one way or another soon."

"Yes," he said sourly, "I suppose we will. And then, at some point, we're going to have to turn around and make our way out of here."

Laura took pity on him. "Did Joseph tell you anything about Vincent Bickham?" she asked, trying to distract him from his worries.

"All I know is what you said on Saturday. That Joseph spent months negotiating to win the estate."

"He did. It was touch-and-go for a long time. The heirs wanted to ensure that Vincent and Serena's belongings—Serena was Vincent's wife—were treated with the proper respect. It's my understanding that Joseph did a lot of fast talking and made a lot of promises."

"Does he intend on keeping those promises?" Michael asked.

Laura gave what she hoped was a nonchalant shrug. "With Joseph one never knows for sure."

"Meaning he might not."

Michael had just touched on one aspect of working undercover that Laura was growing to hate. Vincent Bickham's heirs had negotiated with Joseph in good faith. By all rights he should honor, to the letter, every promise he made. She had no idea whether he intended to uphold his end of the bargain. Even if she were aware that Joseph planned to renege on some of his promises, there was nothing she could do about it. She certainly couldn't blow her cover by informing Vincent Bickham's heirs.

What she could do, however, was everything in her power to ensure that the valuation and cataloguing of the estate was done properly. The rest would simply have to be left to chance.

That she worried about it at all served to underscore her need for a long vacation. There had been a time, not so long ago, when she wouldn't have questioned anything. A time when she had believed unreservedly that the ends, the bad guy being put behind bars, had entirely justified the means, her actions as an undercover cop. And she'd never worried about any innocent individuals who might get caught in the middle. At that time nothing, and no one, could have pulled her out of character.

The truth hit her squarely between the eyes, and she quickly looked down at her lap before Michael could see her face change and ask her what was wrong. What was wrong was that, after three long years of associating primarily with felons, she was tired of being around bad people. She was tired of spending every waking hour with men and women whose morals were lower than those of an alley cat. Instead she craved peace and quiet and the company of people who actually cared about someone other than themselves.

And she was stuck for at least three more days, out here in the middle of nowhere, with Michael Corsi.

"Joseph is a businessman, first and foremost," she explained. "His interests always supercede anything else."

"Even promises?"

"Even promises."

"Joseph isn't the most moral fellow, is he?"

Odd, she thought, how his words mirrored her thoughts so precisely. "Something, I believe, you understand completely."

He met her gaze without flinching. "As do you."

Laura couldn't argue with him there. Ruby's lack of morality was her defining characteristic.

"By heirs," Michael said, "I assume you mean Vincent Bickham's children?"

Laura shook her head. "Vincent and Serena had no children. To my knowledge there are no other relatives. Believe it or not, he left his entire fortune to the surviving employees of his marble factory. The factory itself closed its doors sixteen years ago when he retired, but apparently Vincent kept in touch with them."

"How many are left?"

"Thirteen."

"And they say thirteen's an unlucky number."

"Not in this case. When all of Vincent's property and his stocks and bonds are liquidated, before taxes they should each receive a little over four million dollars."

Michael gave a low whistle. "Now I know why they were so careful about who they chose to dispose of Vincent's belongings."

"You would think that, wouldn't you? But Joseph told me they were more concerned with how Vincent was presented to the public than they were about how Joseph would handle the distribution of the proceeds. Joseph couldn't get over it. Frankly, I can't, either. Here were these thirteen men, each of them staring a small fortune in the face, and they would quibble endlessly about what was to be written about Vincent in any promotion surrounding the sale of his property. According to them, Vincent made it a pleasure to go to work each day.

He always greeted each employee by name, and he paid them well and provided generously for their retirement. They insisted he be treated with no less respect, now that he was gone."

"Not many employers inspire such devotion in their employees," Michael commented.

Joseph surely didn't, Laura thought. Oh, he paid his workers well enough, but only because he himself was ignorant of the work to be done. Any devotion he inspired was through fear of how he might retaliate if displeased.

Of course, she wasn't about to say that out loud. Ruby wouldn't waste more than a second or two thinking about the welfare of anyone but herself. Laura knew exactly what her alter ego would say in response to such a comment.

"No, they don't. Nor should they need to. You ask me, Vincent was a fool. He should have paid his employees the minimum he could get away with. And he should have spent every penny he had. You might not be able to take it with you, but you can sure have fun with it while you're here."

There was a grimness to the set of Michael's mouth, but his voice sounded light and unconcerned when he spoke. "I can't disagree with you. I'm sure Joseph doesn't, either."

"Trust me. He doesn't."

"Marble," Michael mused, his brow furrowing. "I thought the bulk of the marble quarried in this country was in Vermont."

"Vincent didn't make his fortune quarrying marble. He came home from World War II and built a factory that produced marbles. Plural."

"Marbles?"

"Marbles," Laura confirmed. "Little, round, multicolored spheres. The kind kids play with. The kind you shoot with your thumb and forefinger."

Michael burst out laughing. "Marbles?"

She couldn't help laughing herself. It did sound ridiculous. "I kid you not."

"Just how many marbles would a man have to manufacture in order to make a fortune?"

"A frightening number of them. But in Vincent's case, he was also a canny investor."

Michael shook his head. "So the man made marbles."

"He did indeed. And in his spare time he worked in his garden. It's my understanding that people came from miles around to see it."

"He must have been some gardener for people to travel this road."

"I only know what I was told," Laura said. "Besides, maybe the road was in better shape then. Apparently, after his wife died five years ago, Vincent lost interest in pretty much everything. He and Serena were devoted to each other for more than fifty years."

"Not many marriages last five years these days, let alone fifty."

She stared off into the distance, recalling a time when she'd hoped to spend fifty-plus years with Jacob. It didn't hurt as much as it used to, to think of him and the plans they had made, the dreams they'd shared. She was slowly learning that there was a kernel of truth in the old saying about time healing all wounds. Whether she wanted it to or not.

Of course, she didn't dream anymore. And she didn't plan much beyond the next job. To do either was to risk having them snatched away, cruelly and without warning. It went without saying that she'd cordoned off her heart, as well, the way a theater reserved its best seats, to be offered by invitation only. It hurt too much to love, to feel, so she didn't do either anymore. The only feeling she nurtured was her need to rid the streets of bad guys.

And now that need was fading. What would happen if it disappeared altogether? Would she actually consider dreaming, planning, maybe even—and her heart faltered at the thought—allowing herself to fall in love again? The notion seemed as incredible as it was disloyal. Especially since, barring her contact officers, the only men she'd associated with in recent years had hardly been glittering examples of the male species. Case in point was the man at her side.

"That's true," she said, her voice subdued as she recalled the unwanted emotions Michael Corsi stirred in her. "They don't."

After what seemed forever, they reached the crest of a hill. Abruptly the forest disappeared and a clearing came into view. In the center sat a huge mansion enclosed by an iron lattice-work fence. Michael brought the truck to a halt. For a long minute both of them just sat there, staring.

"Incredible," he murmured.

"You can say that again," Laura replied.

"I've never seen anything like it."

"I have. In late-night horror movies."

"Talk about your fixer-uppers," Michael said. "This one is a doozy."

"And a half," she agreed.

Rust coated the spikes of the iron fence. The hinges of the main gate had obviously rusted through, because it slanted inward at a drunken angle. The house itself, a three-story edifice, was straight out of a Gothic novel, its stone weathered to a dull black. Drawn shutters, dark-green paint flaking, made it look even more dank and gloomy. Ivy crawled everywhere along the walls, looking for all the world like a widow's shroud. Or, in this case, a widower's.

Laura let her gaze rove to the rounded turrets. She half expected to see bats circling. The gardens and the circular driveway, what was left of them, anyway, were a tangle of shapeless hedges, weeds and, here and there, thigh-high grass. One lone rhododendron bush, at least six feet tall and just as wide, sat to the right of the front door. Amazingly it was in bloom, the splash of brilliant violet adding color to a mostly monochromatic scene.

She wondered how long it would take for the encroaching weeds and ivy to reclaim the remainder of the grounds, and shivered. In a year or two, maybe three, it would look just like the pictures of Sleeping Beauty's castle she'd seen in the storybooks she'd read as a child.

"Hard to believe people used to come from miles around to view this garden," Michael murmured. "You sure there's electricity and running water?"

"That's what the caretaker told Joseph."

Michael gave a harsh laugh. "Caretaker? If I was the caretaker of this place, I wouldn't admit it in front of witnesses."

"He was appointed after Vincent's death," Laura said.

"So Vincent Bickham made his fortune manufacturing marbles." Michael shook his head. "You ask me, somewhere along the way he definitely lost his own. How could he let this place get so run-down?"

"I've heard grief can do that to people," Laura murmured.

"Let me get this straight," he said. "*This* is the estate Joseph spent months negotiating for? These grounds, and the contents of that mausoleum, are worth millions of dollars? In my opinion, somebody has just pulled something big over on our boss. Not to mention those thirteen heirs, who, by the looks of things, are going to be receiving a good deal less than four million dollars apiece."

Laura surveyed the scene in front of them again. She could only imagine Joseph's anger if he had been lied to.

"If those directions of yours were correct," she said, "this is it. The man Joseph sent to check out the place assured him that, even though it was a little run-down on the outside, the contents inside were immaculate."

"If this is what he calls a little run-down, I'd hate to think what he calls immaculate."

"All I know is what he told Joseph."

"Let's hope, for his sake, that he wasn't exaggerating."

Apparently, Michael had had the same thought she had.

"You know," she said, cocking her head and studying the house once more, "at second glance, it really isn't all that bad. Some spit and polish, and this place could be a showcase."

Michael gave a contemptuous snort. "More like a couple of backhoes, a dozen machetes and some sandblasters." After giving the place the once-over the same way she had, he added, "But maybe you're right. With the proper work, it could be stunning."

"Something we actually agree on."

"Will wonders never cease?"

Laura sat up straight in her seat. "This might sound outlandish, but give it some thought before you make your decision. Maybe *you* should consider snapping this place up."

"Me?" He looked taken aback.

"Yes, you."

"Trying to get rid of me?"

She gave him a blithe smile. "Why would I want to do that?" Not waiting for a response she didn't expect him to offer, she said, "I'm serious, Michael. A place like this would give you the status you crave. It would show people how well you're doing."

"I don't think so."

"Why not?"

"Status means nothing, if no one can find their way out here to see how well I'm doing."

"I bet the price is right," she said.

"Even if it was, and even if I could afford it, I'm not interested."

"Can I ask why?"

"It's a little too permanent for me."

She studied him for a minute. "No permanent things and no permanent people in your life. Is that it?"

"That's it," he agreed.

"Because…?" she prompted.

He shrugged. "It's not exciting."

"Do you own your own home now?"

"No, I rent. That way if I get bored with a place I can just move. Plus, someone else has to pay for the upkeep."

"Variety is the spice of life?" she asked.

"Absolutely."

And the man said he didn't have commitment issues. Someone was seriously deluded here, and it wasn't her.

"You feel that way about jobs, too?" she asked.

"I go where the top dollar is. Money is the one thing that never bores me."

She gave him the response her role required. "Another point we agree on."

"At this rate we'll be bosom buddies by the end of the day."

She crinkled her nose. "I wouldn't count on it."

Michael's laughter held genuine enjoyment. "Neither would I."

In spite of his faults—and they were legion—Laura couldn't help admiring his sense of humor. Not many people possessed the ability to laugh at themselves.

Thankfully, he spared her any further introspection by pointing out the Mercedes that was parked to the right of the front door. A man sat in the front seat.

"Someone waiting for us?"

"That would be Howard Bracken," she said. "He's the lawyer in charge of the liquidation. He should have some keys for us."

"Why bother locking up?" Michael muttered. "Who in their right mind would come all the way out here, just to rob the place? I doubt many people even know it exists."

"Why don't we just go get the keys from Howard Bracken?" Laura suggested.

Michael carefully drove past the leaning front gate and around the circular driveway. He parked behind the Mercedes, and they both climbed to the ground. After so many hours spent sitting, Laura was grateful for the opportunity to stretch.

Howard Bracken, a stern-looking, middle-aged man wearing a perfectly pressed gray suit, met them at the foot of the steps leading to the front door. Laura watched his sternness fade after he got an eyeful of her short skirt.

"Miss O'Toole," he said with a delighted smile. "It is indeed a pleasure to meet you." Turning to Michael, he added, his greeting noticeably less warm, "And you must be Mr. Corsi."

Laura turned Ruby's practiced charm on the man. "I can't tell you how much we appreciate you going out of your way to meet us here. Especially considering the state of things."

"Don't be discouraged," Howard Bracken said. "I have a feeling that Mr. Merrill will be very pleased with what you find inside. Very pleased, indeed. Would you care to follow me?"

The lawyer preceded them up the stone stairs, inserted a key and pulled on the heavy oak door. With a loud creaking noise that sounded suspiciously like a shriek, it slowly opened.

She had taken only one step, when Michael closed a hand around her upper arm, forestalling her. Ignoring the questioning look she shot him, he called, "Mr. Bracken? Mind if I confer with my colleague for a minute?"

A look of annoyance crossed Howard Bracken's face in the instant before he composed it into a mask of urbanity. He bowed his head.

"Of course not, Mr. Corsi. Take your time."

Steering her by the elbow, Michael led her over to the truck.

"What's the point of all this?" she hissed, glaring at him.

Michael leaned forward. Speaking in a low voice, he asked, "You sure you want to go in there?"

She blinked. "Why wouldn't I?"

"Doesn't he seem a little too eager to you?" He nodded to where Howard Bracken stood, pointedly gazing at his watch. "To show us around, I mean."

The citrusy aroma of Michael's aftershave tickled her nose, and the warmth of his skin made the hairs stand up on her arm. Laura took a step back. Michael was getting a little too close for comfort. Her comfort.

"Of course he's eager. Like us, he's traveled miles to get here. And our detour made us late. He probably wants to get back to his office as soon as possible. I don't blame him."

"Well, I have a different take on the situation."

Laura heaved an exasperated sigh. "And what take would that be?"

"Ever see the old Bugs Bunny cartoon, where the evil scientist invites Bugs into his dark, creepy mansion and then proceeds to try to use him in his vile experiments?''

Laura just stood there, staring at him. ''You're kidding, right?''

''Why should I be kidding? We are in the middle of nowhere, aren't we? And we do live in a violent world. Neither one of us has ever seen Howard Bracken before. Who knows? Maybe that man on the steps is an imposter, and the real Howard Bracken is gagged and bound in the trunk of that Mercedes.''

She opened her mouth, but no words emerged. Neither she nor Ruby had any idea what to say. Surely he couldn't be serious. Could he?

Michael's lips twitched, and the truth suddenly dawned on her. He *was* making fun of her.

''You have a warped sense of humor, Corsi,'' she snapped. ''And a terrible sense of timing.''

His eyes actually had the nerve to sparkle. ''I have to take my enjoyment where I can find it.''

He was throwing her own words back in her face. What was worse, she knew she deserved it.

''Why are you doing this?'' she asked.

''I just wanted to liven things up.''

''And you chose *now* to do it?''

Michael shrugged. ''No time like the present.''

''Joseph is paying Howard Bracken by the hour, you know.''

''He can afford a few spare moments. Besides, since small talk usually gets us into trouble, I thought I'd try humor. You smile a lot, Ruby, but I don't think you laugh all that much.''

It surprised her that he had noticed. Her internal warning system went on alert. Michael Corsi was, in all probability, the most dangerous opponent she had ever faced. More dangerous than the mythical terrors he'd described awaiting them inside the Bickham mansion. More dangerous, even, than Joseph. Because every time he annoyed her, or otherwise sent her emotions spiraling, she promptly lost her professionalism.

The best defense, she told herself, was a good offense. "You've been doing precious little laughing yourself."

"All the better to laugh now."

"In case you haven't noticed, I'm still not laughing."

"That's because you won't let yourself," he chided. "You have to admit it's more fun to laugh than to cry."

She couldn't imagine this man crying over anything. Unless, that is, he was sent back to jail.

"And since we're going to be stuck with each other for the next few days, we might as well laugh? Is that what you're saying?"

"By George, I think she's got it!" He smiled broadly at her.

Oh, no you don't, Laura told herself fiercely. You're not going to charm me into liking you. Not today. Not tomorrow. Not ever.

Framing his hands around his mouth, Michael called, "We're ready, Mr. Bracken."

Even though she knew he had only been pulling her leg, even though she knew that the stern man in the gray suit waiting for them was a lawyer and not a mad scientist in disguise, Laura couldn't help peering cautiously around the door as they went inside.

From behind her came a low, knowing chuckle. Gritting her teeth, she suppressed an extremely childish urge to kick Michael in the shins. Then, shaking her head, she chuckled at her own foolishness. Ruby might not have a sense of humor, but Laura did. If ever there was a time to laugh at herself, this was it.

"See?" she heard him say. "It's always better to laugh."

Chapter 5

They worked straight through dinner. Exhaustion had Laura's feet dragging and her shoulders slumping as she climbed into Michael's truck for the drive to the motel Joseph had booked for them. More powerful than her fatigue, however, were the hunger pangs squeezing her stomach. She couldn't wait to eat.

As the crow flies it was only ten miles from the Bickham estate to the nearest town. Given, however, the condition of the road leading from Vincent Bickham's property to the main road, and coupled with Michael's caution driving it, it took them nearly thirty minutes to get there. By that time Laura was nearly salivating.

The town proper featured a lovely tree-shaded park, a square replete with gurgling fountain and statues of founding fathers and a main street lined with quaint Victorian storefronts boasting names like Blue Bonnet Bakery, Kunst Five and Dime and Joe's Butcher Shop.

"Oh, stop, please," she cried, her delight forcing her hunger from her mind.

Michael slanted a glance at her. "It's been a long day,

Ruby. Could we save the window-shopping for another time?''

She stemmed a surge of impatience. She didn't want to shop; far from it.

''Indulge me, Michael. Please?''

''You're the boss.''

With a long-suffering sigh he pulled to the curb. The truck had barely come to a halt when Laura climbed out, smoothed down her skirt, and, despite her aching feet, set off down the street. She moved from store to store, her pace picking up as she avidly studied every detail of the gaily colored buildings. To her surprise, halfway down the block Michael fell into step beside her.

''Interesting place,'' he said.

''For the record,'' she said, ''I'm not window-shopping. I'm studying the architecture.''

''I realize that. Now.''

As apologies went, it wasn't much, but it would have to do. Her hand swept out, indicating the store in front of them. It was painted a pale lilac and outlined with intricately carved gingerbread molding.

''I just love old things, don't you?'' she enthused.

''That's why I auction off antiques,'' he replied dryly.

Except for a few people strolling here and there, the street was empty. Apparently, according to the signs in the windows, everyone closed up shop promptly at 5:00 p.m., and it was now almost eight.

Ignoring his sarcasm, she moved on to the next store. ''I feel like we've driven through a time warp. Any minute now I expect these doors to burst open, and we'll see ladies come strolling out in long skirts and bustles, accompanied by men in dark suits and high hats.''

Unable to conceal the depth of her excitement, Laura smiled up at him. Michael didn't smile back. Instead, his body seemed to tense, and he went utterly still. A sudden emotion blazed in his eyes, causing her smile to falter and her heart to skip a beat. Powerless to look away, she watched in fascination while his throat worked and a nerve pulsed in his temple.

"You're so beautiful." He spoke as if he were in the midst of a revelation.

Had he uttered the words in his customary insolent drawl, and with that knowing smirk that never failed to send her temper soaring, she wouldn't have felt a thing. But the absolute sincerity in his voice, and in his eyes, told her he meant every word.

Laura's breath caught, and something deep inside her unfurled and went all soft and malleable. A pulse of pleasure, pure and unadulterated, the strength of which she hadn't experienced in years, radiated slowly outward from her center. It left her feeling hot and definitely bothered as they both continued to stand there awkwardly, neither seeming to know what to do. Or say.

Don't! she wanted to cry. Don't look at me that way. Because if you do, I won't be able to…

To what? Do her job? Handle it? Resist him? Walk away? Ridiculous notions, each and every one of them.

What had happened to the man who had practically bent over backward assuring her he didn't find her in the least attractive? What had happened to the woman who thought he was the most annoying creature on the face of the earth? And why, oh, why, had she ever asked him to stop? First it was his hand on her breast, now this. What could possibly happen next? Her knees nearly buckled at the thought.

The last person to tell her she was beautiful had been her husband. And the look in Jacob's eyes when he spoke those precious words had been tender, and loving. The look in Michael's eyes wasn't tender, and it wasn't loving. It was hot and needful and demanding. For Laura to respond to it, the way she had, seemed like a betrayal of everything that had been good and honorable about her marriage.

It was just hormones, she told herself, as what was becoming an all-too-familiar guilt filled her. It certainly wasn't her admiration for the man at her side. Her reaction was purely chemical, with no underpinnings to give it any meaning or depth. As such, it was meaningless to her.

Sincere or not, she couldn't let him get to her like this. Not only did it complicate matters unnecessarily, she was simply not in the market for even the most fleeting of relationships. And he had made it more than clear that fleeting was all he would ever offer. When the time came that she did begin looking for a suitable candidate—*if* she ever did—the man would not only have to stimulate her sexual nature, he would first have to earn her admiration and respect. He would have to have scruples. And goals more far-reaching than making an easy buck.

In short, not Michael.

Finally, mercifully, she found her voice. "Th-thank you," she stammered.

Immediately she wished she could call the words back. Th-thank you? Had she actually said, Th-thank you?

It didn't help that she had fallen totally out of character yet again. Nor did it help, knowing that Ruby would have handled the situation with aplomb. She would have said something light and meaningless to dispel the tension. That, in turn, would have elicited one of two reactions from Michael: laughter or irritation. Either was preferable to the way he was looking at her now.

Thank goodness her contact officer couldn't see—and hear—her. If he could, she had no doubt he would pull her off the case faster than she could draw her gun. That is, if she had been wearing it, instead of stashing it away in a suitcase.

She was making too many mistakes. She really needed that vacation.

One thing was certain. The next time she went undercover, she was going to create a character just like herself. This was one folly she didn't care to repeat.

Michael gave a strangled laugh. "Sorry about that. I don't know what came over me. It must be this place. It gets to you, doesn't it?"

"Yes," she agreed, eager to grasp at any excuse to change the mood. "Yes, it does."

He tore his gaze from hers and looked at the sign hanging above their heads. "This store looks interesting."

Still unsettled, Laura read the sign hanging below a black-and-white-striped awning. E. J. Fulton, Haberdasher.

"I've never seen an actual haberdashery before," she said. "I thought they disappeared years ago."

"Apparently this one hasn't."

Though she had lost all interest in the local architecture, she continued walking down the street. Michael followed, staying a pace or two behind. The distance didn't stop her from feeling the heat emanating from his body or from smelling his scent, which, after the long day they'd just spent, was not of soap and aftershave but of perspiration and hard work. Surprisingly, she didn't find it at all unpleasant.

Every now and then Michael would stop to point out an item of interest—once he even openly ogled an attractive woman who passed them. Laura, still so distracted she barely heard half of what he said, would simply nod in reply and move on. At the end of the street they turned around and headed back to the truck.

She felt somewhat composed by the time she engaged her seat belt. For his part Michael seemed to have forgotten the incident entirely. He seemed relaxed, unconcerned. What was he thinking? Feeling?

The man was such a mass of contradictions. Would she ever understand him? Did she even want to try?

For reasons of his own that she couldn't begin to fathom, except that maybe he was bored, Michael was deliberately trying to keep her off balance. It was the only explanation that made sense. The only explanation that accounted for his rapid, and unsettling, mood swings.

He was toying with her, like a cat with a mouse. Every time she thought she'd escaped, he'd come bounding around a corner and pounce on her again. Well, she had news for him. She was no longer going to serve as his source of entertainment.

This mouse was going on strike. If he needed to be amused, let him watch television. Or read a book.

If he could read.

For some reason, the uncharitable thought made her feel better.

Laura stared out the windshield and made a mental vow. She was tired, hungry and cranky, and definitely prone to making a serious misstep. Until she got some food in her belly and a good night's sleep, until she felt more centered and in control of both her actions and her reactions, she was going to keep her gaze pointed straight ahead and her thoughts a careful blank.

And if Michael came at her sideways, out of the range of her peripheral vision? She'd reach out a hand and swat him. Hard.

Buskey's Motel was located a half mile outside town.

The sun was just beginning to sink below the horizon when Antonio pulled into the parking lot. Despite the favorable light that softened the focus of the building, like pantyhose over a camera lens, it was readily apparent that the place possessed none of the charm of the town they had left behind them. Across the road, the convenience store, with its gas pumps and gravel parking lot, looked more inviting.

Instead of being depressed by the sight, he actually felt relieved. At least this place wouldn't inspire him to make any more stupid moves or remarks. Or so he fervently hoped.

Buskey's might be rustic. It might even be a little bit seedy. But it was definitely hopping. By all appearances it not only housed out-of-towners, it also served as the local watering hole. In a place where every other establishment closed its doors promptly at five, it and the convenience store held exclusive rights to the night crowd. While only one or two cars were parked in front of the actual rooms, the spaces were filled in front of the main building, where a neon sign reading Lounge blinked in the window.

Antonio shot a hooded glance at the woman at his side. Ruby hadn't spoken a word since they'd left town.

His hands tightened around the steering wheel, and he felt a nerve pulsating in his temple. What, after all, was there left for her to say? He'd certainly said a mouthful.

What was she thinking? He sure as hell couldn't tell.

Her silence was disturbing on more than one level. Not only did it leave him feeling naked and exposed, the way he had in the minutes following his impulsive utterance, it downright worried him. Because he had fully expected the Ruby he was coming to know to have laughed in his face at his romantic foolishness. Instead, she seemed as rattled by the whole episode as he was. And that didn't compute. Not at all. Ruby O'Toole was not a woman who was ever at a loss for words where a man was concerned.

Until now, that is. He hadn't even been able to elicit a snide remark from her by openly ogling a woman on the street—the one action, ironically, that had been appropriate for him in his role as Michael to make.

Antonio still didn't understand what had gotten into him. All sorts of explanations sprang to his mind when he tried to reason and rationalize it out. The way the fading sunlight had silhouetted her face, making her look like an angel. The glow of almost childlike enjoyment in her eyes as she moved from store to store. His sheer exhaustion from driving all day, having his truck batted around on that shameful disgrace for a road, and then putting in several hours of toil at the Bickham mansion. The toll of having to remain in character for more than twelve hours straight. Temporary insanity.

Even more insane was the realization that those three little words—you're so beautiful—were the most honest words he'd ever spoken to a woman. In the dim, distant recesses of his mind, he couldn't escape the ridiculous notion that, when he had offered them up to her, he'd been saying so much more.

It was one thing to want Ruby physically. It was quite another to offer her a piece—not of his heart, surely, but of himself. Antonio wasn't in the position to offer a woman anything; even a woman like Ruby. And neither was Michael.

If only she had blithely dismissed his words, the fragile, unfledged emotion that had consumed him would have died a merciful death.

But she hadn't. And so that feeling still had its hold on him. As a result, he was terrified for them both.

Because there was only one explanation that made sense. On some level, whether Ruby was willing to acknowledge it or not, she wasn't as immune to him as she professed to be. She might even, he thought, his heart thudding, be attracted to him.

Antonio gave himself a mental shake. If he was susceptible to her dubious charms and she was to his, it could only spell trouble with a capital T. For him, because he could no longer maintain his objectivity around her—hell, he wondered if he ever could. And for Ruby, because if Joseph ever suspected that her loyalties were divided... That thought didn't bear finishing.

No matter what he was feeling, or whether that feeling was reciprocated, he had still been wrong for speaking so impulsively. Never before had he said something so foolishly stupid, especially while on a job. With three carelessly spoken words, he had put the entire case in jeopardy. To act any further on his feelings would only invite disaster.

He had to make things right between them again. Which meant he had to kill any positive feelings she might have for him. Even if it made getting information from her difficult if not next to impossible.

Antonio climbed out of the truck. He heard the slam of Ruby's door, followed by the tap of her heels across the pavement. She met him in front of the main office. He knew exactly what he had to do.

"*This* is the suitable accommodation Joseph found for us?" he asked, pasting a look of revulsion on his face.

Ruby looked down at the paper in her hand, then over at the sign on the edge of the parking lot. "This is it."

"It isn't exactly a four-star hotel."

She shrugged. "I've stayed in worse."

He allowed his lip to curl. "Alone or with company?"

"Both."

When she didn't rise to his bait, Antonio knew he had to do something to shake her out of her distraction, but fast. The less she analyzed, the better off they both would be.

He raised an eyebrow. "But it's a motel."

"So?"

"It's a motel, Ruby," he repeated, stressing the *M*. "Motel not hotel."

"Yes," she replied, her voice still dangerously impassive. "I realize that."

"You mean you're actually going to stay here?"

A sigh of impatience was his reward. "Why shouldn't I?"

"Don't take this the wrong way, Ruby, but you're just not the motel type."

She turned to him then. "Unless, that is, as you already insinuated, I was with someone who was renting the room by the hour?" she said sweetly.

Yes! Now they were getting somewhere. He held up his hands, as if in surrender. "I didn't say that."

"You didn't have to. Your meaning was more than clear."

Instead of trying to deny it, he said, "You sure there isn't any other place for us to stay?"

Ruby extended an arm, encompassing their surroundings. "In case you haven't noticed, we are in the middle of nowhere. Few, if any, major hotel chains build in the middle of nowhere. Not enough customers, you see."

"I'm aware of that." Antonio tried to make his voice as ingratiating and grating as possible. "Believe it or not, I was thinking of you."

"And just what were you thinking of me?"

"You, Ruby, are a woman who likes her creature comforts. Do you deny that?"

"Of course not."

"Motels aren't renowned for their creature comforts."

Suddenly she seemed weary. "I'm a realist, Michael. I didn't expect to be spending the next few days in the lap of luxury."

"So you really won't mind staying here?" he pressed.

"I believe I told you when we met that I'm deadly serious about my work. For the sake of that work, I can endure anything for a few days."

Her pointed look told him he was one of those things.

Antonio felt a surge of triumph. A few seconds later, the triumph receded, leaving a peculiar hollowness in its wake. Unaccountably he felt a vague intuition that, by his actions, he had just lost far more than he'd gained. Although what it was he could have lost remained hidden from him.

Ruby settled her hands on her hips. "And I'm not going to let you stand there and get away with telling me that *my* reaction to staying here was your only concern."

"Okay, so I'm not into self-denial any more than you are," Antonio replied, shaking off his ambivalence. He'd gotten what he wanted, and it was time to exploit it further. Ruby might as well learn up front that Michael was as vain, self-centered and fond of creature comforts as she was. Truth was, they'd make a great pair. If she wasn't so loyal to Joseph, that is. And if Michael actually existed.

But the pairing that made absolutely no sense and defied rational explanation, no matter how hot and bothered she made him, was Ruby and Antonio.

A bored-looking clerk checked them in. After parking in front of their appointed rooms, Michael wrestled Laura's suitcases from the back of his truck and followed her to her door.

She wasn't surprised that Joseph had booked them adjoining rooms, but she had hoped to achieve more space between them. Oh, well, a wall was going to have to suffice. She was exhausted, and once she'd filled her empty belly she should have little trouble falling asleep. At least while she was sleeping, Michael wouldn't be able to disturb her equilibrium. Unless, that is—and at this point she wouldn't put anything past him—he somehow managed to invade her dreams.

The possibility made her shudder.

"Cold?" he asked.

Anything but. "Just an unpleasant thought."

Laura decided there was no way he could disturb her dreams if she didn't want him to. She would simply put pleasant images into her brain in the moments before she fell asleep, and she would have nothing to worry about.

It took several twists of her key to get the lock to yield to her efforts. She was reaching for the door handle when she heard Michael say, "I don't think the surprise waiting behind this door will be nearly as pleasant as what we found at the Bickham estate."

While the outside of the mansion had been a preservationist's nightmare, the inside had been surprisingly immaculate. The rooms had all been full of uncounted treasures. Laura had been more than a little relieved to discover that Joseph would, indeed, be pleased with his acquisition.

They had asked Howard Bracken about the apparent contradiction between the outside of the building and its interior. According to the lawyer, Serena Bickham had not only worked with the architect to design the home, she had furnished and decorated every room personally. After her death, Vincent had been adamant that it continue to be kept as she intended. As for the lawn and garden, they were his, and nobody but himself was going to work them. He would get back to them someday, he had always insisted. But someday had never come.

Laura understood only too well. For a year after Jacob and Jason died, it had been such an effort simply to breathe, let alone move. It was only over the past two years—and very gradually at that—that she had started reclaiming the joy in treasured activities like reading and sketching.

Yes, loneliness and grief *could* do strange things to people. It had turned Vincent Bickham into a virtual recluse. And it was making Laura search for character in a man who had none.

"What?" she said, keeping her voice light. "No jokes about boogeymen hiding in closets or under the bed?"

The distaste on his face was plain for her to see. "Not even a comedian could joke about this place."

"Give it up, Michael," she said, pushing the door inward and reaching for the light switch. "We're staying here. Accept it."

She was beginning to think she'd imagined that moment on the street in town. At least with Michael back to his old, irritating self, she no longer felt that traitorous weakness.

The interior of the motel room was as she had expected. Two double beds covered by matching polyester bedspreads that were patterned in a forest print. A worn green carpet underneath her feet. A long, scarred dresser lining one wall, with the television bolted to it. A round table and two chairs in the corner.

What she hadn't expected—but now realized that she should have—was the connecting door to the adjoining room. Michael's room.

Joseph was certainly doing his best to throw the two of them together. And to give them the chance to get much closer, if they so desired. Discreetly, of course.

At least the room was clean. Next to some of the tenements her police work had taken her to in New York City, it might even be called a palace. She certainly wouldn't have to worry about cockroaches and other assorted creatures scurrying across the floor while she slept.

No, the only creature she needed to worry about was the two-legged variety holding her luggage and looking decidedly weary. Though she fought it, the sight of his tired eyes tugged at her heartstrings.

"Where do you want me to put these?" he asked.

She nodded to one of the beds and placed her purse on the table. "There, please. I'll unpack later."

"Don't waste your time," he said under his breath. "There's probably not enough drawer space."

Laura was too tired to have Ruby's temper rise to the comment.

With a grunt of effort, Michael heaved her suitcases onto the bed. Then, placing his hands in the small of his back, he stretched, arching his back and neck. Laura angled her head down at the floor and pretended she wasn't watching.

The growl of her stomach was loud in the quiet room. She didn't want to ask, but she knew politeness required it. Michael had toted her luggage all the way in here.

"Would you like to join me in the lounge for dinner?"

To her relief, he shook his head. "I'm not really hungry. I think I'll go for a quick jog to unwind, and then I'm going to bed. What time do you want to get started in the morning?"

"Eight o'clock okay with you?"

"Fine. Do you want to meet for breakfast at seven?"

"Seven it is."

He headed for the door, then turned back. Yet again he asked, "It really doesn't bother you to stay here?"

Laura was tired and cranky. All she wanted was a bite to eat so she could get out of this silly, impractical outfit and into her nightgown and that bed, even if the mattress did sag in the middle and the pillows were as plump as an unleavened loaf of bread. Why did he insist on going round and round over a conversation she'd thought was over long ago? Enough was enough already.

"Look, Michael, we're here to do a job. We'll only be using these rooms to shower and sleep. For that small amount of time, I'll be just fine. After all, it's not like I'm planning to conduct a wild affair here."

He looked around the room. "Trust me. A man would need a good dose of Viagra to want to conduct a wild affair here."

She didn't want to respond—with all her heart she yearned to remain mute—but Ruby, no matter how exhausted, never would have let that remark go unchallenged.

"You mean, if I did a striptease right here and right now, you would be totally unaffected?"

Michael's face went blank, and a heavy silence settled over the room. Endless seconds passed as the two of them stood there, neither quite meeting the other's gaze. Then he drew a ragged breath and thrust a not-quite-steady hand through his hair.

"I'm too tired for any more verbal sparring right now, Ruby. Would you mind if we continued this conversation in the morning?"

The relief she felt that he hadn't taken her up on her challenge wasn't as great as she had expected it to be. Even more surprising was the loneliness that filled her when he walked to the door.

"Good night," he said without turning. "Don't forget to use the chain." He closed the door softly behind him.

Laura stared after him, bemused, as the realization hit her. She'd scared him off. She'd actually scared him off. Apparently Michael Corsi had reached his limit. Interesting.

Unfortunately, now was not the time for further analysis. No matter how badly she wanted to eat, no matter how desperately she wanted to change into something more comfortable, both activities would have to wait. She had work to do.

Five minutes later she heard Michael's front door open and close. Cautiously she parted the curtain and peeked outside. Clad in shorts and a T-shirt, a pair of running shoes on his feet, he stretched in the darkened parking lot.

"Come on, come on," she muttered, and let out a long breath when he finally took off. When his retreating figure disappeared from sight, she let the curtain fall into place and got busy working on the lock to the connecting door.

Chapter 6

She found the gun tucked beneath his Hanes briefs.

The briefs were in the suitcase lying open on one of the double beds in a room that, except for the furniture being on opposite walls, was identical to hers. Further inspection revealed the ammunition that had been tucked into the toe of one sock.

Frowning, Laura picked up the .45 and examined it closely. It was big but flat, thus easily concealed under almost any clothing.

A shiver raced up her spine. The reaction had nothing to do with her being squeamish about guns. Quite the contrary. She was comfortable with their heft and with the feel of their cool metal. She was even comfortable with firing, when necessary, and was a crack shot. Her knowledge of firearms, and her respect for their power, was the source of her unease. The gun she held was one you didn't fool around with. While, in the wrong hands, any weapon could be lethal, this one was lethal to the extreme. It asked no questions and took no prisoners.

Two things immediately came to her mind. The first was

that, as a convicted felon, it was illegal for Michael to possess any type of firearm. Which meant he didn't have a license to carry it. The second was that he had transported it over state lines, also illegal without a license. Of course, neither offense was likely to bother him. He'd made it more than clear that he was willing to skirt the law whenever it served his purpose.

So what *was* his purpose for packing a gun? Was it a macho thing with him, or was he anticipating trouble? They were out in the middle of nowhere. What trouble could he possibly expect to find here?

A sudden thought unsettled her. Michael had gone for a jog. Alone. Was he meeting someone? If so, was that someone involved with Joseph and his drug dealings? How could she have been so foolish as to let him out of her sight? Tired or not, hungry or not, she should have followed him. But then, when would she have had a chance to search his room?

Laura gave an impatient shake of her head. It didn't make sense. Michael hadn't taken his gun with him. Surely, if he was meeting someone about an illegal activity, he wouldn't have gone to that meeting unprotected. It was possible he had another gun with him. But where he could have concealed it beneath those short shorts of his was beyond her.

Placing the .45 in the exact position she had found it, she crossed to the chair and picked up the jeans Michael had draped there. Whatever he was up to, and the gun in his suitcase proved it had to be no good, it was her job to discover it. She would have to keep a much closer eye on him from now on. And stick as close to him as his shadow.

As she thrust her hand into a pocket, a different kind of shiver from the one she'd felt when she'd picked up the gun traveled up her spine. She told herself it was because she was handling an item of clothing that, just minutes before, had rested intimately against his body. It certainly wasn't because Michael still had the power to affect her on a sexual level. The veil had been ripped from her eyes. She was no longer capable of nurturing any more illusions about him. And that was a good thing.

His wallet was still in his back pocket. No surprises there. Michael carried several hundred dollars in cash, a valid Pennsylvania driver's license and a platinum master card. She wondered if the credit card had been obtained legally.

The only other item of interest in the room was the book on the bedside table. Laura reached down to pick it up and got the shock of her life when she saw the title. *The Grapes of Wrath* by John Steinbeck. Inexplicably, they were both reading the same book, although Michael appeared to be about fifty pages ahead of her.

She shouldn't be surprised that he was a reader. After all, he was a crossword puzzle devotee. A person didn't get to be proficient at crossword puzzles without doing extensive reading. Still, she never would have pegged him as the type to read classics. And she was honest enough to admit her dismay that they actually did have something in common.

It just proved how full of surprises people could always be. Goodness knew, since she had met him—was it only three days ago?—Michael had been full of endless surprises, most of them dangerous to her peace of mind.

A glance at her watch produced a sense of urgency that had her quickening her movements. After replacing the book on the bedside table, Laura checked the rest of the room to make sure that everything was as she had found it. Then, after closing and locking the dividing door behind her, she headed for the truck. If Michael discovered her there, she could always claim she had lost an earring and was searching for it.

Five minutes later, having discovered nothing else except that Michael had a penchant for Baby Ruth candy bars and bluegrass music, she made her aching feet drag her across the road to the convenience store. Stomach growling louder than a mother grizzly defending her cub, she used the pay phone located beneath a streetlamp to call her contact officer.

Because they weren't secure, no calls were ever made on cell phones. Hotel room phones were likewise off-limits, as their use left an easily followable trail. Only pay phones offered the near-perfect security an undercover officer required while on the job.

After reporting her findings and the events of the day, Laura limped across the street to the lounge. It was dinnertime—finally—and woe be to anyone who got in her way.

Antonio ran hard through the streets of the town that had so captivated Ruby. He raced past the Victorian storefronts, past the gurgling fountain and the statues of the founding fathers, past the park, past two-story homes with lights blazing in the windows. Finally he was out in the quiet countryside on the road he'd traveled earlier to the Bickham estate. There were no more lights and no traffic, and the only sound, other than insects, was the pounding of his feet against the pavement.

He ran until sweat poured down his face and molded his T-shirt to his back. He ran until his sides ached, his knees screamed in protest, and he thought his lungs were about to burst. He ran as if the devil himself was on his heels.

With every step, he told himself that if he ran hard enough and fast enough and far enough, he would forget how Ruby had looked in that skintight outfit of hers. He would forget the way her hips had swayed when she'd climbed up into his truck. He would forget the sound of her laughter and the light in her eyes when she'd stared up at him in the middle of town while telling him how much she loved old things. He would forget what a fool he had made of himself.

And he would forget her offer, even if it had been made to get a rise out of him—pun intended—to do a striptease for him.

Abruptly he stopped running. Bending over, he balanced his palms against his thighs and gulped in deep breaths of air. Then, squaring his shoulders resolutely, he turned and, heart still racing, began a slow jog back to the motel. Because the simple truth was that there weren't enough miles between here and the edge of the world to drive *that* image out of his mind.

Besides, punishing his body for its weakness to Ruby wasn't

going to get the job done. And in the meantime, she was several miles away. Alone. Getting into who knew what kind of trouble.

Thirty minutes later Antonio stood at the pay phone outside the convenience store. After checking in with his contact officer, he dialed his older brother's phone number.

"It's about time you called," Carlo said. "We were starting to worry."

We were Antonio's five brothers and his sister. His was an extremely close family. Weekly dinners and daily phone conversations were the norm with them. Though they had grown accustomed to his frequent absences, and the silences that his undercover work necessitated, they had never liked it.

"Sorry, Carlo, but I was just sent in on a new job. I couldn't call any sooner."

"Where are you?"

Antonio fixed his gaze on Ruby's motel room. The lights were on, and he wondered if she had already finished her dinner. Was she at that very minute getting ready for bed? He refused to take his speculation any further. Thoughts like that would definitely rob him of his sleep, and he desperately needed the restorative powers of a good night's rest.

"Somewhere in southeastern West Virginia. That's all I can tell you."

"Job going well?"

Just how was the job going? Not the way he had expected it to, that was for sure. As a matter of fact, if he had to give himself a grade for his performance so far, it would be a dismal C-plus. On the positive side, he wasn't bored. He couldn't imagine himself ever being bored in Ruby's company. Irritated, yes. Exasperated beyond all measure, definitely. So aroused he thought his body might explode, absolutely. But never ever bored.

"As well as can be expected."

"Then what's bothering you?"

Antonio blinked. He should have known better than to think he could hide anything from his older brother. Not only was

Carlo chief of police in the town where he lived, he had practically raised Antonio after the death of their mother. There was precious little that escaped Carlo's sharp eyes and ears. None of his childhood antics had, anyway.

"You're a happily married man, right?" Antonio asked, already knowing the answer. Whenever he saw them, Carlo and Samantha appeared the picture of bliss.

"Yes, I am. Why do you ask?"

"I just assume that, as a happily married man, you should understand women."

It took Carlo a full minute to stop laughing. A full minute during which Antonio had to hold the phone away from his head to keep his ears from ringing.

"Okay," he muttered when silence finally reigned once more. "So that was a stupid assumption."

"Who is the woman you want to understand?" Carlo asked.

Without giving any particulars about the job, Antonio told Carlo about Ruby and all her seeming contradictions.

"You like this woman, don't you?"

A loaded question if Antonio had ever heard one. "*Like* isn't exactly the word I would use. We don't have that much in common." He thrust his fingers through his hair. "Hell, I don't even respect her."

"But she keeps you off balance."

"Put it this way. If I were a tightrope walker, I would definitely need a net."

"And you're attracted to her."

Antonio gave a long sigh. "That's the hell of it."

"Why does it bother you so much to feel that way?"

"Wouldn't it bother you?"

There was a brief pause. "Well, I am married."

"Seriously, Carlo. You're a cop. If you found yourself attracted to a woman who was the antithesis of everything you found admirable in a person, wouldn't it upset you?"

"Yes, I suppose it would."

"Well, there you have it."

''Especially if I were interested in something other than a one-night stand,'' Carlo added.

Antonio felt his back go up. ''What's that supposed to mean?''

''It means you've never asked my advice about a woman before.''

''So?''

''Don't you think that's significant?''

There were many advantages to coming from a large family. One of the major disadvantages was that his siblings tended to stick their big noses in his business whenever it pleased them to. And it pleased them a lot.

''No,'' Antonio replied with exaggerated patience, ''I don't. But obviously you do.''

''I do indeed.''

''You know I'm not into long-term relationships. My job doesn't permit it.''

''That's what Marco said, and look at him.''

''I'm not Marco.''

''No, you're not.'' Carlo's tone turned reflective. ''Maybe this woman who fascinates you so isn't what she appears to be. Have you ever thought of that?''

''And maybe,'' Antonio replied, ''that's just wishful thinking on your part.''

''You going to tell me you haven't wished the same thing a time or two?''

The door of the lounge opened, and a man sauntered over to one of the cars parked in the lot. Antonio didn't want to be standing there, in plain view under the convenience store's lights should Ruby be the next patron to exit. Nor did he want to continue the current conversation.

''Look, Carlo,'' he said hurriedly, ''I've got to go. I'll call you again as soon as I get the chance. Tell everyone I said hello.''

''Take care, brother. And watch your back.''

''I always do.''

Antonio crossed the street to the lounge. Choosing a window that was off to the side and away from the parked vehicles, he framed his face with his hands and peered inside. Whether by luck or by internal radar, the first person he saw was Ruby.

She was sitting in the rear of the room, well away from the crowded bar, whose patrons were mostly men. Her back was to the wall, and her attention was focused solely on her plate. The plate itself held a half-eaten steak, a large portion of broccoli and a baked potato. Even through the grimy window and the cigarette smoke filling the air inside like a low-lying fog, he could see the sour cream overflowing the slit that had been cut into the top of the potato. He licked his lips and even imagined he could taste it.

Contrary to popular belief that exercise released chemicals in the body that blunted hunger, his stomach growled. Loudly. And his mouth actually watered. Pavlov's dogs had nothing on his response to the sight of Ruby O'Toole digging into her dinner.

The way she was eating didn't help matters. As she had at lunchtime, she attacked her food with a gusto and an appreciation that made it hard for him to look away.

How could any one person enjoy eating so much?

His stomach growled again, and he had his answer.

Why had he told her he wasn't hungry? Because he had been desperate to get away from her, that was why.

He could always head inside and announce he had changed his mind. He could even pretend he didn't see her and sit at another table, if he didn't think he was ready just yet to handle her company. But he had something else to do, a task far more important than feeding his empty belly. He had a box of Baby Ruth bars stashed away in his truck. And, if he got desperate, there was always the convenience store.

Antonio was about to turn away, when he saw the two men approach her. He tensed and drew in a harsh breath. There was no mistaking their intent, just as there was no mistaking their youth and the cocky swaggers that life hadn't yet knocked out of them.

He didn't know what to think as he watched them flank her on either side before leaning toward her to deliver their spiel. He had a fair idea of what they were saying. He should; he'd uttered similar words, quite successfully, often enough himself.

Hey, gorgeous. What you doin', sittin' there all by your lonesome? The night's young. We're young. What say, after you're finished with your meal, the three of us cosy on up to the bar for a drink or two?

A part of him wanted to shoulder his way in there, grab them by the scruffs of their necks, then toss them out the door. Another part—the more sane part—waited breathlessly to see how Ruby would react.

To his surprise, she barely looked up from her plate. She didn't smile, and she didn't preen. Instead, she said something around a mouthful of steak that had the men heading straight back to the bar. They didn't even protest, just turned on their heels and walked meekly away, like scolded puppies with their tails between their legs.

What on earth had she said to them?

Even more interesting, the incorrigible flirt was no longer flirting. At least not tonight. The woman who had said she needed a man to take care of her had more than adequately taken care of herself.

Carlo's words echoed in Antonio's head. *Maybe this woman who fascinates you so isn't what she appears to be. Have you ever thought of that?*

He was thinking it now. Big-time.

There was a logical explanation for what he had witnessed, Antonio told himself. After all, she was a woman on her own in a strange town. Incorrigible flirt or not, she'd been around the block enough times to know that picking up two strangers in a bar was a fast ticket to getting raped. It was one thing for her to flirt outrageously with a man while in the safety of her lover's company. It was another thing altogether to do so here, while on her own.

As far as any relief he had felt when she'd sent those two

jerks packing, it was simply gratitude that no action had been required on his part. Because if they had given her trouble, he would have had to summon energy he didn't possess to straighten things out.

Antonio turned away from the window and headed back to their rooms. He had work to do, and time was running short. He had no idea that he was whistling.

He took one look at the still-unopened suitcases on the spare bed in Ruby's room and sighed. He sure as hell hoped she would order dessert, because it wasn't going to be easy going through all that.

Thank goodness she'd left her lights on. At least he wouldn't have to worry that she'd see them from the lounge and come to investigate.

The first suitcase he opened was filled with lingerie. Antonio made his mind a careful blank as his fingers sifted through slippery, silky underthings. Jaw clenched, he uttered a few choice epithets. For Pete's sake, he thought, gritting his teeth, did the woman have to order every item in the Victoria's Secret catalogue?

It was with more than a sense of relief that he moved on to the second suitcase. The items it contained were intriguing in a different way. He puzzled a bit over the worn pair of jeans and the sketch pad he found. Why had she brought them along? Both seemed out of character for her. When he found the book, he sat down hard on the edge of the other bed. What was Ruby doing reading *The Grapes of Wrath?*

If he had to imagine her reading material, he would have limited it to the area of glossy fashion magazines, maybe *Reader's Digest.* But a classic like *The Grapes of Wrath?* No way, no how would that ever have occurred to him.

When his fingers encountered the gun, he forgot all about the jeans, the sketch pad and Steinbeck.

Disbelieving, he raised the .44 to the light and examined its crudely shortened barrel. It was not a weapon typically preferred by women, or, for that matter, by any self-respecting cop. Nor was it for amateurs. Had Joseph given it to Ruby so that she could protect herself? Did the perceived threat come from the people Joseph was dealing with?

Did Ruby know how to shoot? It was hard to picture her at a shooting range. After all, she might break a fingernail. But she was, in all likelihood, involved in a dirty and dangerous business. And she was—appearances aside—a survivor. She would do what she had to do, even if it meant using this gun.

He'd be a fool to forget that.

Antonio was already in bed when he heard Ruby return. He knew he should record his thoughts and impressions in his journal, but he was simply too exhausted. Switching off the light, he fell into a restless sleep.

He woke once, around 3:00 a.m., and saw the lights blazing beneath Ruby's door. Was she still awake? He strained his ears for any sound coming from her room, but heard nothing. Too tired for further speculation, he closed his eyes.

When he got up at five-thirty to write in his journal, her lights were still on.

Chapter 7

She was gone. Ruby was gone.

After knocking on her door and calling her name for a full five minutes without a response, and after receiving an earful from the couple he'd awoken two doors down, Antonio went back in his room and picked the lock to the connecting door.

As they had been all night, her lights were on. The bathroom door stood ajar, its lights also ablaze. Her suitcases were open on one bed. Ruby was nowhere to be seen.

Had she been taken against her will? But by whom? And when? He hadn't left his room all night. If she had been abducted, it had to have been shortly after six, while he was in the shower. He certainly hadn't slept soundly enough to have missed the entrance of an intruder, and he couldn't believe that Ruby would have gone anywhere against her will without putting up a fight.

He'd been working undercover for too long, Antonio told himself. That was why he was jumping to such crazy and sinister conclusions. Ruby was absolutely fine. She had to be.

Yet no matter how many times he repeated the words, he

couldn't quite make himself believe them. These weren't ordinary circumstances. Ruby was involved with Joseph, and Joseph was involved with some very nasty characters. Who knew what they were capable of? If she wasn't part of the scheme, all it would take would be for one of them to think she had seen or heard just a little too much, and her life would be in jeopardy. She would "disappear," the way his predecessor had.

They were certainly in the perfect location to make someone vanish. Excluding the town and its outskirts, they were surrounded by untold miles of undeveloped forestland. A person or persons could hide a body in the midst of that land and feel fairly confident it wouldn't be found.

Antonio drew a shaky breath and pulled the emergency brake on that train of thought. He absolutely wasn't going to go there. Not yet. Not until he'd exhausted every other alternative. He was a cop. It was high time he acted like one. His first order of business was to analyze the scene of the crime. If, indeed, a crime had been committed.

There was no evidence of a struggle, which was a good sign. Another good sign was that Ruby's bed had definitely been slept in. The sheets and the pillow she had used still bore the imprint of her body and her head, although they were no longer warm to the touch. Her nightgown was tossed haphazardly across the foot of the bed, and the clothes she had worn yesterday lay in a heap on the floor.

The bad signs, and there were two of them, were ominous. Her gun was still in the suitcase, where he had found it the night before. And her purse sat smack in the middle of the dresser, wallet filled with money, credit cards and identification still inside. Though he looked, Antonio couldn't find her room key.

He tried to convince himself there was a logical explanation for her absence. Maybe she had gone for an early-morning walk, although she hadn't struck him as the early-morning walk type. Maybe she was a sleepwalker, and this very minute was out wandering down the middle of the road. Did sleepwalkers change out of their nightclothes and into other attire before setting out on their nocturnal journeys? Not to mention, it was nearing seven-thirty and the sun was up.

Maybe, despite her assertion of loyalty to Joseph, she hadn't blown off those two men from the lounge. Maybe she had arranged to meet them under cover of darkness, when no one else would see, and she was having such a good time she hadn't yet returned.

That thought left an extremely nasty taste in his mouth.

Maybe—and it galled him to admit she had so easily succeeded—she had simply snuck out on him. It wasn't outside the realm of possibility that she had scheduled a meeting with someone she didn't want him to know about. In all likelihood, instead of meeting those two punks, she was out doing Joseph's work.

Still, the point of sneaking out was to return before the person you were sneaking out on discovered your absence. So if Ruby did have an early morning assignation, surely it was only logical to assume she would have returned by now. And surely it was only logical to assume that, at the very minimum, she would have taken her purse with her. Ruby was not the type of woman to go anywhere without her purse.

Antonio's stomach growled. Nor was she a woman to ignore her appetite.

Her appetite. He experienced one of those ah-ha! moments that had him shaking his head at the depth of his own stupidity. Of course. It was so obvious, he couldn't believe he hadn't thought of it first.

After closing and locking the connecting door, Antonio headed for the lounge. Even though they were supposed to meet at seven o'clock for breakfast, considering her hunger the night before, it wouldn't surprise him if she hadn't been able to wait for their appointed hour to eat. As to why she hadn't informed him of that decision, all he could suppose was that she hadn't wanted to wake him if he was still asleep. It would have been nice if she'd slipped a note under his door, but they were work colleagues only. Ruby didn't owe him an explanation as to her movements.

The lounge was filled to capacity, the aroma of frying bacon and eggs overpowering the cigarette smoke that perpetually hung on the air. Ignoring the painful growling of his stomach, Antonio allowed his gaze to run over the seated diners. Ruby was not one of them.

His earlier dread came back full force after he'd asked at each table, and no one had seen her. He was ready to race back to his room and load his gun—to do what, he had no idea—when a man emerging from the rest room told him he'd seen a woman fitting Ruby's description headed toward town. On foot. And, thank heavens, alone.

His tires spun as he raced the truck out of the parking lot. After leaving the vehicle in front of the haberdashery, Antonio ran down the empty main street. Where was she?

He finally found her in the park, sitting on a bench. Her back was to him, her head bent over something in her lap, and she didn't see him approach. Chest heaving from exertion, Antonio braced a hand against a tree and watched her in silence. Funny, he thought, how relief really could leave your knees weak. This was a new experience for him. As was the panic he had felt when he'd thought someone had harmed her. The strength of that reaction didn't bear analysis. Not yet, anyway.

Ruby was safe, and that was all that mattered. Still, he had never wanted to strangle anyone more than he did at that moment.

When his emotions were under control, he moved closer. As he neared, he began noticing things he had missed in his first giddy rush of relief. Incredibly, Ruby was sitting cross-legged on the bench, and her feet were bare. She had on the worn pair of jeans he had seen in her luggage, and the sketch pad that had so puzzled him lay on her lap. A piece of charcoal was lodged between her smudged fingers, and a pair of high heels sat on the bench beside her.

He felt his lips twitch at the thought of her hobbling all the way here on those heels. No wonder she'd taken them off. Her feet had to be killing her.

Careful not to make a sound, he stood directly behind her. What he saw on the sketch pad literally took his breath away. On the surface, it was a simple charcoal rendering of the park itself. But there was a confidence in each stroke of the charcoal across the page, a depth to the images portrayed there, that drew the eye and held it, refusing to let go. Ruby had talent. Real talent.

He leaned forward, and his shadow fell across the sketch pad.

Ruby turned her head to peer over her shoulder. There was a faraway light in her eyes, and Antonio realized her thoughts were miles away from this quiet, peaceful place. It was almost as if she were in a trance.

Her face was bare of makeup, the angle of her cheekbones and her obstinate chin as sharply defined as the lines she had drawn across the page. There was a streak of charcoal on her cheek that he found highly alluring. She looked, somehow, in the early-morning light, incredibly young and vulnerable. He got a lump in his throat just staring at her.

It took a minute or two, but the unfocused light faded from her eyes. Slowly she came back to earth. Back to him.

"Good morning," he said.

"Good morning."

He moved to the front of the bench so she wouldn't have to crane her neck to look at him. "Mind if I sit here?"

She inclined her head, then eyed him cautiously as he settled his body next to hers.

"What are you doing here, Michael?"

"Looking for you."

She frowned. "For me? Why?"

"I thought we had a date."

"A...d-date?" she stammered, her eyes widening.

Lord, but she was lovely. She had the most incredible skin. It was a crime to ever put makeup on that face.

"I might be mistaken, but I distinctly recall you agreeing

to meet me at seven o'clock." When she still looked blank, he prompted, "For breakfast."

"What time is it?"

"Almost eight."

"Eight!" She jumped to her feet, and the charcoal and sketch pad fell to the ground. "I'm sorry, Michael. I've made us both late for work."

"Not a problem," he dismissed. "We'll just stay a little later tonight."

He leaned over and picked up the sketch pad. "I was worried about you."

That got her attention. "You were worried about *me?*"

"Yes. What would I say to Joseph, if anything happened to you?"

Her eyes went blank of all emotion. "Of course," she said dully. "That would be put you in a difficult spot, wouldn't it?"

"Yes," he was forced to agree, although his immediate response was to wish he could take the words back. Anything to return the light to those incredible eyes of hers. "It would."

He was about to extend the sketch pad to her, when something caught his attention. Down at the bottom of the page, almost hidden by the drawing itself, were the initials *LL,* along with the date.

"What's this?" he murmured.

Ruby snatched the sketch pad from him and clutched it protectively to her chest. "Nothing."

"The initials at the bottom of the page," he pressed. "*LL.* What do they stand for?"

She wouldn't meet his gaze. "*LL* is a pseudonym I use when I sign my drawings."

"I thought pseudonyms were just for writers."

Her chin jutted out. "Lots of people besides authors use pseudonyms. Actors do. Musicians do. Why not artists? Besides, I was only twelve, and I hated my name. I chose a pseudonym in case my drawings ever made me famous."

"So you've been drawing since you were twelve?"

"I've been drawing for as long as I can remember."

"What does *LL* stand for?"

Her hesitation was barely noticeable, but it was there all the same. "Lois Lane."

He bit back surprised laughter. "Lois Lane? As in *Superman? That* Lois Lane?"

Antonio had expected his skepticism to make her grow even more defensive. But she totally disarmed him by grinning saucily.

"I was twelve, Michael. What do you expect?"

"It's a wonderful drawing, Ruby."

Her grin disappeared, and she eyed him closely, as if judging his sincerity. Then she disarmed him even further by biting her lip and shifting awkwardly from one bare foot to the other.

"You really like it?"

He had never heard her sound so tentative. Apparently, while she was self-assured in every other area of her life, Ruby had doubts about her abilities as an artist. Although how that was possible he didn't understand.

"I really do. You have a rare talent, you know that?"

"Thank you," she replied quietly.

"I'm curious. Do you show your work?"

She seemed to have regained her composure. After stooping to pick up the piece of charcoal, she sat back down on the park bench. "Why would I do that?"

"You did say you used to dream of becoming famous, didn't you? The only way I know of for an artist to become famous is if she shows her work."

"I was a child, Michael. Children dream impossible dreams."

"Tell me I'm wrong, but when I arrived, you were so absorbed in your drawing you had no idea where you were, what time it was or even who I was."

She didn't bother denying it. "Your point is?"

What was his point? Why was he pressing so hard? Because he hated seeing talent, any talent, go to waste. Ruby was already wasting her life on Joseph. It would be a crime to waste her talent, too. The crime fighter in him wanted to prevent that, if at all possible.

"You could have sat here all day, drawing, couldn't you?" he said. "You love it."

"Yes." The admission was reluctant.

"More than anything else in your life."

"Yes."

"And I'm not the only person who has told you that you have talent."

She clutched the sketch pad tighter. "No."

"Then why haven't you tried making a living off your art? Do you know how many people go to work, day after day, in despair because they hate what they're doing? You've actually found something you love, yet you're ignoring it."

"I'm not ignoring it, Michael. Whenever I have spare time, like this morning, I draw."

"And how much spare time do you average in a week?"

She shrugged. "I don't know. An hour. Two. Maybe three."

"If you worked at it full-time, you could have forty hours. Fifty. Even sixty, depending on how much of a workaholic you wanted to be."

"It's a nice thought, Michael. There's only one problem."

"What's that?"

She tossed her head and flicked her hair back off her face, then smiled that empty smile of hers that every man but him seemed to find fascinating. "I wouldn't be able to maintain my wardrobe on a starving artist's pay. That's why I valuate art for a living, instead of creating it. Maybe, though, after Joseph and I are married, I'll give it some more thought."

He didn't know what infuriated him more: the coy look in her eyes, or her words. Here, he'd thought they were sharing a rare moment of honesty, and she went and ruined it by reminding him how shallow she truly was. Apparently, his hopes for her were higher than the ones she held for herself.

He had to stop building her up in his mind as something other than what she really was: a young woman obsessed by wealth, beauty and fashion to the exclusion of all else. A woman of no substance.

For a moment, he could even take pity on her. One day her looks would fade, and all the fancy clothing and jewelry in the world wouldn't be able to disguise that fact. Nor would cosmetic surgery. What would she do then?

Antonio studied the woman who was such a puzzle to him. To his amazement, as he replayed each of their encounters in his mind, one of the pieces slid into place. The words were out of his mouth before he could even consider the wisdom of uttering them.

''It's all an act, isn't it?''

Trying not to hyperventilate, Laura stared at Michael in stunned disbelief. Her heart pounded so hard she thought it would burst from her chest. Alarm bells, the magnitude of a submarine's warning system, clanged in her head. It was over. All her hard work, not to mention the work done by the Pittsburgh police, had been for nothing. Her cover was blown. Worse, far, far worse, was the knowledge that *she* was the one who had blown it.

Think, Laura, think. What do you do now?

The problem was, Michael had thrown her off balance with his unexpected arrival in the park. Okay, so he had thrown her off balance from that first moment when his gaze had met hers across the auction floor.

Still, wearing blue jeans and getting charcoal under her fingernails was not an activity in which Ruby would willingly participate. It was only natural he would question her appearance. She'd compounded her error by apologizing for making them late, something Ruby would never do, and by initialing her drawing. Thank goodness she hadn't signed her real name. But Lois Lane? Sheesh. How lame could you get? Small wonder his suspicions had grown.

She had brought the sketch pad with her, and the jeans, because she considered them her good-luck charms and took them with her on every job. She hadn't intended to use them—not out in the open, anyway.

But when she had parted her curtains that morning and seen the way the rising sun had played over the landscape, she hadn't been able to resist. Sketching relaxed her, and with the tension she had been feeling since Michael Corsi's advent in her life, she had desperately needed to relax. She had fully intended to be back in her room before he had even known she was gone. Instead, she had succumbed to the joy she always felt when she held a piece of charcoal in her hand, and had lost all track of time. An unforgivable error, one of many she had made that week.

Face it, she was losing her touch.

Michael had further confused her by complimenting her drawing and by sounding sincere while doing so. Then, when she had tried to respond in a manner she felt Ruby would, his questions about trying to make a living from her art had hit too close to home. His obvious disappointment in her—in Ruby—had stung more than she cared to admit. Because, as far as her drawing was concerned, Ruby's truth was Laura's truth. She had always been too fearful of criticism and failure to even show her work.

None of it mattered now, however. She could make a thousand excuses, and it wouldn't change a thing. Because the job, her very life perhaps, was in jeopardy, and she was the one who had placed it there.

"Well?" Michael insisted, when she continued to stare at him stupidly, and the silence threatened to stretch into next week. "I'm right, aren't I? It is all an act."

For one insane second, Laura wished she could tell him the truth. She was so tired of the lies. So tired of pretending to be someone she wasn't. Still, if there was any chance to rectify this mess, she had to take it. She was the one who had thrown it all in the dumpster. She had to be the one to dig her way out.

She moistened her dry lips with the tip of her tongue. "What is?"

Ordinarily, she would have gone on the attack, in an effort

to throw Michael equally off balance and to make him question his assumptions. Before she could do that, however, she had to know exactly what he was thinking, exactly what conclusions he had drawn. Then, and only then, would she be able to form a response that would, hopefully, allay his suspicions.

"The dumb, helpless female bit. Face it, Ruby, you're as helpless as a life preserver. And you're as dumb as a fox. For some reason, though, you don't want people to know just how capable and smart you truly are. Why?"

Relief coursed through her, and she had to fight not to let it show on her face. She hadn't blown her cover. Not totally, anyway. She could fix this, so long as she didn't let her emotions make her do or say anything more stupid than she already had that morning. What would Ruby say in answer to this?

"Men don't like women who are smarter than they are," she said.

Michael's brow furrowed. "Who told you that?"

"My mother."

"And you believed her?"

"Didn't you believe the things your mother told you?"

"Yes. But in your case, your mother was married to a man who, according to you, was cold and unfeeling. A man who, also according to you, has sent you on a life-long quest for male attention. I would think you would find any advice she gave you, about men anyway, suspect at best."

Laura allowed herself to relax, just a little. She was back on familiar territory. At last.

"She had my interests at heart."

"As does your brother, yet you haven't listened to him about changing your lifestyle."

"It made sense to me, Michael. Still does."

His gaze raked her from head to toe. "So the tight clothes, the makeup, the Marilyn Monroe act, they're all for a man?"

"It works, doesn't it? I've never been without a man in my life."

"And, as we've already established, you need that."

Her chin went up. "Yes, Michael, I do."

"Even if you have to play dumb to get him?"

"Trust me, I'm not acting that much. I'm not exactly Einstein."

"You're not Betty Boop, either."

She widened her eyes at him. "Who's Betty Boop?"

"Very funny."

She grinned unrepentantly, which only seemed to make him grind his teeth. Good. So long as he stayed irritated with her, he wouldn't waste his time trying to figure her out. And before she patted herself on the back too hard, she had to get herself out of this conversation and back to the motel. Once in her Ruby gear, uncomfortable or not, impractical or not, she would feel much better. She would feel more in control and less...vulnerable.

"What does your father do for a living?" Michael surprised her by asking.

"He's an accountant." Laura mentally apologized to all the accountants in the world. Still, their stereotypical image of being staid, humorless and uptight lent credibility to the story of her father being emotionally remote.

"And your mother?"

"She's a homemaker."

"The kind who does housework wearing a dress and cultured pearls, and who always greets her husband at the door with a smile on her face when he comes home from a long day at the office?"

"Not even close."

"She doesn't meet your father at the door?"

"Oh, she meets him."

"She's not a good housekeeper, then."

Laura shook her head. "My mother keeps an immaculate home. I don't recall her ever sitting down. She's always busy doing something."

The question formed in his eyes before he spoke the words. "What are you so carefully not saying, Ruby?"

"My mother waits on my father hand and foot. Not because she wants to, but because she's afraid not to."

"How does she behave when he's around?"

"Like a frightened little mouse, scurrying from place to place to keep out of the way of the cat."

"But not you," Michael commented.

This was exactly where she had wanted the discussion to go. "I learned early on to stand up for myself."

"Did you get any bruises for your efforts?" he asked softly.

She looked down at her lap and traced one bare foot across the top of the cool grass, the way she suspected Ruby might, if actually confronted with the question. "A few. They faded quickly."

"Did they really, Ruby? Did they really?"

He sounded like he really cared, but that had to be her imagination. Ruby struck as many sparks off Michael as he did off her. If he cared anything, it was that they would have to work overtime to make up for the time they had already lost this morning.

He was waiting for an answer, but what answer did he expect? Of course the scars wouldn't have faded. That was why she had given Ruby the history she had. But would Ruby herself, intelligent or not, be enlightened enough to realize that? Would she even care? Laura didn't think so.

She looked up. "Are you trying to psychoanalyze me, Michael?"

For half a second he seemed taken aback, then he grinned. "Would it bother you if I were?"

She tilted her head and waited a beat. "Didn't think I'd be so deep, huh?"

His laughter was filled with both surprise and appreciation. It flowed over her like an unexpected ocean wave, leaving her trembling and sputtering in its wake. He'd thrown his head back, exposing the column of his throat. For one brief, crazy second, she had to fight the urge to lean forward and press her lips to it.

How could a man who was morally bankrupt have such a wonderful laugh? she wondered, dismayed. And how could she let herself respond to it?

"Do you see them much?" he asked.

She stared at him, not comprehending. "Who?"

"Your parents. Do you seem them much?"

His words reminded her of how much she missed her mother and father. And Jacob and Jason. "As little as possible."

"How old were you when you left home?"

"Eighteen."

"Couldn't wait to get away, could you?"

"No, Michael, I couldn't."

He nodded as if she had answered a question he hadn't asked. "This is only a wild guess here, and probably more personal than you'd care for, but you linked up with your first man then, didn't you?"

"Psychoanalyzing me again?" she said lightly.

"I'm right, aren't I?"

"And if you are?"

"Who was he?"

There was a bite in his tone she didn't understand. "Just a man. A man who taught me many things. A man who was far more gentle and loving than my father had ever been."

She drew a deep breath and flashed him a brilliant smile. "Anything else you care to know? Because it's getting late, and we really should be heading back to the motel."

"Just about your brother," he said.

She was surprised, and grateful, that he wasn't prying further into Ruby's love life. "What about him?"

"Has he cut your parents out of his life?"

"Of course not. He's a priest. He's into forgiveness."

"But you're not."

"Are you?"

Instead of answering, he said, "I assume, since you mentioned him on the drive down, that you're still in touch with him."

Laura felt her lips curl in a fond smile. How wonderful it felt to finally be able to speak the truth, to not have to worry about being tripped up on an inconsistency.

"We see each other whenever we can. The parish he's assigned to is in New Mexico, so it isn't as often as we would like."

"When you do get together," Michael said, "he prays for your mortal soul?"

Laura chuckled. Whenever they got together, Alex nearly turned blue in the face trying to talk her out of being a cop. "Fervently."

"That doesn't bug you?"

She shrugged. "Sometimes. But I know he loves me. He only wants what he thinks is best for me."

"And you love him?"

"Unconditionally."

"Changing your lifestyle would give him peace of mind, wouldn't it?"

"Yes, I suppose it would."

"Yet you're not about to change it, are you?"

"No, I'm not. Tell me, Michael. Would you change your lifestyle for anyone, no matter how much they loved you?"

"No, I suppose I wouldn't."

She had no business feeling disappointed, Laura told herself. After all, it wasn't as if she was going to ask him to change his lifestyle for *her*.

"Look, Ruby. Why don't we make a pact? For the time that we are here, away from the auction gallery, you drop the dumb brunette act. You'll get a chance to let your hair down—metaphorically speaking, of course—and I won't grind my teeth down to the gums."

"You're really serious about this, aren't you?"

"Yes, I am." He stood and stuck out his hand. "Do we have a deal?"

She thought for a long minute. They would be spending many hours in each other's company. It sure would be nice to talk about something besides fashion or the weather.

Standing, she slid her hand into his. Ignoring the way the contact shot a tingle of awareness up her arm, she gave it a vigorous shake. "Deal."

Quickly withdrawing her hand, she ran it down her thigh. Ostensibly the motion was made to look like she was brushing something off her jeans. What she was really trying to do was wipe the feel of him off her. It didn't work.

"We really do need to be getting back, Michael," she said, making her voice no-nonsense. "Did you walk here or drive?"

"I drove."

Thank God. It was only a mile, but if she had to hobble all the way back to the motel in her high heels, she just might find herself begging for mercy.

"Can I tell you something?" Michael asked.

Laura reached for her shoes and thrust her aching feet into them, trying not to wince as she did so. "Can I stop you?"

He leaned close, as if confiding a secret. "You look far more comfortable in those jeans than you ever did in that tight skirt you had on yesterday."

Reaction set in when she stepped into the shower. Replaying the moment when she thought Michael had figured it all out on the viewing screen of her mind, Laura sank to the shower floor, wrapped her arms around her knees and gasped in deep, gulping breaths while the hot water pounded down on her bent head.

Her near unmasking wasn't the cause of her distress. She'd come close to being unmasked numerous times. She had also been in more immediate danger on those occasions than the one in the park. The difference between this morning and every other time was the fear that had jolted her, or more specifically her reaction to it.

While she had felt fear before, hundreds of times, it had never incapacitated her. This morning, however, when Michael had uttered those fateful words, fear had literally struck her dumb. Oh, she'd managed to pull it off, just barely, but in the process she had totally lost her cool.

What was wrong with her? Why was she feeling so raw, so close to the edge? She had a reputation for having nerves of steel, and this morning those very same nerves had turned to gelatin.

When the truth hit her, she shivered. Before today, on each case she had worked, she hadn't cared whether or not she came out alive. And because she hadn't cared, any fear she felt had seemed, if not unimportant, definitely secondary to the job she had to do. But she cared now. What did it mean?

It meant that the changes she had felt inside herself over the past few months were growing and mutating. First the rage had gone, then her hormones had reawakened and now her immunity to fear had disappeared. What would be next? Laura had no idea. But she did know that, when this job was over, she would have to assess whether she was still fit for undercover work.

She huddled on the floor of the shower stall for a full five minutes. Then she gathered what was left of her composure, climbed to her feet and got on with the business of showering.

Okay, so she wasn't at the top of her game anymore, and might never be again. She'd also made some inexcusable—some might even say sophomoric—mistakes. But all wasn't lost. She could still pull this job off. And the next time she was in a situation that produced fear? It was a handicap that, now she had acknowledged and accepted it, she would deal with appropriately. She wouldn't allow it to catch her off guard again.

A fine tremor shook her hand as she applied mascara to her eyelashes. Though she felt a renewed urgency to hurry—her actions that morning had already cost precious time—she forced herself not to rush. After all, when it came to applying the face she wore in public, Ruby would never allow herself to be rushed.

For the first time since she had undertaken the job of playing Ruby, Laura didn't resent the time and effort it took to put on her makeup. This morning it felt like a layer of protection between her and Michael Corsi's knowing eyes. If she couldn't wear a Kevlar vest, at least she could put on foundation.

When she emerged from her room a full hour after their return from the park, she wore hot-pink Irish linen cropped pants and a matching sleeveless square-necked top. On her feet were a pair of pink leather sandals. At least with her toes open, and with the heels only an inch off the ground, her feet shouldn't be in agony by the end of the day.

There was no telling, however, what the state of her emotions would be.

Michael was pacing impatiently in the parking lot, but he halted in his tracks when he saw her. The look on his face, and the gaze he raked over her, told her more loudly than words that any care she might have taken in prettying herself up for him was totally wasted. Not that she was trying to impress him. She might be undergoing some inner transformation, the extent of which she couldn't yet predict. Her hormones might have awakened with a vengeance. Still, it didn't mean the changes she was undergoing encompassed a relationship with this man. The last thing she wanted on this morning that had so shaken her confidence in herself was for Michael to notice her as a man would a woman.

And if she told herself that enough times, she just might start believing it.

"You should have kept the jeans on," he said, practically snarling. "It would have saved some time."

He was obviously spoiling for a fight. Well, she wasn't going to give it to him. Not yet, anyway. Not until she was feeling a lot more collected. She couldn't risk making any more stupid mistakes.

"I always dress for the job, Michael. I told you that before."

"Glad to know you remembered we have a job to do."

Ouch. "Trust me, that is one thing I never forget."

"I'll have to take your word for it." He headed for the truck. Over his shoulder, he added, "Ready?"

As she'd ever be. Squaring her shoulders, Laura let out a long breath.

"Let's get this show on the road."

Chapter 8

By the time they arrived at the Bickham estate, Laura had regained her composure. Michael, on the other hand, seemed positively morose. He hadn't spoken a word since they'd left the motel, and had driven, grim-faced, down the long, winding, bumpy road to the mansion with total disregard for any damage his truck might sustain.

The first thing she saw when they entered the huge living room was the portrait hanging above the stone fireplace. Fascinated, she placed the laptop and the box of sequentially numbered tags she carried on an elegant Victorian sofa before crossing the room to stand beneath it.

"Serena Bickham, age forty-two," she read aloud from the brass plaque fastened to the frame.

Moving back, she studied the oil painting with a critical eye. The artist was a man who had enjoyed quite a bit of notoriety during the 1960s, for both his flamboyant lifestyle and his uncanny ability to capture the essence of his subjects. From an artistic standpoint, it was an excellent rendering and should fetch a good price at auction. Joseph would be pleased.

Laura, however, was more interested in the woman the painting portrayed. Serena Bickham wasn't beautiful, she wasn't even all that pretty, but her spirit radiated from the canvas; so much so, it was almost possible for Laura to imagine she was viewing the actual woman in the flesh.

There was a light in Serena's eyes, and a serenity to her bearing, that was compelling and true to her given name. Laura had no doubt she was gazing at the face of a supremely contented woman. Apparently Vincent was as devoted to his wife as Joseph had described, and it showed.

Lucky Serena.

"So this is the woman who inspired Vincent Bickham's everlasting devotion," Michael murmured.

She'd been so absorbed in her study of the portrait, she hadn't heard his approach. Sparing him a glance, she asked, "Are you speaking to *me?*"

"You're the only other person here. Who else would I be addressing?"

He still sounded grumpy. And his remark about everlasting devotion had definitely held a snide undertone. Because he didn't believe in lasting love? Or because he was out of sorts? Probably a combination of both.

She turned to face him. "Just thought I'd ask, since I got the distinct impression I was the last person you wanted to talk to."

He shrugged. "It's either you or the walls."

One thing was certain. She was in no danger of getting a swelled head whenever she was with him.

Laura waved a hand at their surroundings. "I suppose I should be grateful you find me more interesting than the walls. I mean, look at this wallpaper. Have you ever seen such an interesting pattern? And is that real gold leaf painted on it?"

Michael made some sort of grunt she assumed signaled his agreement. Then again, it could have been indigestion, although how he could be suffering from that particular ailment on an empty stomach was beyond her.

"Keep frowning so fiercely, and your face will freeze that

way,'' she warned, using a phrase she had heard countless times as a child.

This time he didn't even grunt.

Putting her thumbs in her ears, Laura stuck her tongue out at him and wiggled her fingers.

His brows furrowed even closer together. ''What are you doing?''

''What do you think I'm doing?'' She lowered her hands. ''I'm trying to inject a little levity into the situation. Notice the big words, inject and levity? As you can see, I'm keeping my end of the bargain. I'm no longer pretending to be vocabulary impaired. We're going to be spending the next three days together in this house, Michael. We might as well try to get along. Wasn't it you who said, just yesterday, and I quote, that it's more fun to laugh?''

''Hoist by my own petard.'' His smile was rueful. ''And yes, Ruby, I'm grateful you're not going to pretend you don't know what a petard is.''

Laura chuckled. ''Since you brought it up, I know what the phrase means. But what, exactly, *is* a petard? Have you ever seen one?''

Laughter sparkled in his eyes, and her stomach did a weird little flip-flop. ''Damned if I know, either.'' He sobered. ''I'm sorry, Ruby, about my behavior this morning. I guess skipping breakfast didn't do much for my disposition.''

Scouting out her whereabouts and then waiting another full hour for her to get ready when they were already late hadn't helped matters, either. Michael wasn't used to waiting on a woman, she would wager. Most likely he crooked his little finger at one and said woman came running. On the double. These next few days would most likely prove a further test of his disposition.

And, undoubtedly, hers.

''I told you I didn't mind if you wanted to stop and eat,'' she said.

He shook his head. ''We wouldn't make up any time that way. I can wait for lunch.''

Since she hadn't eaten, either, by all rights she should be ravenous. This morning, however, perhaps because of her inner turmoil, the mere thought of food made her nauseous. As things stood, she sincerely doubted she'd be hungry when lunchtime rolled around. Maybe not even by dinner.

"If you insist," she said.

"I insist."

Laura wondered if perhaps she shouldn't revise her opinion of Michael, just a little bit. After all, a man who could laugh at himself and who apologized for being ill-tempered, couldn't be all bad. Could he?

"Mind if I ask you something that's been bugging me?" he said.

"Go ahead."

"When I got back from my run last night, I saw you in the lounge. I also saw the two men hit on you."

"Yes?" she said cautiously, wondering where this was going.

"What did you say to make them hightail it away like that?"

She relaxed. "You really want to know?"

"I really want to know."

"I told them it was my first night out after my sex change operation, and I couldn't wait to try out the new equipment."

He gave a hoot of laughter. "That's priceless."

"I thought so, too."

Still chuckling, he nodded to Serena's portrait. "So, what do you think of her?"

He was standing close enough for them to rub shoulders, and she had never been more aware of his presence. He smelled good, too, a combination of lime-scented aftershave and deodorant soap. The skin of his cheeks looked temptingly soft and glowed with disgusting good health. Worse, he had the most incredibly long eyelashes. Ruby, Laura knew, would kill to have eyelashes that gorgeous. As for his mouth…

The painting, Laura, she reminded herself. He asked you about the painting.

"She's not very pretty, is she?" she offered, knowing this was how Ruby would have evaluated the woman, and that Michael was just waiting for her to point out the obvious.

"No, she's not."

Picking up the laptop, Laura searched for a place to plug it in. She set up shop with it on the opposite side of the room, on a mahogany desk located between a pair of twelve-foot-high windows that were draped in green velvet.

"I haven't seen a picture of Vincent," she said, "but maybe he wasn't all that good-looking, either."

"Does it matter?"

Michael had moved to a Chippendale corner chair and was studying it intently. She knew he was formulating the preliminary dollar amount they would enter into their records to use as a reserve, the minimum amount Joseph would accept at auction before withdrawing the piece from consideration. If they had any problem coming up with a valuation, they would simply hook up to the Internet and do the necessary research to get what they needed.

"Of course it does." She brought up the program they would use to record the estate's inventory. "Because if Vincent had been handsome, he would have gone after a much prettier woman."

"You think so?"

Laura liked to believe men were attracted to women for more than their outward appearance. In a perfect world, they would consider intelligence to be the ultimate aphrodisiac. At least, on second glance, anyway, after the pheromones had dissipated somewhat on the air. Ruby, on the other hand, was far more realistic.

"Don't you?"

"He had a lot of money, Ruby. He could have had his pick of women, pretty or not. And still he chose Serena."

Michael took a tag and affixed it to the chair. Laura moved aside while he recorded the description and dollar value he'd assigned to it.

"I don't know whether I told you or not," she said, placing

a tag on Serena's portrait. "But Vincent didn't make that money until after he and Serena were married."

"That changes things, then." Michael moved on to another chair. "Believe it or not, some men actually look beneath the surface to the person inside. Maybe Vincent was one of them."

"Are you?"

Michael's smile was sardonic. "I said some men."

She was not disappointed, Laura told herself. This was exactly what she would have expected from him. In fact, she would have been astonished had he said anything else.

"So you wouldn't have given Serena Bickham a second glance?" she pressed.

"Probably not."

At least he was honest enough to admit it. "But Vincent did."

"Obviously."

"Why, do you think?"

He shrugged. "Why is the sky blue?"

Because, she thought, blue light gets scattered around more than all the other colors from the sun.

"What kind of woman do you give a second glance?" The words were out of her mouth before she could call them back.

Michael's head came up, and his gaze collided with hers. For a tense, heart-stopping moment, he stared at her searchingly.

"Want to know if you qualify?" he finally asked.

"Who, me?" Laura hoped he'd chalk up her breathiness to surprise. It took all the skill she possessed to widen her eyes at him in mock innocence. "I have Joseph. Remember?"

She didn't know who she was trying to remind more: herself or Michael.

"And you are one hundred percent faithful to him."

"I turned down those men in the lounge, remember? I'm as faithful to Joseph as Serena was to Vincent."

"How do you know she was?" he challenged.

"Look at her, Michael." Laura indicated the portrait with a sweep of her arm. "She was faithful."

"Why?" There was an unmistakable bite to his voice. "Because she was plain? Because you assume her plainness meant she never had the opportunity to cheat?"

"No," she corrected, not caring that her answer was more suitable to her way of thinking than Ruby's. "Because she looks so supremely happy to be the lady of *this* manor. Besides, if she had cheated on him, Vincent wouldn't have been so devoted to her. He wouldn't have stopped living when she did." The way Laura would have done after Jacob and Jason died if she hadn't poured all her energy into police work.

"That's assuming he found out she cheated."

"When you're that close to a person, Michael, you know."

His gaze seemed to sharpen on her. "And the reason *you* know this is because of your relationship with Joseph?"

"Of course." She'd been thinking of Jacob, and the depth of the love they had shared, but she could hardly tell Michael that.

She began entering information about the portrait on the laptop. "As for my question." She shrugged. "I was just passing the time, Michael. Consider it idle chitchat. You don't have to answer—" Laura left a deliberate, provocative pause "—if you don't want to."

She hoped he would take her words as a challenge, and he didn't disappoint her.

"What kind of woman makes me take a second look? That's what you asked, isn't it?" He stroked his cheeks as if pondering. "I like blondes. I like blondes with blue eyes, narrow waists, round hips, long legs and big..." He shut his mouth as heat crept up his throat.

It was the second time he had blushed in her presence. As she recalled, the first time he had actually had his hand on the body part he was so judiciously not mentioning by name.

Asking him how a man who had spent two-plus years behind bars could still blush would definitely increase his discomfort level. But she could think of another way to increase it more.

''I believe the term you're looking for is breast,'' she supplied sweetly. ''You like women with big breasts.''

''I was going to say feet,'' he replied.

She knew she should have laughed out loud at the blatant lie. She should also have felt a spurt of triumph that she had succeeded in making his flush deepen. But right now she didn't feel in the least like laughing or celebrating. Oddly, what she felt was...depressed. And outraged. Once again, as was the norm with them, their conversation had deteriorated.

''Know what you just described?'' she said, unaware of the accusatory note that had entered her voice.

''What?''

''Every adolescent's fantasy. Your perfect woman is a dream. Congratulations.''

''Something wrong with dreams?''

Yes, if real women could never hope to measure up to them. Laura's physical attributes certainly didn't come close, a fact over which she had agonized many an hour during her youth. Nor had it escaped her notice that Michael had mentioned nothing about character or intellect. The man was totally superficial, a perfect match for Ruby.

But not for Laura. Not that she was looking.

So why was she spitting mad? Because, on behalf of all the intelligent, thinking, *real* women in the world, who were much, much more than the sum of their body parts, she felt she needed to take a stand. And she couldn't take a stand; not without stepping out of character. While Laura always struck out against perceived injustices, Ruby never did, unless her own welfare was at stake.

She expelled a long, long breath. ''Nothing's wrong with them.''

''What do you look for in a man?'' Michael asked.

''Money,'' she snapped.

''Just money?''

''Just money.''

They worked in silence for several minutes. Whenever they passed each other on their way to enter information into the laptop, she studiously avoided his gaze.

"Something bothering you?" Michael finally asked.

"No," she lied.

"You seem awfully quiet all of a sudden."

Her objective when she'd initiated the conversation had been to lighten the mood. And maybe, if she was being totally honest, to pull his chain just a little.

Laura summoned a carefree laugh. "I guess I am a little piqued. Even if she's not interested, when a man rhapsodizes about his fantasy woman in front of a woman who will never look like her, well..." She spread her hands. "You'll have to forgive her if she tends to get a little out of sorts."

"Would it make things better if I told you I found your figure to be quite...adequate?"

She felt her lips give a wry twist. No woman, interested or not, wanted to be told that she was merely adequate. And no matter how much she ranted and raved on behalf of all the real women in the world, he wouldn't get it.

"I appreciate the thought, Michael. But right now the only thing that would make things better is if we concentrated all our efforts on making up for lost time."

"In that case," he replied, "wouldn't it be more efficient if you and I worked in separate rooms?"

If only that were possible. She didn't bother looking up from the computer.

"We work together. That way we keep each other honest."

"Or we collude and pocket some extra cash for ourselves."

The silence that fell after his remark was deafening. At first Laura thought she hadn't heard him correctly, but the look on his face told her otherwise. The man certainly had guts, she would give him that. He was also taking an awful risk that she would report his offer to Joseph. Why?

And here she'd been about to rethink her opinion of him. She should have known better. Especially after his description of the perfect woman.

"Joseph trusts me not to do that," she said carefully. "I value our relationship too highly to risk it. For anything."

"I wasn't suggesting you should," Michael answered smoothly. "I was just pointing out the obvious weakness in the arrangement."

Okay, so maybe she'd been wrong. Maybe he hadn't been suggesting what she thought he'd been suggesting.

"There's no weakness, if there's no collusion."

"No," he replied. "There's not."

She was busy studying another portrait when she heard him ask, "So you've never been tempted?"

"To do what?" she replied, distracted.

"To collude with someone while on the job."

It was there in his eyes, plain for her to see. No mistake this time. If she was willing, he would form an alliance with her. An alliance to steal from Joseph.

Why was she so surprised? Laura asked herself. He'd already admitted he was looking for a way to make some easy money. And he'd spent over two years behind bars for thumbing his nose at the law. Instead of being angry and outraged that he should suggest such a thing to her, what she really felt was an absurd desire to cry.

"Maybe, a time or two."

"But you never did?"

Had Joseph put him up to this? Or was he simply searching for another way of lining his pockets? Where, exactly, did Michael Corsi's loyalties lie?

"Why collude with someone, when all I have to do is ask, and Joseph gives me anything I want?"

He shrugged, as if to say he couldn't care less. "Why, indeed?"

Laura turned back to her work.

"I guess that's the end of the idle chitchat," Michael murmured in a low voice.

She didn't answer.

Lunchtime found them in the massive dining room, eating the meal Laura had arranged to have delivered. The remainder of the morning had passed swiftly, if silently. They'd finished cataloguing all the items in the living room and Vincent's study, along with three other rooms on the first floor.

It was amazing, she reflected, exactly how much they had accomplished. Despite his other character flaws, there was no denying that Michael was a hard worker. At this rate, and with minimal overtime, they should have no problem finishing up by Friday.

Since they were working in the dining room when their lunch arrived, they decided the most efficient thing to do would be to eat on the intricately carved mahogany table that had been crafted to seat fifty. As she sank her teeth into a BLT, Laura kicked off her sandals and let her toes sink into the oriental carpet, the pile of which was thicker than the heels of her shoes. An enormous crystal chandelier hung above their heads, a cleaning nightmare if ever she had seen one. Portraits of men and women, long gone on to their heavenly—or otherwise—rewards, lined the walls.

She wondered why Vincent, or perhaps it had been Serena, had purchased them. They were all over the house—dozens of portraits of people who, according to the nameplates, were not family members. Most had been painted in the mid to late 1800s by varied artists. Had the Bickhams simply collected portraits, the way some people collect coins or stamps? Maybe lining the walls of almost every room with the paintings was their way of populating this huge, old place, since they'd seemed to have no family besides themselves.

As she took another bite of her sandwich, Laura half imagined that the long-dead men and women were glaring down their patrician noses at her for despoiling the gleaming table with paper plates and cups instead of using fancy china, cut glass, fine linens and gleaming silver. She didn't care. The sandwich, the baked potato chips, the ice-cold lemonade, even the apple, plain as they were, were entirely delectable. Surprisingly, since she was still upset with Michael, her appetite had returned. With a vengeance.

"Can you imagine eating in a place like this?" Michael asked around a bite of sandwich.

"We are eating in a place like this," she pointed out.

He gave her a patient look. "You know what I meant. I was just searching for a subject that wouldn't set one or the other of us off."

Their voices echoed hollowly in the cavernous room. Laura placed her sandwich on a paper plate and reached for her lemonade.

"You think such a subject exists?"

He grinned. "Put it this way. I haven't entirely given up hope."

She refused to let that engaging grin of his soften her up. Although she was in no mood to smile back, she decided proper manners dictated that she behave in a civil way.

"Neither have I. Yet."

Settling more comfortably into her chair, she stretched her legs out in front of her. Her first impulse, when she saw Michael's gaze follow the motion, was to pull them back beneath her and sit upright. The only thing that stopped her was the sure knowledge that, once aware of his regard, Ruby would have taken the opportunity to stretch languorously. Plus, she was wearing pants. Even though they were cropped above the ankle, it wasn't as if he was getting an eyeful of leg.

While she couldn't quite pull off the languorous part, Laura did manage to stay put. "Why did you become an auctioneer, Michael?"

It took him a heartbeat or two to raise his gaze to her face. When he did, the look in his eyes made her hot all over.

"Your effort at finding a neutral topic of conversation?" he asked.

Her effort at trying to concentrate his attention on something other than her. Slowly, and as naturally as possible, she slid her feet back into her sandals before crossing her legs at the ankles and tucking them beneath her chair.

"Just trying to do my part."

He opened his bag of potato chips. "So you're just making polite conversation. You don't really want to know."

"No, Michael. I'm curious. I really would like to know why, out of all the careers you could have chosen, you became an auctioneer."

"As opposed to a mafioso, you mean?"

He was teasing, she knew, but sometimes it was downright scary how close he came to reading her mind. "As opposed to anything else."

"I don't know if I told you, but I have five brothers and a sister."

Since previously he had only mentioned his sister, the five brothers were a revelation. "Go ahead," she encouraged with a nod.

He shrugged. "In order to give each of us special time that belonged to us alone, my mother chose seven different activities to share with us. One Saturday every seven weeks, beginning with my sixth birthday, she and I would go to an auction together."

His voice had grown nostalgic with his memories, and Laura found herself listening in fascination. She was no longer killing time. She really wanted to know about Michael and those Saturdays he spent with his mother.

"Please," she said. "Tell me more."

"There's not much else to tell. We avoided the big auction houses. Instead, we spent all our time at small estate sales, where we focused on the furniture. My mother taught me all about the different grains of wood and what to look for when judging a particular piece. It became a game for us to find the most undervalued item at each auction we attended."

Laura found it astonishingly easy to picture him as a six-year-old, his thin legs poking out beneath a pair of shorts, his small hand thrust trustingly into his mother's, his brown eyes sparkling with eager curiosity as he gazed at the wonders around him. Could the Michael Corsi she knew ever have been so young, so eager, so innocent?

"What special memories for you," she murmured.

"Yes, they are," he replied. "Do you have any memories like that with your mother?"

Laura did. Warm, happy memories of baking cookies together and then taking them to shut-ins. Of drawing endlessly with chalk on the sidewalk in front of the house she had grown up in. Of tea parties where they would dress up in old clothing and pretend to be from a bygone time. The childhood she had fashioned for Ruby, however, had been far different.

"My mother did things for me, Michael. She never did things with me."

"But those things," Michael pointed out, "were done with love, weren't they? That made them special in their own right."

"Yes," she said, as if realizing it for the first time, "I suppose they were. Thank you for pointing that out to me."

And how extraordinary that he would think of it in the first place. There were, it appeared, more facets to his personality than there were to a brilliantly cut diamond.

"So," she said, adding the new information she'd learned about him to the stockpile she was amassing to be evaluated at a later time, "you became an auctioneer because of those Saturdays you spent with your mother?"

"Not at first."

"What does that mean?"

"It means that, in my early twenties, I worked as an investment analyst."

He had such an affinity for money, that choice made complete sense to her. Of course, since he'd started searching for other outlets to increase his cash flow, maybe he hadn't been so good at it. Or maybe the funds he'd invested in simply hadn't accrued at a fast enough rate for him.

"That's what you were doing when you got caught..." She trailed off.

"Dealing drugs," he supplied with a nod. "Yes. When I got out of prison, there weren't too many job openings for an investment adviser with a record. I bounced around from place to place for a bit. Then I remembered those times I spent with my mother, and I went to school and learned how to be an auctioneer.'' He spread his arms. ''The rest, as they say, is history.''

''I bet your mother's really proud whenever she sees you conduct an auction,'' Laura said. Especially since he had managed—so far, anyway—to avoid further incarceration.

Michael looked down at the bag of potato chips. ''She's never seen me conduct an auction.'' Regret laced his voice.

''Why not? Does the thought of having her there make you nervous? Have you asked her to stay away?''

When he raised his head, the pain in his eyes pierced her heart.

''I would love to have her there. The reason, Ruby, that she has never been to one of my auctions is that she died when I was eleven.''

Death, and its impact on survivors, was something Laura understood far better than she had ever wanted to. She couldn't help feeling a kinship to him. They'd both known terrible loss.

''I'm sorry, Michael. That must have been hard on you, on your entire family.''

''It was.''

''It was fortunate you had each other to help you through.''

He nodded. ''We each developed different coping mechanisms for dealing with it. Kate, the baby, became fiercely independent. Franco retreated behind his books. Bruno refused to talk about it, as if ignoring it meant it didn't happen.''

She was surprised he was telling her so much. Then again, they truly had seemed to stumble upon a subject they could talk about without immediate argument. Maybe he was as reluctant as she to spoil the mood. Or maybe he just needed to talk about that time in his life.

''What about you, Michael?'' she asked. ''What coping mechanism did you develop?''

He mulled the question over, as if he'd never given it proper thought before. ''People used to say I was a daredevil. I'd do anything—and I do mean anything—someone dared me to do.''

"Tempting death?" she asked.

"Probably."

"What kind of things were you dared to do?"

"Playing Evel Knieval with my bike. Jumping off the roof of my house onto a mattress." His mouth curved. "I broke an arm and a leg that time and was grounded for a month."

Laura chuckled her appreciation. "What else?"

"Skateboard wheelies in gullies. I bought my first motorcycle when I was sixteen. And on my seventeenth birthday, I got my private pilot's license."

"You can fly a plane?"

He nodded. "A friend of mine owns a Cessna Skyhawk. He lets me borrow it whenever I want. Flying relaxes me."

She'd totally forgotten her earlier irritation and her disappointment in him. Like his affinity for animals, this was a side of Michael she had never expected existed.

"What about your father? How did he handle your mother's death?"

Michael gave a long sigh. "As you can imagine, he was pretty much torn up about the whole thing. He didn't function well the first year, so my brother, Carlo, stepped in."

How well Laura remembered the paralysis that had taken hold of her that first, agonizing year. "Is Carlo the oldest?"

"No, Roberto is. But he had just gotten married, and his wife was pregnant."

"So Carlo stepped in."

"Yes."

"How old was he?"

"Seventeen."

"He must be a remarkable person."

She was beginning to believe in the nature part of the nature versus nurture argument. Because, with all the love and support he had been given as a child, Michael had still ended up in jail. It was a pity he didn't share more of his older brother's admirable traits.

But then again, as she well knew, loss could do strange things to people. Maybe Michael's forays into illegality were less about money and more about his subconscious shouting, the way it had when he'd jumped off that roof, "Look at me! I'm here, and I'm alive."

"He is," Michael said. "I owe Carlo more than words can express."

His mother's early death explained so much, Laura realized. Not only did it hold the key to understanding his character, but it also clarified why he flitted from relationship to relationship, as well as why he only looked to the physical when entering into those relationships.

She didn't want to think of him as a little boy, crying into his pillow each night because he missed his mother. Nor did she want to think of him haunting auctions in the vain hope that he could recapture the magic of the time they had spent together. And she knew the minute her head hit the pillow tonight and she closed her eyes, she would forget all about his murky past and do just that.

Worse, she was feeling way, way too sympathetic toward him, which left her only a step or two away from, what? Nursing warm, fuzzy thoughts about him? Forming an alliance with him against Joseph? Throwing herself into his arms? Ludicrous.

"I thought you'd never been burned by love," she said.

He blinked, obviously confused by her abrupt change of subject.

"I haven't."

"Oh, yes, Michael," she stated confidently, "you have."

"When?"

"The day your mother died, you got burned." Seared was more like it.

"Your turn to psychoanalyze me?" he said.

"Ever hear the old saying, 'Turnabout is fair play'?"

He gathered up his lunch wrappings and stuffed them into the paper bag they'd been delivered in. "I thought we were looking for a subject that wouldn't push either of our buttons. This isn't exactly it."

"I know," she replied. "But it...interests me."

''And it makes me...uncomfortable.''

''What can I say? Better you than me.''

''How about neither one of us.''

''Did I hit a nerve, Michael?'' she asked with mock innocence.

''Okay, Ruby.'' He acknowledged her challenge with a wry smile. ''I'll indulge you. For a minute or two, anyway. As I recall, when we had that discussion you're referring to, we weren't speaking of a mother's love.''

''Loss is loss, Michael. It would only be natural if you put up barriers.''

''To women, you mean?''

''Of course.''

''The way you did to men when your father ignored you?''

She applauded. ''Very good.''

''You're wrong, you know.''

''I don't think so. You going to try to make me change my mind?''

''Is that possible?'' he asked.

''Only one way I can think of.''

''And that is?''

''Have a relationship with a woman that lasts longer than a date or two.''

''And who do you propose I have that relationship with?'' he returned. ''You?''

Chapter 9

"Me?" Her voice came out a high-pitched squeak.

"Yes, Ruby. You."

Laura's heart fluttered like the wings of a bird preparing for its first solo flight. Her powers of speech also took wing as a host of emotions swept through her. She couldn't begin to identify half of them, but the top two were plain enough to decipher: dismay and a terrible, traitorous longing.

It served her right. She was the one who had taken the most pleasant conversation they had ever had, and—because it had aroused emotions in her she didn't want to deal with—turned it into a challenge. Michael, she knew, would no more back down from that challenge than would Ruby.

"Makes sense, don't you think?" he went on, seemingly unaware of her inner turmoil. "I mean, if you wanted tangible proof that I can sustain a relationship for a certain period of time, it would be a whole lot easier for you to verify that proof if you were the woman I had the relationship with. Don't you agree?"

He had to be joking. Yes, that was it. Michael was just

pulling her chain. He was paying her back for her eagerness to pursue a topic that he'd admitted gave him discomfort. But when she searched his face for the teasing gleam in his eyes and the uncontrollable upward twitch of his lower lip, he stared straight back at her, his expression deadly serious.

And when she racked her brain for the flip response that Ruby would make to such an outrageous suggestion, it wouldn't come.

"Now you're trying to make *me* uncomfortable," she said. And succeeding admirably.

"I might be," he agreed. "Then again, I might not."

She should have known better. Each time she tried to turn the heat up under him in an effort to make him squirm, she was the one who inevitably wound up on the burner. The better question to ask herself was, Why did she feel such a need to see him squirm?

Subconsciously she knew the answer, but she wasn't ready to face it on a conscious level. Not just yet.

Standing, Laura began gathering up her lunch fixings and shoving them hurriedly into the brown paper bag. "Would you look at the time? We'd better get back to work if we don't want to lose all the ground we made up this morning."

"I never took you for a coward, Ruby."

She froze with one hand inside the paper bag. When she looked over, his gaze hadn't moved from her.

"What's that supposed to mean?"

"It means you started this, you have the guts to finish it."

He was right, damn it. She was Ruby O'Toole, and Ruby didn't back down without a fight. She sank back into the chair, her back rigid, and folded her arms tightly across her middle.

This time his lips did twitch. "Glad to see you're keeping an open mind."

She forced herself to relax. "You really think you can do it, don't you? Have a relationship with a woman, I mean. A real relationship."

"I really do."

"By relationship, I don't mean sex," she felt compelled to explain.

"I'm aware of that."

"What I'm describing is a meeting of the minds, a true sharing of thoughts and goals, hopes and dreams." She paused. "Time spent together. Talking only."

"I'm aware of that, too."

"A lot of time, Michael."

"How long?"

She shrugged. "A year."

"I'm game. Are you?"

The man was impossible. "You can't be serious."

"What if I am?"

He sat there expectantly, as if waiting for her to agree with him. "You're forgetting one thing," she said.

"You mean Joseph," he supplied.

"Yes."

"Forget about Joseph."

"I can't."

Folding his arms on the tabletop, he leaned forward. "We're two of a kind, Ruby, you and I. Haven't you realized that yet? It might be interesting to see what would happen if we joined forces."

Was this another calculated risk on his part? If he couldn't get her to form a working alliance, maybe he could get her to form a romantic one. Behind Joseph's back? What did he hope to accomplish by doing that?

"Thanks for the offer, but I'm not interested."

He stared her down. "You're a terrible liar."

To a woman who was living a lie, whose very life depended on everyone else believing that lie, Michael's words were not exactly music to her ears.

"Why would I lie to you about that?"

"Maybe you have something more important at stake."

"Like what?"

"Like your illusions."

"What illusions?"

"That you're better off with Joseph."

"As opposed to who?" She forced a laugh. "You?"

"Yes, me, Ruby. Are you going to sit there and tell me you don't enjoy our little...interactions?"

He was right, she admitted. She did enjoy them. Even when he made her mad enough to spit. They were a guilty pleasure, like the chocolates she craved once a month.

"Face it, Michael. If I took you up on your invitation, you'd run for the hills."

"You'll never know unless you try. I already told you I was game."

"And I already told you that I'm quite happy with things the way they are, thank you."

There was nothing teasing or lighthearted about the way he regarded her. As a teenager, she'd seen the same look of concern on her parents' faces just before they'd launched into one of their lectures on life's hard-earned lessons.

"Maybe, for once in your life, Ruby, you should be with a man because you enjoy interacting with him, instead of being with him because you want the security his money can buy."

She was Ruby, Laura reminded herself. She had to respond the way Ruby would. "Joseph is a very attractive man. Any woman would want to be with him."

"He's old enough to be your father," Michael pointed out.

"He's only forty-eight."

"And you're, what, twenty-eight? The symbolism isn't lost on me. Most wealthy men tend to be older and more established. Father figures."

He'd figured Ruby out. How long till he figured Laura out, too? That thought didn't bear thinking about.

She stared mutinously at him. "What do you want from me, Michael?"

"The truth. Just the truth, Ruby. That you find me as attractive as I find you."

Her pulse leaped, and her breathing grew erratic. It took an effort of will not to look away. "All right, if that's what you want. You're an attractive man. I'd be a fool not to notice.

But if you're looking for anything else, it just isn't going to happen."

"Because of Joseph," he stated.

This was exactly what Joseph had wanted. This was why he had thrown them together. Ruby would have had no compunction using Michael's admitted attraction for her to get what she needed from him. But Laura couldn't. She just couldn't. There were certain things she just wouldn't do. For any job.

"Yes."

"Because of the things he can give you? The things I can't?"

"Yes."

His mouth drew into a tight line, and a nerve pulsed in his temple. "What if things changed? What if I could give you all the things Joseph can and more? What then?"

Laura drew a long breath. "That's a big *if,* Michael."

"You didn't answer my question," he replied.

Ruby, Laura was sorry to say, would be fickle and amoral enough to switch alliances without a second thought. But in this case, Laura couldn't allow her alter ego to do so. She had a job to do, and that job depended on Joseph's trust in her. She wouldn't let anything jeopardize that. Not even a reluctant attraction that Joseph himself had sanctioned.

"I think, Michael," she said slowly, "that you and I would be a huge mistake."

Antonio closed his journal and placed it in the secret compartment in his suitcase. It had taken him a long time to record the events of the day. He did this with every case he worked. Often the very act of putting into words what had happened, without any corresponding emotion to cloud the issue, helped him find a break in a case.

He knew exactly what he had hoped to find tonight: evidence that he wasn't losing his edge. But the facts didn't lie. It was all down on the page, in blue and white. He had let his emotions get the best of him, to control his actions, something he had never permitted before. "Before" meaning before he met Ruby.

Turning the lights off, he lay back in bed and cradled his arms beneath his head. When his eyes grew accustomed to the darkness, he watched the play of shadows across the ceiling.

All in all, he acknowledged, it had been a lousy day. First Ruby had scared the life out of him when he'd thought she'd disappeared. Then, when he had gotten a little too much into character and forgotten he was talking to a woman, she had made him blush. She had followed that embarrassing demonstration by analyzing his love life and declaring it lacking. The coup de grâce had been her assertion that, no matter how attractive she found him, she would never want him enough to leave Joseph, even if he could offer her everything Joseph could and more.

And he, poor, stupid fool that he was, was still totally besotted by her. He knew what she was, and still he wanted her. He admitted it now. There was no use denying it any longer.

Just as there was no use denying he had pushed things too far. He had started out trying to pay her back for the anxiety she'd caused him, and things had escalated from there. He had been totally out of control when he'd tried to get her to admit he wasn't the only one struggling with feelings he didn't want to have. So much in his life of late was make-believe. Was it so bad to want just one little thing to be out in the open for both Ruby and him to see? There was, in the final analysis, only so much a man could take, and he had definitely reached his limit.

All the justifying in the world wouldn't change the fact that he was teetering on the edge of blowing this whole operation. He had to get control, and he had to do it now.

On the bright side, his ineptitude had served a purpose. In a very roundabout way, he had taken a step toward achieving his objective. He had planted the seed that he and Ruby form an alliance, either financially or romantically. Now he just had to sit back and see if that seed would take root and grow. He didn't delude himself that, just because he was besotted by her, she would automatically turn into the woman he wanted her to be. Ruby was a person who looked out for number one first. She would do whatever it took for her to stay on top, even if it meant choosing Michael over Joseph.

The question Antonio had to answer was, given his feelings for her, what would he do in the unlikely event she took him up on either offer? There was only one correct answer: his job. He would do his job.

Still waters run deep. The phrase his mother had been so fond of echoed in his mind. At first meeting, he never would have thought it would apply to Ruby. But now he knew better. She was not the woman she wanted the world to think she was. Far from it.

Who was Ruby O'Toole? Antonio wondered if he would ever really know. She was definitely an enigma. Sometimes she seemed like two different people. There was the Ruby who, without a hint of makeup on her face, sat cross-legged and barefoot on a park bench, sketching the local scenery. Then there was the Ruby who seemed to care solely about showing off her legs and figure, and who was a practiced flirt.

The Ruby who was unable to hide her intelligence and the depth of her knowledge fascinated him. The Ruby who put money and physical appearance before all else irritated the hell out of him. Both Rubys turned him on more than he had ever believed possible, something he was determined to ignore from this point on. Better to focus on the question of how Joseph was receiving and distributing drugs and to put her totally out of his mind.

One thing was certain. She wasn't lying awake, obsessing about him. His gaze traveled to the connecting door and the faint light that seeped beneath its lower edge. Or was she?

Antonio raised himself up on his elbows and listened to the silence. It was after midnight, and he hadn't heard a peep from her room for a couple of hours now. Was she lost in the Joads' efforts to escape the dust bowl, or had she fallen asleep while reading?

He wished he felt relaxed enough to read. So much for putting her out of his mind.

An hour passed while he pounded his pillow and tossed and turned in a futile effort to sleep. Every time he looked at the door, the light still burned.

At one-fifteen, he started pacing. At one-thirty, he silently opened his side of the connecting doors. At one forty-five, he placed his ear to Ruby's door and listened. There was no sound; no muted television volume, no rustling of bedclothes, not even the turn of a page.

Acting on an urge he felt powerless to resist, Antonio silently picked the lock and slowly pushed the door inward. As he had anticipated, she was fast asleep, the bed sheets pulled securely beneath her chin. *The Grapes of Wrath* lay firmly closed on the bedside table, which meant she hadn't nodded off while reading. As far as he could tell, for the second night in a row, Ruby had deliberately snuggled down under the covers and closed her eyes with every light still blazing.

Her back was to him, her figure curled in a fetal position, her brown hair a wild tangle on the pillow. She looked impossibly small and vulnerable. As he stood in the silence, watching the even rise and fall of her shoulders, every protective instinct he possessed roared to life.

Why did Ruby sleep with the lights on? And why did he feel a compulsion to climb into bed beside her and cradle her close? The urge wasn't even remotely sexual, but instead a desire to protect her from whatever demons obviously haunted her dreams to the point where she didn't feel safe sleeping in the dark.

Quietly, before he made an even bigger fool of himself, or found himself arrested for breaking and entering, as well as being a Peeping Tom, Antonio closed and relocked the door. Then he went back to bed.

''You seem tired,'' Ruby said.

Tired wasn't the word for it, Antonio thought. Wiped out was more like it. It was three o'clock in the afternoon, he'd been up for eight hours, and still he felt as exhausted as he had when, after a paltry two hours' sleep, he'd jerked awake to the shrill ringing of his alarm.

Since he couldn't look at her without recalling how slight and vulnerable she had appeared in her bed, he concentrated on the full-length Victorian cheval mirror he was evaluating.

"Do I? I guess I didn't sleep all that well last night."

After spending the bulk of the day on the second and third floors of the Bickham mansion, they had finally made their way to the attic. Antonio was doing his best to keep his distance from Ruby, a feat made much easier due to the sheer size of the room.

The downside was it was hot and stuffy, and he was forever stifling a sneeze from all the dust on the air. Though they'd flung open several windows, there wasn't much of a breeze to cool things down. Antonio could feel his T-shirt clinging uncomfortably to his chest.

He chanced a glance at her. It hadn't taken Ruby long to shed her jacket. At present she knelt in front of an old steamer trunk, seemingly oblivious to the streaks of dirt coating her hands and knees, as well as her pale-blue sleeveless silk dress. That was one outfit Joseph would definitely have to replace. He hoped it cost a fortune.

"What about you, Ruby? How did you sleep?"

"Me?" Glancing over her shoulder, she shrugged. "Like a rock. To tell you the truth, Michael, I haven't slept so soundly in ages."

Since he couldn't recall when he'd slept less soundly, her confirmation of what he had already known only served to worsen his sour mood. Her unflagging cheerfulness hadn't helped matters, either. She'd kept up a steady stream of idle chatter all day. If yesterday's events had had any impact on her, he certainly couldn't tell.

"No dreams?" he asked.

"None that I can remember."

At least now he could rest assured that a niggling suspicion of someone being in her room wasn't lurking in the back of her mind.

"Lucky you," he muttered.

"You say something?" she called, her head back in the trunk.

"Just talking to myself."

"Oh, wow," she said a minute later, sitting back on her heels.

"Find something?"

Standing, she dusted herself off, then held up a bundled sheaf of letters for his inspection.

"What are they?" he asked.

"Letters Vincent and Serena wrote to each other." She riffled through them. "They're dated 1942 through 1945. They have to be from the time Vincent served in World War II. What a great find."

He couldn't see what she was so worked up about. "They're just letters. No one cares about them. They're not worth anything, Ruby."

"You're wrong," she disagreed. "A historian, particularly one compiling a biography about either Serena or Vincent, would be highly interested."

"Interested or not, if Joseph does include them in the auction, I can't see them bringing more than fifty dollars, and even that's a stretch."

She stood her ground. "You and I both have seen worthless items go for outrageous sums because bidders got caught up in auction fever and didn't know when to back down."

"True. But I can't imagine that happening here."

She closed the lid of the trunk and sat down on top of it. "They're the history of a relationship, Michael. As such, they're priceless. Want to read them with me?"

The excitement in her voice was unmistakable, as was the quickening of his pulse. "Why would I want to do that?"

"Aren't you interested in learning more about Vincent and Serena? After all, we've been poking about in their things for two days now. I should think you'd want to get inside their heads as much as I do.''

Not if it meant putting his head together with hers. Dusting off his hands, Antonio moved over to a maple dry sink that looked as if it dated from a time before Vincent made it big.

''If it's all the same to you, I think I'll keep on working.''

''Don't be such an old stick-in-the-mud,'' she chided, then patted the trunk lid. ''Sit here with me, or pull up a crate, if you'd like. We both need a break. I insist. You especially, Michael, since you only took a couple of minutes for lunch.''

It was obvious she wasn't going to take no for an answer. Unless he wanted to face a whole host of questions he didn't want to answer, he'd be better off just giving in.

''I'll stand here, if that's okay with you.''

Ruby shot him a curious look, but refrained from further comment. After loosening the ribbon that had been tied around the bundle of letters, she picked up the first envelope and extracted the pages it contained. Handling the thin sheets carefully, she read:

''January 15, 1942.
Darling,
You have been gone but an hour, yet already it feels like years. I walk through our little home, and I see touches of you everywhere. Your magazines and your books. Your guitar propped in the corner. The gloves hanging in the garage that you always wear when you work in the garden. The cup you drank your coffee from at breakfast this very morning, and which I cannot bring myself to wash. Each time I look at these things that remind me of you, I get a huge lump in my throat, and it is all I can do not to burst into tears.

This is the first time we have been apart since our fateful meeting in the children's home fourteen years ago. Is that memory still as vivid for you as it is for me? It seems like only yesterday that I saw you, and you pulled my hair and called me midget. To my everlasting shame,

I kicked you in the shin. Oh, how I hated you!

I used to pray every night—of course, we all did—for a family to step forward and adopt me. After your arrival, I prayed even harder. Then suddenly my prayers changed, and I pleaded with God that no one step forward and adopt either one of us. Because that would have taken me from you, and you from me.

I know most people would scoff that, at eight and ten, we couldn't possibly have fallen in love, that we were too young and naive to know the way of our own hearts. But they are the ones who lack understanding. They are the ones who are naive. Though separate and distinct, in spirit we are truly one. Others find it odd that we are so devoted to each another. Sometimes I think they are even threatened by our closeness and, perhaps, somewhat resentful. I certainly find it sad how most of the married people we know don't devote more love and attention to the person with whom they have chosen to travel this journey through life.

Speaking of journeys… Right now, beloved, as you travel to North Carolina for your training, there are only two states separating us. Soon, all too soon, however, there will be an ocean, and guns and bombs. How my poor heart quails to think of it! I should hate the army for taking you from me, but of course I can't. The cause is a just and righteous one.

If only God had seen fit to bless us with a child, it might be easier for me with you gone. But I haven't yet given up hope that, after your return, we will be thus blessed. In the meantime I take comfort in all the good things He has already bestowed upon us. If this is all I am to have, it will be more than enough.

I know, darling, that my letters to you are supposed to be cheerful, but please indulge me just this once as I express my grief at being apart from you. After this one day of feeling sorry for myself, I promise to keep my chin up and to think only good thoughts. After all, my sacrifice is insignificant in comparison to what you and your fellow soldiers have given up to fight for our country. I am so very proud of you, Vincent, and I will do everything in my power to keep the home fires burning brightly until your return.

Your devoted wife,

Serena"

Ruby slowly lowered the letter to her lap. There was a faraway light in the eyes she raised to him.

"So they were both orphans," she murmured. "That explains so much."

Despite his intention to remain aloof, Antonio had found himself caught up in Serena's words, and in the rise and fall of Ruby's voice as she read them out loud. "You mean, why Vincent left his estate to his former employees."

She nodded. "Since he and Serena never did have children, I suppose there was no one else to leave it to."

"There was charity," he pointed out.

"Maybe," Ruby ventured, "he thought of his workers as family. They certainly thought highly of him."

Antonio recalled her telling him how they had insisted that Joseph handle the disposition of Vincent's estate in a certain manner. He also tried—and failed—to picture Joseph leaving his estate to his employees. And as much as he liked and respected his superiors, he would be astonished if one of them left him anything in their wills.

"Perhaps," he said, "Vincent identified with his workers, and that's how they grew close. How did he make his living before he opened his marble factory?"

"It's my understanding he worked in a coal mine."

Antonio found himself smiling. "From lumps of coal to marbles. Not such a huge leap, I suppose."

"But a profitable one," Ruby said.

"And a lot easier on the lungs."

She picked up the next envelope. "This one's from Vincent," she said, extending it toward him.

Her intent was plain. "You want me to read it?"

"You can read, can't you?"

"Of course."

"Then what's the problem? Aren't you even curious to find out how it all ends?"

"I know how it ends, Ruby. Vincent makes it home safely. He builds a marble factory and earns a fortune. They live happily ever after. Then she dies, and he loses all interest in life until he finally dies, too. What else is there to know?"

"For starters," she challenged, "why you're so reluctant to read one little letter out loud. What are you afraid of, Michael?"

That if he let himself get all caught up in her excitement over her find, he'd do something stupid. "That if we don't get this work done, we'll be stuck out here in the middle of nowhere for an extra day or two."

"Is that all?" she asked.

"What else could it be?"

She tilted her head and studied him. "Maybe you're just a sentimental softy, and you're terrified someone will find out."

"That someone being you?"

"You see anyone else here? Don't worry, Michael. I'm good at keeping secrets. I won't tell."

His fellow cops, Antonio knew, would roll on the floor laughing their heads off at the thought that he was either sentimental or a softy. His family, on the other hand, might be inclined to agree with Ruby. It was a certainty that Michael would definitely be offended to be considered, either.

Then there was the mention of secrets. Ruby might be keeping a few that it would be to his advantage to uncover. Which meant he had to placate her.

"I'm not sentimental," he said. "And I'm definitely not a softy."

She waved the letter at him. "Prove it."

Antonio moved to stand at her shoulder. Reluctantly he plucked the pages from her fingers.

"'January 15, 1942,'" he read slowly. "'Somewhere in

Virginia.' " He looked up. "That's the same day Serena wrote her letter. The day Vincent left."

"And you said you weren't interested," she chided gently.

Ignoring her, Antonio kept reading:

"Beloved wife,

Please forgive the unsteady penmanship, but I am on a moving train. I suppose I should wait until I arrive at my posting to write this, but I find that I cannot. I have never considered myself to be a sentimental man. Nor have I been a man to speak of his feelings with flowery words and fanciful images. You know me, Serena. I'm more likely to tug on your hair and call you midget than to bring you flowers and quote the great poets. Yet, as I leave you for an unknown length of time, I now understand what inspired those poets. Love.

I watched you waving goodbye to me today at the train station, your face pinched and worried, the tears threatening to fall from your beautiful eyes, and all I could think of was the little girl I met fourteen years ago in an orphanage. Did I ever tell you how terrified I was that day? I was ten years old, my parents had just died, and I had no other family to take me in. Though I had always felt somewhat set apart, even when my parents were alive, never had I felt so alone.

Then I saw you standing there, staring at me. Your long brown hair was braided, you had freckles on your nose and cheeks, and your big brown eyes were so solemn. I just couldn't resist. I reached out and tugged on your braids and called you midget. And you glared at me and kicked me in the shin.

In that orphanage, Serena, I found the part of me that had always been missing. I found you, the love, the meaning of my life, and it all but tears my heart out to leave you behind. If you had asked me to stay, I don't know if I would have found the strength to board this train.

Even now, halfway into my journey, part of me wants to get off at the next stop and return to the loving comfort of your arms. However, I could not, in all good conscience, enjoy the precious freedoms we cherish in this land if I did not take a stand to preserve them. I will try to do my duty with courage and skill, as I know you will do yours here, at home.

And so, my beloved, I go off to war. But I do not go alone. At my side are hundreds and thousands of fine, upstanding young men. And in my heart is you. It is your sweet, beloved face and the memory of the heaven to be found in your embrace that will carry me through the difficult times that I know are coming. God willing, I will return to you soon. Until then, I impatiently count the hours.

Your husband,

Vincent''

''Now that,'' Ruby said softly, and on a sigh, ''is what I call a love letter.''

It was what Antonio called sheer bravery. The letter had affected him deeply. When Vincent wrote of how he had felt when he had first seen Serena, Antonio had immediately recalled his first glimpse of Ruby across the crowded auction floor.

Of course, any similarity between Vincent and Serena, and Ruby and himself ended there. Not only had Ruby pledged herself to another man, but Serena and Ruby were two entirely different women. It wasn't just because Ruby was a much more attractive woman. There was no doubt in his mind that, inwardly, Serena Bickham had the leading edge on beauty. The most compelling evidence for that argument was that she had stuck by Vincent's side when he was nothing but a poor coal miner, and she hadn't seemed to care whether or not he wanted to do anything else with his life. Antonio couldn't imagine Ruby doing the same.

"He sure put it out there in the open, for everyone to see," he said.

Ruby's gaze was curious. "You mean the way he told Serena what she meant to him? You think that's not manly?"

"As a general rule, men don't exactly share their feelings like that." He leaned back against a support beam and crossed his legs, trying to appear nonchalant. "Vincent did write that he wasn't a man prone to the use of flowery phrases. I suppose, though, when he was staring death in the face on his way to war, he felt it was important to let Serena know exactly what he was feeling."

"And he probably didn't think anyone else besides Serena would ever read his words." Ruby fingered the pearls at her neck. "That letter kind of makes all our problems seem trivial, doesn't it?"

"Sure does," he agreed.

She seemed to hesitate. "Have you ever been that honest with a woman?"

He was living a lie, yet Antonio couldn't deny that his conversations with Ruby, despite the way they never failed to infuriate him, had been the most honest discussions he had ever had with a woman. Even so, he couldn't imagine baring his soul to anyone the way Vincent had to his wife.

"I'm the one who's never had anything other than a fleeting relationship, remember?" he said.

"How silly of me," she replied, a wry twist to her mouth. "I can't imagine how I forgot."

"What about you, Ruby? Have you been that honest with Joseph?"

Her fingers went still. She dropped them from the necklace to her lap. "Joseph knows what my feelings are where he is concerned."

Which told him nothing. He nodded at the pile of letters. "I believe it's your turn."

They continued on that way, Ruby reading Serena's missives about rationing and war bonds and Serena's taking a job so that she could accumulate a nest egg in anticipation of

Vincent's return; Antonio reading Vincent's censored words about battles, wartime friendships and the sudden violent losses of the same, and the thrill and expectation that surrounded D-Day and both V-E and V-J days.

Underneath each written word, though never expressly spelled out, he could feel both Serena's and Vincent's need and desire for each other. That need and desire grew with each letter, until it became almost a physical thing, a third presence in the room with them.

Time passed, but neither he nor Ruby seemed aware of it. It was as if they were caught up in some magical spell that refused to let them go. At some point, he couldn't exactly recall when, he actually sat down next to her on top of the trunk.

"This is the last letter," she finally said, holding it out to him.

As if coming out of a trance, Antonio slowly raised his gaze to hers. For the first time he realized how closely they sat atop the old trunk, so close in fact that their legs touched at thigh and calf. A faint sheen of perspiration dotted her upper lip, and a smudge of dirt streaked her forehead. The heat of her skin seared him, and the fragrant aroma of her perfume cut through the mustiness on the air. Suddenly the temperature in the attic seemed to shoot up at least ten degrees, and he felt the fierce sweetness of desire beginning to unfurl deep inside him.

"Aren't you going to read it?" she asked.

It was either that or kiss her, which would be a mistake of monumental proportions.

Antonio managed to tear his gaze from her and gave a halting nod. With fingers that weren't quite steady, he pulled the letter from its envelope. Drawing a ragged breath, he read:

"October 28, 1945.
Dearest Serena,
At last, the news we have waited so long for. I'm coming home! By Thanksgiving Day we should be reunited,

never to be apart again. It is all I can think of, and I walk around all day with a big, goofy smile on my face. Of course, I'm not the only one. Most of the men in my unit who got the same word I did are sporting the same silly grin.

Now that I know I will be seeing you soon, I can let myself think of all the things I would not allow myself to think of, because they made me too homesick. These are probably not things I should be writing in such a public forum, but I have a feeling that, since all is said and done but the shouting, the censors aren't as worried about military security as they used to be. Maybe this letter will reach you, unseen by other eyes. If another pair of eyes does happen to chance upon my words, I hope he has someone as wonderful as you waiting for him at home.

My darling Serena, I can't wait to take you in my arms again, to feel the softness of your lips against mine. I hope you're not planning on wearing clothes for the first few weeks, sweetheart, because I don't plan on letting you out of my arms or our bed. Making love to you and with you is the only thing I can think of. The rest—a job, our future, the world—can wait until later. Much, much later. Until Thanksgiving, I am as ever,

Your husband,

Vincent''

There was a long, taut silence after Antonio finished reading. It wasn't so much that Vincent's words had put certain images into his mind—although they were definitely there—but Ruby's reaction to them that got to him.

The eyes she trained on him were huge and shone a little too brightly. Her lips trembled, and a lone tear slowly made its way down her cheek. She didn't bother to hide the emotion or to brush the tear away, and he was deeply touched by how much she truly seemed to care about two people she had never met.

Never had she seemed more beautiful to him. From that point on, Antonio knew he would forever hold that image of her in his mind.

"I guess I'm the one who's the sentimental softy," she said, her smile a little misty.

"Maybe," he admitted, "we both are."

"Watch out, Michael," she teased. "If you're not careful, soon you'll be whispering sweet nothings into my ear."

He knew she was trying to lighten the mood. Still, he couldn't keep his heart from thundering and his gaze from focusing more intently on her.

"Would you like me to?" he asked softly.

He heard the swift catch of her breath, saw the unmistakable parting of her lips.

"I said it once before, Ruby, and I'll say it again." He leaned in close to her. "You are so incredibly beautiful."

"Michael."

The word was both a protest and an invitation. Antonio reached out a hand and slid it along the smooth line of her jaw. When his fingers reached the back of her neck, he pressed them gently into her skin. Slowly, with their gazes locked together, he drew her toward him. When finally only mere millimeters separated them, and he could feel the sweetness of her breath on his face, he closed his eyes and dropped his mouth to hers.

Unheeded, the letters fell to the floor.

Chapter 10

He never meant for the kiss to get out of hand. When his mouth closed over Ruby's, Antonio expected the experience to mirror every first kiss he'd ever exchanged with a woman. Somewhat tentative at first, while they grew accustomed to the taste and feel of each other. Then nice. Pleasurable. Maybe even a little passionate. And ultimately, when all was said and done, forgettable.

But when Ruby turned into him, wrapping her arms around his neck and opening her mouth to him, responding with a fervency he had hardly dared dream of, Antonio felt himself consumed by a searing heat that had nothing to do with the closeness of the air in the attic. That was when he lost all semblance of control.

With a groan he threaded both hands through her hair and pressed her closer. He traced the tip of his tongue over the outline of her lips, then ran it across her teeth. Seemingly impatient with his exploration, she uttered a low, dissatisfied growl before tangling her tongue with his, and he felt himself drawn even further under her spell.

Restlessly his hands left her hair to wander down her bare arms and over her back. With a growing sense of wonder, he felt the press of her small breasts against his chest, along with the fragility of her bones beneath his fingers. She felt as delicate as the Spode china she had marveled over in the dining room, yet Antonio sensed in her an inner core that was as strong and lasting as the dry sink he'd just valued. One thing was certain: she tasted like heaven and the sweetest elixir ever offered up to a man. And he never wanted to let her go.

When his arousal began throbbing painfully, he started sifting through the back of his mind for alternatives on how to get closer to her. In the end, the awkwardness of their position atop the sloped lid of the trunk, as well as the impossibility of seduction in a room with nothing resembling a bed, not to mention hardwood floors that hadn't been swept in years, brought him to his senses.

What was he doing? He was kissing the woman who was sleeping with his boss, and she was kissing him back. Passionately. Worse, she was also, if he was reading her right, giving him every indication that she would take the kiss as far as he wanted it to go. And damn his very soul to hell, he wanted it to go all the way.

Joseph finding out, and then firing him for his offense, was the least of Antonio's worries. His actions were jeopardizing the job he had been assigned to do. It had taken untold hours and effort on the behalf of his colleagues to arrange for him to be hired by Joseph, not to mention all the work that had gone into detecting the truth beneath the extensive cover—that Joseph was a big player in the drug trade— and here he was, allowing his hormones to rule his actions.

The sad truth was, Antonio couldn't think of a single thing he had done right since he'd started this job, but he sure could think of dozens of things he'd done wrong. The first, and biggest, mistake he had made was letting Ruby get under his skin.

Hadn't he worried, earlier, that reading those letters with

her would lead him to do something stupid? If this wasn't stupid, the pope wasn't Catholic.

Somehow he found the strength to push her away. Breathing heavily, he rubbed his hand over his mouth, not that anything could ever wipe the taste of her from him. Even though he knew he was doing what he had to do, regret squeezed thick fingers around his heart.

"This isn't going to happen," he said, far more roughly than he had intended. "We're not Vincent and Serena, and we never will be."

She stared at him blankly for an endless stretch of time. He knew exactly when his words penetrated, because she paled. With a proud tilt of her head that spoke more loudly than words of the hurt he had caused, a hurt he was powerless to make better, she climbed carefully off the trunk. After taking a few unsteady steps, she whirled to face him.

"Do you believe in a love like that, Michael?" she demanded, an unusual urgency in her voice.

Expecting condemnation, Antonio felt a momentary surprise. When the meaning of her question registered, his thoughts automatically turned to his parents. Even as a child he had been able to understand that the love they shared was special, a love as deep and abiding as the one Serena and Vincent had expressed in their letters.

He thought of the relationships he had had over the years. Not once had he come close to feeling that way about a woman. Since his mother's death had nearly destroyed his father, Antonio couldn't help being thankful. He could still recall, all too vividly, the awful years when Lorenzo Garibaldi had simply gone through the motions of living, his eyes haunted and dead. If it hadn't been for Carlo, the family would have fallen apart. Then there was Vincent. Hadn't he merely subsisted for five long years after Serena passed away?

That kind of love he could definitely do without. As could Michael.

"No, Ruby," he replied. "I don't."

"That's what I thought," she said flatly.

"What about you?" he asked. "Do you believe in it?"

As in that moment when their gazes had first met, Antonio saw myriad emotions swirling in her eyes. Remembrance, loss, emptiness, a haunting yearning and a deep, long-buried pain. And, like that first moment, after allowing a glimpse of her feelings, her face went blank. Ruby laughed that brittle laugh of hers and gave a negligent shrug of her shoulders.

"I'm a realist, Michael. That kind of love only happens once in a lifetime, if then. I'd rather stick to the kind of relationship that provides more material rewards. The pay is a whole lot better."

The outrage he felt at her assertion lacked any real heat. Because there was a question he needed to ask. A question only a heel would voice. Michael wouldn't have hesitated to ask it, and Antonio couldn't, either. They both needed her answer, though for very different reasons.

"Are you going to tell Joseph?"

Ruby sucked in a harsh breath and went still. A taut silence made the already heavy air seem even heavier. Defiantly she thrust out her chin, her throat working convulsively. At her sides her hands clenched and unclenched.

Antonio stayed where he was atop the old trunk, while she fought her inner battle, and awaited the dressing down that was inevitable. The dressing down he deserved. Never had he felt like such a complete bastard.

"What don't you want me to tell him, Michael?" she finally said, the emotion blazing from her eyes belying the calmness of her voice. "That you asked me to help you steal from him? Or that you asked me to have an affair with you behind his back? Maybe it's just the kiss you don't want me to tell him about."

Good points, each one of them, he conceded. To tell Joseph about any of them would put his job in jeopardy. Antonio—no, Michael—had to make things right here.

"You do know, don't you," he said, "that I wasn't serious about us stealing from Joseph or having an affair? I was just trying to get a rise out of you. I thought you understood that at the time.''

If the look on Ruby's face was any indication, she knew, as well as he, that his words were only a half-truth.

''And the kiss?'' she asked. ''Was that a joke, too?''

No matter how much he wanted to, Antonio couldn't lie about the kiss. ''No. It wasn't a joke. I'm sorry, Ruby. I stepped out of line. My only excuse is that I got caught up in the moment. I think we both did. I promise you, it won't happen again.''

There was another long silence before she said, ''If I told Joseph about the kiss, I'd also have to admit I got as caught up in the moment as you. Don't worry, Michael. I'm not going to say a word. About anything. Your precious job is safe.'' Turning her back to him, she went to work.

The relief he'd anticipated didn't come. Instead Antonio found himself puzzling over Ruby's response. It would have been so easy for her to lie, so easy for her to tell Joseph that Michael had taken advantage of her, and that she hadn't responded to his kiss. She wouldn't have had to lie at all to tell him about his other offers.

But she wasn't going to do any of that. Why? Could she actually—improbable though the thought seemed—be protecting him? Ruby never looked out for anyone but herself. Despite her response to his kiss, and despite her response to Vincent's and Serena's letters, the most likely explanation for her closemouthedness was that he didn't mean enough to her to bother herself, or Joseph, over.

A glance at her stiff back confirmed that for him. With a sigh, and with a heart that felt unusually heavy, Antonio resumed his work.

Laura held the dress up to the light, twisting it so she could view both the front and the back. There was no denying it was a total loss. Along with the streaks of dirt, there were also a couple of spots that looked suspiciously like fingerprints.

Michael had left his prints on her, both literally and figuratively.

With a disgusted grunt, she tossed the dress onto the bed, strode into the bathroom and began removing her makeup. When her face was clean, she dashed it with cold water and toweled it dry. Leaning into the mirror, she studied her reflection. It was time to stop fabricating excuses. Time to stop hiding from reality. Time to face the truth, head-on, and to take action.

"Face it," she told the woman in the mirror. "You want the man. You want him bad. No matter how wrong it is. No matter how guilty it makes you feel. No matter that he's no good for you. No matter that you're not now, and may never be, ready for another relationship. That's why you lost yourself in his kiss the way you did, why you asked him about his belief in love. You want him. And if he hadn't pushed you away, you would have made love with him."

With a groan, Laura dropped her head into her hands.

Wanting him physically was bad enough. That was simply hormonal. Worse was the knowledge that, try though she might, she simply couldn't dislike the man. Even though he often made her madder than a wet cat, she enjoyed being with him. She definitely enjoyed their verbal sparring. She even admired a lot of things about him, like the fact that he was a hard worker, that he worried himself sick over a pair of abandoned puppies, that he read the classics and worked crossword puzzles. She liked that he appreciated art and had taken the trouble to try to encourage her efforts.

But the best thing about him was that, when she least expected it, Michael made her laugh. She hadn't laughed much these past four years, and it had felt good to rediscover the part of her that responded to humor.

And when it came to her, the only thing he was concerned about was his job.

It was like a hostage situation, she told herself. She'd read about it countless times. The hapless kidnap victim, dependent on the charity of her captor, begins to identify, even to sympathize with and support his goals. It was the only explanation that could explain why she found herself enamored of a man who had no moral center.

Laura wished she had someone to talk to, a sympathetic ear to bounce her troubles off. But there was no one. She realized it now, for the first time. That first awful year after Jacob and Jason had died, she had been so immersed in the pain that she'd pushed away everyone who tried to help. The past three years she had immersed herself in her police work, even furthering the distance. Invitations to join this friend or that had stopped coming long ago.

Was that why she was identifying so closely with Michael? Because, other than her brother, she was all alone?

"Understanding a problem is halfway to solving it," she told her reflection. When this was all over, when she was back in New York, she vowed to revisit those friends she had sadly neglected and try to rebuild the bridges she had destroyed. As far as her larger problem—Michael—was concerned, she might not be able to stop herself from wanting him, but she could stop herself from giving in to that want.

Now that she had faced the truth about her feelings for him, she could take whatever precautions were necessary to keep her distance. The first of those was to finish up the job so that they could return to Pittsburgh and normalcy, or as normal as her life got these days.

All she had to do was get through one more day. Once she was back at the auction gallery, when the two of them weren't alone together for nearly sixteen hours every day, not only would Laura be able to devote her time to the job she'd been sent to do, she would be able to look at Michael more objectively. She'd be able to see him for what he truly was.

Not for her. Never for her.

The atmosphere at breakfast was highly strained. After exchanging the most basic of pleasantries, Ruby lapsed into silence, and for the first time Antonio saw her only pick at her food. She spent the bulk of the mealtime looking down at her plate, at the walls of the lounge, at the ceiling, at the other diners—anywhere but at him. To the casual observer, he supposed they resembled a long-married couple who, sadly, had nothing left to say to each other.

After checking out of the motel—Ruby had broken her silence long enough to insist they both leave a large tip for the maid—they made their final trip to the mansion. When Antonio crested the last hill on the long, winding, bumpy road, he saw that the moving vans had already arrived. Once they finished cataloguing the few remaining items, and once Howard Bracken arrived to supervise the loading process, he and Ruby could head back to Pittsburgh.

He wished he felt happier about the prospect.

There were five vans in all. Each bore the name and logo of the Merrill Auction Gallery. Joseph was certainly doing well if he could maintain his own fleet of moving vans. Antonio wondered if they were involved in the drug operation. There was only one way to find out. He had to get inside them.

He made his move at lunchtime, when, along with Howard Bracken, the drivers all trouped into the kitchen at Ruby's invitation to share the lunch she'd had delivered. Saying that he needed to recheck a few pieces of furniture one last time and that he'd rejoin them in a minute, Antonio excused himself.

Since the loading process had already begun, the rear doors of all five vans stood open. Peering over his shoulder to make sure he wasn't being observed, he climbed into the first van and threaded his way through the already loaded furniture.

Though he searched the interior of each van carefully, he found nothing out of the ordinary. If Joseph was using them in his drug operations, there wasn't so much as the faintest residue of powder to prove it.

Disappointed, he returned to the kitchen, where he sat across from a woman who wouldn't look at him, and ate a lunch he didn't taste.

* * *

Crouching low and bouncing from foot to foot, Antonio pounded his fists into the ceiling-mounted, fifty-pound punching bag as hard and as rapidly as he could. It wasn't long before sweat poured down his face and his breathing grew labored. He kept punching.

It was just a kiss, he told himself. Just a kiss. It didn't mean anything.

So why couldn't he stop being tormented by the memory of his mouth on Ruby's, by the feel of her warm, soft body in his arms, the scent of her in his nostrils, and the heady euphoria of her response?

His jabs grew harder and faster.

"That bag got a face on it?"

Surprise had Antonio turning his head. When the bag rebounded and threatened to knock him on his backside, he braced his legs and thrust his arms out to still it, then stepped out of the way for another man to have a turn.

"What are you doing here?" he asked his older brother as he removed his gloves and headgear.

"Looking for you."

"Why?"

"You called me," Carlo said. "I decided to return the call in person."

"I just wanted to let you know I was home. Didn't Samantha tell you that?"

"She did."

Antonio bent over to pick up the towel he'd dropped on the mat. After wiping the perspiration off his face, he slung it around his neck. He and Carlo made their way past other exercisers to an empty bench on the far wall, where they both took a seat. Despite the lateness of the hour, the gym was full. It catered to men and women like himself who needed the versatility a twenty-four-hour gym offered.

"How did you find me?"

"When you weren't at your apartment, I drove your normal jogging route and then took the chance you might be here."

Antonio eyed his brother's uniform. As chief of police of

the town he resided in, Carlo's hours could often be as erratic as his own.

"You're working late tonight."

Carlo nodded. "I've got a particularly stubborn case that I'd really like to crack."

"Any luck?"

"Not tonight."

"Sorry to hear that."

"You're not the only one."

"It's almost midnight, Carlo," Antonio said. "I should think you'd want to be at home with your wife and son, instead of sitting here with me."

"Samantha told me to find you before I came home."

That got his attention. "She did? Why?"

"She said she heard something in your voice. She thought you might need someone to talk to."

"I'll be damned." Antonio smiled ruefully.

"What?"

"Here you two are, still practically newlyweds, and already you've turned her into one of us."

Amusement lit Carlo's eyes. "You're referring to our tendency to butt our big noses into each other's business?"

"Is there any other?"

"Not in this family." Carlo gave him an appraising look. "Obviously, you're not nearly as happy to see me as I am to see you."

Sighing, Antonio leaned forward and braced his elbows on his thighs. "I'm sorry, Carlo. The last four days have been…trying, to say the least."

"You don't like the job?"

No offense to Carlo, but if Antonio told his older brother what was really bothering him—that he couldn't sleep because he kept picturing Ruby in Joseph's arms and, even worse, in his bed—the rest of the family would know about it by morning, and then he would have no peace.

"It's proving to be a bit of a challenge." That was certainly the truth, as well as the understatement of the century.

"That's good, isn't it?" Carlo said. "Seems to me, a couple of months ago you were complaining how things weren't challenging enough, and how you really needed a change of pace."

Antonio watched a man bench-press 250 pounds. "I wasn't anticipating this much of a challenge."

"You'll do fine." Carlo reached over and clapped him on the back. "You're a great cop."

He wished he had Carlo's conviction. Of course, if his brother had seen just how badly Antonio had screwed things up this week, he'd be singing an entirely different tune.

"Thanks for the vote of confidence."

"When did you get in?"

"A couple of hours ago."

They had left the Bickham estate shortly after three. The drive back to Pittsburgh had been a silent one, with both Ruby and him seemingly lost in their own thoughts. Since neither of them had wanted to stop for dinner, or for a break of any kind, they had driven straight through, with Antonio behind the wheel. For much of that time he had ignored the posted speed limit. As a result he had managed to shave an hour off their anticipated travel time.

What was Ruby doing right now? he wondered for the thousandth time that night. He'd dropped her off at her apartment shortly after nine. Had she unpacked and gone straight to bed? Or had she rushed over to Joseph, as he secretly dreaded, and into his bed?

He needed to concentrate on the job and to forget about Ruby O'Toole, he told himself firmly. He'd wasted enough time on emotions that had nothing to do with the work he was expected to perform.

It was time for him to face facts. The facts in this case were that, even if Ruby were to leave Joseph for him, even if he could overlook her lack of morality and her difficulty with fidelity, they had no future together. He was an undercover cop, and he still didn't know whether she was involved up to her pretty little earlobes in Joseph's drug dealings. He couldn't compromise the case by getting involved with her.

But what if she was an innocent bystander—if, that is, a woman like Ruby could still be called innocent. What then? Embarking on any kind of relationship necessitated a certain honesty between two people, namely that he wasn't exactly who and what Ruby thought he was. He couldn't break his cover to her. That would put both of their lives in jeopardy.

Which put him right back where he started. By himself. Alone.

The way he had always liked it.

Until he met Ruby.

"So whose lights were you punching out?" Carlo asked.

Antonio started back to reality. "No one's. After four days on the road, I just needed a good workout."

Carlo gave him a "get real" look. "This is me you're talking to, remember? And the way you were going after that bag tells a different story. A man punches a bag like that, he's definitely imagining a face at the other end of his fist. Since I know you don't hit women, I'm assuming it's a man and that he's somehow standing in your way."

"That's a lot of assuming," Antonio said.

"Then tell me I'm wrong."

Antonio wished he could. He could lie like a pro on the job, but when it came to his family, and especially Carlo, there was precious little he could slip by them.

"That's what I thought," Carlo said. "So who is he?"

"My quote-unquote boss. And that's all I can tell you about him."

"What about the woman?"

Antonio blinked. "What woman?"

"The one you told me about on the phone. The one you thought I could help you figure out."

"Oh. She's fine."

"She's really gotten to you, hasn't she?" Carlo said.

Antonio stared down at his hands. "What makes you say that?"

"For one thing, the way you can't look me in the eye."

Raising his head, Antonio did just that. In his brother's eyes, eyes that were almost a mirror image of his own, he saw understanding and sympathy. He was a goner, and Carlo knew it.

"What's she like?" Carlo asked.

How to describe Ruby in twenty words or less? It was an impossible task. Still, Samantha had been right. He had wanted someone to talk to.

"She leaves outrageous tips for service workers. She knows the solution to the most obscure crossword puzzle clues. She loves anything old. And she gets all sentimental over love letters written by people she's never met."

"Uh-oh," Carlo said.

"What?"

"You didn't mention her looks."

"So?"

Carlo spread his arms. "Every other woman you've been with, all we ever heard were the praises you sang about her beauty."

Antonio felt his back go up. "Ruby's beautiful. Very beautiful."

"But," Carlo said, his voice lowering, "her beauty isn't the main reason you're attracted to her."

It was a first for Antonio. "No, it isn't."

"You're a goner, Tonio," Carlo said, speaking the obvious.

Antonio sighed. "I know."

"So what's the problem?"

"My quote-unquote boss."

"The face on the punching bag. What about him?"

"She's with him."

"Ahh." There was a wealth of understanding in the drawn-out word.

"'Ahh' is right."

"She's not married to him, is she?" Carlo asked.

Not yet. "No."

"Then what's the problem? Go after her. Remember what Mom always said? All's fair in love and war."

"You don't understand, Carlo."

"What's not to understand?"

Antonio looked down at his hands again. It was an effort, but he finally spoke the words.

"I don't have the one thing it would take to make her leave him."

"What's that?"

"A six-figure bank account."

There was a pause. "You mean she's only with your boss because he has money?"

Antonio nodded.

"And she will only leave him for you, if you can offer her more money?"

Even though he knew Carlo was just trying to clarify the situation, it felt as if he was rubbing salt into an already open wound. Antonio swallowed hard.

"Yes."

"Why would you want a woman like that?"

Good question. He wished he had the answer. And he really wished he knew what Ruby was doing that very minute.

Chapter 11

"Sorry to be calling so late, my dear," Joseph said, "but a business dinner ran longer than I had anticipated."

Blinking fiercely, Laura sat up in her bed and clutched the telephone receiver to her ear. Using her free hand, she pushed the hair from her face and tried to clear the fog from her brain.

A glance at the clock told her it was half past midnight. Amazingly, since she'd expected to spend the night tossing and turning, she'd been asleep for more than two hours.

She hated feeling at such a disadvantage, and she had the niggling suspicion that Joseph had called so late to put her at one. "You know you're welcome to call me anytime."

"That's what I like to hear."

That's why she'd said the words.

"Did I wake you?" he asked.

She could flatter him, tell him she'd missed him and had been sitting up, awaiting his call. That line might even have had a chance of working, if Joseph wasn't gay. And if she hadn't already sounded like a swimmer who, after diving to the bottom of the pool, was slowly making her way to the surface.

Laura struggled to pull her wits together. She must have been deeply asleep if it was taking her this long to fully awaken. Now, more than ever, she needed to be on guard. Given the still-confused state of her mind, it wouldn't take much to trip her up.

"Yes, Joseph, you woke me."

"I hope this unexpected intrusion isn't too unsettling for you."

"Not at all," she replied blithely. "After all, that's what you pay me for, isn't it? To be at your service when you need me?"

"It is indeed." His chuckle was low and appreciative. "That's what I like about you, Ruby. You know your place. I can always count on you to do what you're supposed to do. The challenge is going to be figuring out those secrets you say you're not hiding from me."

Laura felt a jolt of fear. Not a large jolt—it was almost like the shock a person got while walking across a carpet in stocking feet—but it was definitely there. Another sign she wasn't the cop she used to be.

She would have to keep an eye on the feeling. She certainly would have to conceal it from Joseph. Hopefully, if she used it to her advantage, this new awareness would sharpen her reactions.

He'd said he had a business dinner. A long business dinner. Laura wondered if this was something she should know about, something she should report to her superiors.

"I take it, by the length of it, that your meeting was successful?" she asked.

"Beyond my wildest imaginings." Joseph sounded triumphant. "If things go according to plan, very soon the Merrill Auction Gallery is going to be riding on a huge wave of cash."

To Laura's disappointment he didn't elaborate. Unfortunately, she couldn't arouse his suspicion by asking who the meeting had been with. Instead she'd have to keep her eyes and ears open around the gallery and try to learn more that way.

"I hope this means I'm going to get a huge bonus," she said.

Joseph chuckled. "I'll see what I can arrange." After a brief pause he added, almost as an afterthought, "How did the estate valuation go?"

This, she knew, was the real reason for his call. Joseph was checking up on both her and Michael.

"Very well. I think you'll be pleased. You should definitely get your money's worth, plus a good percentage more."

"Excellent. Excellent. And Michael? Everything work out fine with him?"

She didn't want to think about Michael, let alone talk about him. "He did a very thorough job. He knows furniture, and he's a hard worker."

"I wouldn't have expected any less from him after reading the recommendations that accompanied his résumé."

"He came highly recommended?" she asked.

"Very highly."

By whom? Laura wondered. Others in the auction community, or the men with whom Joseph worked in secret? Men who lived on the fringes of society and preyed on people's weaknesses. Men only concerned with the money to be made, and to hell with anyone or anything else.

Men like Michael himself.

Joseph's next question interrupted her thoughts. "What about you two? Anything going on there?"

Laura drew a deep breath. She'd known this was coming, had spent the moments before falling asleep formulating her response to this very question.

"It's proceeding slowly," she replied with caution. "But I have hope that, in the not too distant future, it will produce the results you desire."

"Excellent." Approval filled Joseph's voice. "One last thing, and I'll let you get back to your beauty sleep. Have you learned anything useful about him? Something I might need to know that wasn't included on his résumé?''

She couldn't tell him about the gun. To do so would be to admit she had been in Michael's room. Even if she revealed to Joseph that she possessed the skills to pick a lock, he would assume she had slept with Michael. And that was even more dangerous than the gun she had found in Michael's luggage. Because the minute Joseph suspected she was having an affair with Michael, even though he had encouraged it, he would begin questioning her loyalty. It was inevitable. She was caught squarely in the middle of a Catch-22.

''He told me he spent two years in prison for possession with the intent to sell.''

''Anything else?''

Joseph didn't sound surprised, so Laura assumed he'd already known about Michael's incarceration. What she didn't understand was why she felt as if she was betraying a friend. Why, all of a sudden, was she feeling so protective of Michael?

''He hinted he wouldn't mind crossing the line when it came to earning some extra money.''

''Think carefully.'' Obviously this was news to Joseph, because his excitement was palpable. ''What were his exact words?''

Laura searched her memory for that particular conversation. Each of them seemed to be indelibly etched on her brain.

''I believe he said that he wasn't going to be stupid enough to get caught again.''

''Well, well, well,'' Joseph murmured to himself, obviously pleased. ''I knew I could count on you, Ruby. Keep up the good work. And keep me posted.''

Instead of feeling satisfied that she had passed another test and moved a step closer to gaining Joseph's total confidence, when she hung up the phone, Laura felt depressed. And not a little alarmed. In truth, the excitement she'd heard in Joseph's voice bothered her. If Michael wasn't already involved in the drug operation, something after this conversation she was beginning to suspect was true, she had a feeling he soon would be. And if he did become involved, when the case broke she would have no choice but to see that he was punished along with Joseph.

Sleep was a long time coming.

''Going once. Going twice.'' Antonio brought the gavel down. ''Sold to bidder number 118 for twelve hundred dollars.''

While he waited for the image on the screen to change to the next item up for bid, he looked out over the auction floor. Every seat was taken. A number of people stood in the rear of the room and lined the side walls.

There was an electricity in the air that was unmistakable, and he felt a surge of adrenaline. This Saturday he was much more comfortable behind the podium. The crowd was with him—he was getting market value and, in some instances, a lot more—and he could feel himself feeding off their energy. This was the one part of the job that he truly did enjoy and would really miss when it was all over.

Though he'd kept his eyes open, he hadn't seen or heard anything suspicious. Nor did there seem to be any additional activity out on the loading docks that would indicate something was going down. According to his contact officer, none of the moving vans had made any unscheduled stops on their return to Pittsburgh, although they would be tailed as they departed for their destinations when they were loaded up with the items he sold today. It was just a gut feeling, but Antonio felt certain that no drugs were being moved during this auction.

One of Joseph's aides approached him. Closing his hand around the microphone, he leaned down to listen to what the man had to say.

When he straightened, he addressed the crowd. ''We seem to be experiencing some technical difficulties.'' Spreading his arms, he smiled ruefully. ''Apparently, despite having the best equipment money can buy, the projector is stuck.''

Heads shook. There was the sound of tittering, some groaning and a few appreciative chuckles.

"I know exactly what you're thinking," he continued, trying to keep the mood light. "All this technology is wonderful, but it's a royal pain when it doesn't work. We apologize for the delay and ask for your patience while we correct the problem. I would sing for you, to pass the time, but I'm afraid that might cause a stampede for the exits."

More laughter. "Seriously, though, folks, I hope you bear with us. The next item up for bid, an exquisite eighteenth-century Windsor chair, is really worth waiting for. You might want to take advantage of the unscheduled break to get a cup of coffee or a glass of freshly squeezed lemonade. I personally can vouch for the Krispy Cremes, as I've eaten more than my fair share today."

The noise level in the room amplified as people stood up, stretched and began milling around. Thankfully, no one seemed in a rush to leave. Antonio looked down at his notes to refresh his mind about the upcoming items. As usual, when he had a spare moment, his thoughts veered to Joseph and Ruby.

Whenever he had caught a glimpse of Joseph in the crowd, he had appeared pleased. In fact, he had appeared more than pleased with Antonio since his return from West Virginia.

Ruby wasn't speaking to him. The only time she seemed to pay him any attention was when Joseph was near. Was she trying to make Joseph jealous? That didn't make any sense.

What had she told Joseph about their four days in West Virginia? Obviously, if his behavior toward Antonio was any indication, she'd kept her word. As a result Antonio still had his job. And he was still in one piece.

Earlier this morning he'd arrived at the gallery and Joseph had greeted him, Ruby by his side. After a first searing surge of jealousy at the sight, he had searched Ruby's face for signs of guilt. He'd seen nothing. Either she was not bothered by her betrayal of Joseph, or the kiss they had shared meant absolutely nothing to her. The truth, he acknowledged wryly, was probably a little bit of both.

Before his arrival he had even half convinced himself that he had succeeded in eradicating her hold over him. One look at her on Joseph's arm, and he knew he'd been deluding himself. Despite everything he knew about her, despite her involvement with another man, he wanted her more than ever. He had to be the biggest fool ever to walk the earth.

A cheer rose on the air, and Antonio glanced over at the screen. The projector was working again. Giving the crowd a couple of minutes to reclaim their seats and settle down, he shoved any further thoughts of Joseph and Ruby to the back of his mind. There would be plenty of time to think about them later. Whether he wanted to or not.

Three hours later the auction was over and the huge gallery had emptied. While during the height of the sale nearly four hundred people had crowded onto the floor, now the only people left were Antonio himself, the twenty or so buyers still awaiting their turn to make final payment on their purchases, the refreshment vendors closing up their stalls and the janitorial staff, who were busily folding up chairs and sweeping away litter from the gleaming hardwood.

He had just gathered up his papers and was preparing to leave when he caught sight of Ruby at the cash register. Before her stood a woman with a baby in one arm. From the opposite shoulder hung a diaper bag and a purse she was awkwardly searching.

He didn't know why he hesitated. Something about Ruby's posture registered on his internal radar, making him take a second look. Though her face was an impassive mask, he recognized the obvious signs of tension. By now he knew them well: the stiff back, the shoulders rigidly squared, the thrust-out chin. Hadn't she looked at him that way often enough, whenever he'd pushed her patience to the limit?

Maybe Ruby was simply eager to keep the line moving, but he didn't think that was the cause of her distress. Something else had her on edge.

Could this be what he had been waiting for? Was the woman standing in front of Ruby the key to unlocking Joseph's secret? Was Ruby awaiting some message from her, maybe even a payment that she in turn would deliver to Joseph? It would be an ingenious way of conducting that kind of business.

Antonio turned his attention to the young mother. With each thrust of her hand through the large purse, she grew more flustered. The baby started to fuss, and she automatically abandoned her search to soothe the child. That was when he knew she was no front. If she was involved with any drug other than an aspirin, he was a monkey's uncle.

She was simply a customer who had forgotten her wallet. Or maybe someone in the crowd had stolen it. A gathering like this, with so many people packed closely together, would be an automatic draw for a thief looking for an easy mark. It would also explain Ruby's tension, as she would obviously be anxious to prevent a scene. Antonio moved closer in case she needed his help.

"I'm sorry," he heard the woman apologize. She sounded close to tears. "You might not believe this, but I used to be the most organized person you would ever want to meet. Since Olivia's birth, though, it's all I can do to get dressed in the morning. My house is a mess. I'm a mess. I can't remember the last time I slept through the night or took a bubble bath or wore a shirt that didn't have spit-up stains on the shoulder. All I wanted to do today was to buy a painting for my husband's birthday, and I couldn't even do that right. And you really don't need me unloading all this on you, do you? What you need is for me to find my wallet."

"Unload on me all you want," Ruby said. "I understand perfectly. Believe me. Please, take your time. You're doing just fine."

Though she sounded calm, even compassionate, Antonio heard an underlying strain. It had cost her to speak those words. Why?

"No, it's not okay," the woman protested. "I'm really

holding things up. Look, could you do me a favor? Could you hold Olivia for me? With both hands free, I'm sure I'll find my wallet in no time."

A look of what Antonio interpreted as pure panic crossed Ruby's face. "I...I don't think..."

"Please," the woman pleaded. "I don't want to put her on the floor. And I don't want to hold up the line any longer. I'm sure the people behind me are in a hurry to get home."

Seemingly lost for words, Ruby simply stared.

A look of comprehension crossed the woman's face. "Look at your nice suit. Of course you don't want to hold her. Why don't I just go to the end of the line. By the time I make it back up here, I should have my act together."

Antonio was about to step in and announce that he would hold the baby, when Ruby stood.

"I'll hold her," she said in a low voice.

"But your suit..."

"Don't worry about my suit. It's stood up to stronger stuff than messy fingers or spit-up."

Antonio received a vivid image of Ruby in the attic of the Bickham mansion, her hair mussed and her suit a total loss from the dirt streaked on it. Whatever was bothering her, it wasn't worry about her suit.

"Thank you." The woman beamed and held out her arms.

There was a noticeable hesitation before Ruby took the little girl. "Why don't you try the diaper bag?" she suggested, her gaze riveted on the child. "Maybe you put your wallet in there by mistake."

"Thanks. I will."

Antonio watched in fascination while Ruby first held the baby away from her gingerly. Then, her throat working, she cradled the little girl to her breast. Dropping her head, she pressed her lips to the child's forehead while chubby fingers reached up and grabbed a lock of her hair. She murmured something low and indistinguishable beneath her breath.

"Found it!" the woman exclaimed in triumph, holding up

the missing wallet. She held out her arms for her child. "Thank you so much for holding her."

As reluctant as she had been to take the baby, Ruby now seemed even more reluctant to relinquish her hold on her. After gently disengaging the little girl's fingers from her hair, she returned Olivia to her mother.

She must have sensed his presence then, because her gaze flew immediately to his. Antonio was astonished to see the shimmer of tears and a deep, private anguish in the depths of her eyes. The look caused a lump to lodge in his throat and made him want to take her into his arms and offer what comfort he could.

Ruby let out a long, shaky breath and turned her attention back to Olivia's mother. "She's a beautiful child. You hold on tight to her, okay?"

"Thanks, I will."

After the woman paid, Ruby pulled her compact from her pocket and repaired the damage Olivia had caused. Then she closed her eyes. When she opened them, she looked directly at Antonio. The anguish, if indeed it had ever been there, was gone. As was all other emotion.

She turned her attention to the people still waiting in line and flashed her patented smile. "Next, please," she announced in a clear, calm voice.

Why had the baby affected her so? He never would have pegged Ruby for the maternal type. He'd been wrong about her before; he could be wrong about that, too. Did she want children and Joseph not want any? Was that one sacrifice she was going to have to make in her quest for money?

He knew the problem was one he would ponder endlessly while lying awake that night. If only he didn't have such a penchant for solving puzzles, he might find himself sleeping better. Who was he kidding? Even if he knew all there was to know about her, he would still find Ruby to be the most fascinating woman he'd ever met.

A tap on his shoulder made him start. Turning, he saw Joseph. Had the man witnessed the scene with Ruby and the baby? Had he witnessed Antonio's complete absorption in it? Worse, had he caught a glimpse of exactly how Antonio felt about the woman he believed belonged to him?

"I'm glad I caught you before you left," Joseph said. "There's something I need to talk to you about."

Damn. He had to have seen something. Might as well get this over with.

"Of course. I'll come straight to your office."

"No need," Joseph dismissed with a wave of his hand. "What I have to say will just take a minute."

Antonio braced himself.

Joseph beamed at him. "You did a good job today, Michael. I'm very pleased."

Antonio blinked. This wasn't exactly what he had been expecting, but he'd take it. "Thank you."

"Ruby told me what a good job you did at the Bickham estate, also. She said you two work well together, that you make a good team."

Had she really said that? "It went...well."

"I just wanted to let you know that you both will be on the road again this week."

Antonio went still. "Oh?"

"I just snagged an estate in Cleveland that I need you two to value for me."

"I see."

"The arrangements have all been made. Ruby has the particulars." Joseph took a step, then halted and turned back. "Oh, and Michael? When you return, we need to have a talk. I think it will be beneficial for us both."

Instead of congratulating himself that he seemed to have gained Joseph's confidence, all Antonio could think about was the following week. He was going to be alone with Ruby. Again. How on earth was he going to keep his hands off her?

In the end it turned out to be much easier than he had anticipated. First of all, they drove separately. Second, they ate their meals apart. And third, she never got close enough to him for them to brush arms, let alone for him to wrap his arms around her.

Though Joseph had, once again, put them in adjoining rooms, this time they were in a sixteen-story hotel in the heart of downtown Cleveland. The only time Antonio saw Ruby was while they were working, and she was studiously polite in his presence. If any of the items they valued thrilled her or if she found any long-lost love letters, she kept it to herself.

The vans arrived on the third day. This time he and Ruby were supervising the loading. As before, in West Virginia, Antonio inspected them. And as before he was disappointed to find nothing incriminating. He was beginning to believe the entire operation was a wild-goose chase.

It was while he was pacing the outside length of one still-empty van that the truth hit him. Excitement mounting, he counted the number of paces it took him to traverse the trailer's exterior. Then he climbed inside and took another count. He was right. The inside of each van was shorter than the outside by a good foot. There must be a false wall at the end of the compartment.

When he knocked, the hollow sound greeting his ears increased his excitement. Since the entrance wasn't on the inside, where it could be seen by someone like himself, it had to be underneath the trailer.

A quick, furtive search confirmed his suspicions. Above the tires was a narrow, sliding door. It was awkward to reach, but when he opened each one and peered up inside, he found enough room to store a large cache of drugs. Bingo.

Laura ducked into an empty room when she heard Michael approach. His footsteps echoed on the hardwood floor as he neared her hiding place. Holding her breath, she plastered her back to the wall. She let it out slowly when the echoes of his footfalls faded away.

Heart thundering, she rushed to the first moving van and peered underneath, the way she had seen Michael doing when she'd come to fetch him before his lunch grew cold. Suddenly, as she looked at the sliding door, everything fell into place. She'd known Joseph had to be transporting the drugs in the moving vans, but she'd always assumed he'd been using the furniture as a hiding place. Now she knew why she had never found any evidence to support her suspicions.

She knew something else, too, and the knowledge made her heart ache. Michael Corsi was definitely involved. He had to be. Otherwise why would he have been looking under the van?

Chapter 12

Hand rubbing the back of his neck, Antonio paced his hotel room. When he tired of that pastime, he moved to the window that looked out over Cleveland's darkened city skyline and the shore of Lake Erie. The view from the twelfth floor was breathtaking, not that he derived any pleasure from it.

With a long sigh he returned to his pacing. A glance at the bedside clock slowed his steps. It was almost ten o'clock, and he still hadn't called his contact officer. Now that he knew how Joseph was bringing the drugs in and shipping them out, he suddenly found himself hesitant to report his findings. Hence the pacing. He was literally dragging his feet; postponing a job he knew he had to do.

As if of its own volition, his gaze traveled to the door connecting his room to Ruby's. Just how involved was she in all this? Would his phone call ensure her an extended stay in a facility of the State of Pennsylvania's choice? He tried to picture Ruby behind bars and failed. She would never survive.

Even if she was completely innocent, it was a certainty she would hate him for taking away her meal ticket.

Stiffening his resolve along with his shoulders, Antonio put his hesitation behind him. He was a cop. He'd sworn to uphold the law, regardless of his personal feelings. To do less would bring dishonor to all the men and women who had served faithfully before him.

It was time—past time—to report his discovery. Joseph Merrill had to be stopped. It was as simple and as complicated as that.

If that brought Ruby down, too, and if it made her hate him, he would have to find the strength to deal with it.

When she heard Michael leave, Laura waited two minutes before picking the lock on the connecting door. Once again she searched his belongings. This time, however, with secret compartments on her mind, she discovered what she'd missed the first time: a hidden partition in his suitcase.

Inside the partition was a notebook. Letting out a long breath, Laura removed it from its hiding place. Her hands shook as she opened it.

The pages were filled with Michael's handwriting and outlined everything that had happened since he started working for Joseph, including his need to gain her confidence to find out how much she knew. It made her shiver to learn he had searched her belongings, just as she had searched his.

The one thing the notes didn't detail was the kiss they had shared, and what exactly, if anything, were his true feelings for her. Nor did they detail why he was looking for the drugs and trying to win Joseph's confidence.

For long minutes she stared at the words filling page after page. Then, carefully replacing the notebook and making sure there was no evidence of her search, she retreated to her room.

She heard Michael return ten minutes later and waited an additional ten before slipping out her door. The pay phone she chose was three blocks away. Her stomach felt as if it was tied in a thousand knots by the time her call was picked up on the other end.

"It's me," she said.

"You have news?"

"Yes. I've discovered how Joseph is distributing the drugs." She explained about the false compartments.

"Excellent work, Laura. I knew you could do it."

"I thought you'd be pleased."

"Is something wrong? You sound rather…odd."

She squared her shoulders and launched her attack. "Yes, as a matter of fact, there is. Who the hell is Michael Corsi?"

The emotions flowing through her made it impossible for Laura to fall asleep. Arms folded beneath her head and eyes wide open, she lay in bed, lights blazing, staring up at the ceiling.

She couldn't believe it. Like her, Michael was a cop. He was a good guy. And she was falling in love with him.

At last she understood the source of the discontent that had plagued her over the past months. She'd attributed it to a need for a long vacation, and while that need still existed, the real reason for her unrest was suddenly clear. Finally, after four long years, she was coming alive again. Undercover work, which had sustained her through the darkest period of her life, was no longer enough. She needed more. She wanted more.

She wanted to paint again.

She wanted to play again.

She wanted to live again.

She wanted Michael.

Slowly but surely, step by step, she was putting the past behind her. While she would never forget her husband and child, and would always feel a residue of pain thinking about them, she finally acknowledged that she had to go on living. Which meant she also had to acknowledge that Jacob and Jason weren't coming back, and that it was perfectly right and okay for her to have feelings for Michael Corsi.

Jacob would have liked him, Laura realized. Even more important, he would have encouraged her to move forward with the relationship.

One question remained in her mind, and it was huge, especially after what she'd read in his notes. Did Michael kiss her because he was truly attracted to her, or was it just for the job? Since she'd been forbidden by her contact officer to tell him what she knew or to reveal who she really was—for safety reasons Erik wouldn't even tell her Michael's real name—it was a question she couldn't ask. Yet.

Things were coming to a head. Hopefully, she would discover both the source and the destination of Joseph's drug operation any day now. And when she did, she would have her answer. She prayed it was the one she wished for.

Laura's gaze wandered from the overhead light to the two bedside table lamps to the bathroom light. She knew now why she had let them blaze twenty-four hours a day for the past four years. She'd been keeping them on for Jacob and Jason.

Slowly she climbed out of bed and, one by one, turned them off. A lone tear traced its way down her cheek when she reached for the last switch.

"Good night," she whispered to the darkness.

"Mind if I join you?"

Antonio looked up from the newspaper he was reading while waiting for his breakfast order to arrive. His mouth nearly fell open when he saw Ruby standing at his elbow. Before he dropped it, he quickly replaced his coffee cup on the saucer.

She wore a pair of navy-blue cropped pants and a crisp white blouse that she'd left untucked. Barring that morning in the park, she was the most casually dressed he had ever seen her. Even more incredible, she was smiling at him. Ruby was actually smiling at him.

"Excuse me?" he said, certain he hadn't heard her right.

She looked amused. "I was wondering if I could join you."

He glanced around the dining room. There were plenty of empty tables. It wasn't as though the place was jammed and she *had* to sit with him.

Surprise had him stammering. "N-not at all. Have a seat."

"Thanks." She pulled out a chair and sat down. Nodding

at the newspaper, she asked, "Anything important I should know about?"

He couldn't remember a word of what he had read. He tried refolding the paper into its original neat rectangle, but succeeded only in making an ungainly mess. With a shrug he thrust it onto an empty chair.

"Murder. Mayhem. Corruption. Scandal. The usual."

"Just another day, huh?" Humor twinkled in her eyes.

This was the Ruby he'd thought he had seen the moment their gazes had first met. The Ruby he'd wanted to get to know. Or, to be brutally honest, the Ruby he had wanted to sleep with. No hard edges. No fake smiles. No tension. No disapproval. Soft. Supple. Warm. He had never seen her so relaxed, so…accepting of him.

If he let it, she would go straight to his head, and that would be a big mistake. Because the only reason he could think of for her sudden thaw toward him was Joseph. Joseph wanted her to sound him out about something, and most likely that something had to do with whatever it was Joseph wanted to talk to him about when they returned. He'd thought it was about the drug business. Now, with Ruby smiling so brilliantly at him, he prayed it wasn't.

Still, unwise or not, when she looked at him the way she did now, all he wanted was to plunge into those bottomless green eyes of hers.

The waitress came and took Ruby's order. When she left, Antonio slid his hands down his jeans-clad thighs. "I take it you're no longer mad at me?"

Crossing her forearms in front of her empty plate, she leaned forward. "No, Michael," she said softly. "I'm not mad."

"Why not?"

Her hesitation was barely noticeable. "A person can only sustain a certain level of anger for so long. I guess mine ran out. To tell you the truth, I've really missed your company these past few days."

He had no business feeling so pleased. Especially after that flimsy excuse. It was painfully obvious that she was sitting across from him on Joseph's orders.

"I've missed yours, too," he found himself admitting. Nodding at her outfit, he added, "What's with the casual attire?"

"I thought it would be easier to load things up wearing pants as opposed to a short skirt."

"We're just supervising, remember? We have big, burly truck drivers to do the loading."

"Things'll move faster if we help," she said.

She had a point. Things would definitely move faster if the loaders weren't focused on her legs. Unfortunately the faster things moved, the sooner everything would come to an end. An abrupt end. And, most likely, an unhappy end.

Their food arrived. Antonio picked up his fork and waited for Ruby to start pumping him. Five hours later he was still waiting, and he and Ruby were waving off the last moving van. Incredibly, she was still smiling at him.

Of course, they had kept their conversation on safe topics, like the weather, furniture, paintings, baseball—although how any self-respecting Pittsburgher could be a New York Yankee fan was beyond him—and music. There was no telling how she would react, however, if he asked her how long she was going to wait before getting to whatever it was Joseph had ordered her to do.

"You were right," he said when the van rounded the corner and disappeared.

"About what?" Turning to him, she lowered the hand she had raised to shield her eyes from the sun.

"About pitching in with the loading. It really did make things move fast. What's left to do?"

"Close up the house and return the keys to the real estate agent. That shouldn't take longer than fifteen minutes."

Antonio felt as if someone had just turned over an hourglass. With each grain of sand that fell, his time with Ruby slipped away. He was close, extremely close, to breaking this case wide open. Once it did, events would begin to move more swiftly than today's loading.

If only he could have some time alone with her, away from the job. Time where nothing and no one else mattered. Time where it was just the two of them. Time where he was accountable to no one.

"It's one o'clock now," he said. "If traffic cooperates, we should arrive back in Pittsburgh shortly after three. Should we go straight to the gallery?"

"Tell you what," she said, as if the thought had just occurred to her. "Why don't we play hooky and take the rest of the day off? We've certainly earned it. Joseph isn't expecting us until tomorrow. There's nothing stopping us."

"What's Joseph going to think when the vans arrive without us?"

"That it took longer than we expected to wrap things up here," Ruby replied. "Trust me, Michael, he won't know any differently. And he won't care. He's gotten a fair day's work out of us. If you want, I can finish up here, and you can be on your way. It's a beautiful day. Enjoy."

So much for his assumption that Joseph had put her up to her reconciliation with him. Had he been wrong? Was it just as she had explained, that her anger had run its course? Antonio's sense of time running out intensified.

"What are you going to do with your free afternoon?" he asked.

Ruby shrugged. "I was thinking about getting my hair done. Maybe even a manicure."

He didn't think it was his imagination that she sounded less than thrilled about the prospect. The words were out of his mouth before he could call them back.

"Do you want to go for a plane ride?"

"Who's the pilot?"

"Me."

There was no hesitation. "I'd love to."

The overwhelming urge to kick himself hit Antonio fifteen miles into his drive. That was when reality intruded. The euphoria of Ruby's acceptance had diminished to a level where he could think logically, and he realized the risk he was taking. His professional life was about to collide with his personal one. If, while he was with Ruby, they ran into someone who knew him and called him by his real name, his cover would be blown. It would all be over.

Which begged the question, exactly why *had* he put himself in such a precarious position? Because she had smiled at him?

He groaned. What had he been thinking?

The smart thing to do, the only thing under the circumstances, would be to tell her that he hadn't been able to arrange the use of the plane and to suggest an alternate activity. But if he did that, there was a good chance she would decide she really should use her unscheduled free time to have her hair styled and her nails painted. Despite the diceyness of the situation, he didn't want that to happen.

Thank goodness he and Ruby had driven separately. Pulling over at the next rest stop, Antonio called his friend from a pay phone. Luck was with him, because not only was the plane available, it turned out that Jack planned on working well into the evening at his office, his wife and kids were at her mother's on Cape Cod, and the household and grounds staff would be long gone by the time Antonio and Ruby arrived. No one who could possibly blow his cover would be within shouting distance.

There was still a chance the whole thing could backfire on him—Jack's wife and kids could return early from their visit, for example—but if it bought him some time alone with Ruby, he was prepared to take the risk. He didn't want to think too hard about what it meant that before he met her, he never would have considered taking such a risk.

He picked up Ruby in front of her apartment. Neither one of them said much on the forty-minute drive. They reached the scenic town of Ligonier shortly after five o'clock. A few minutes later they were out in the rolling countryside. He aimed his truck down a private driveway and past a stone mansion that made the Bickham estate look like a cottage.

"Wow," Ruby murmured. "Your friend lives here?"

"Jack built this place three years ago."

"Impressive."

He looked for signs of envy or want on her face, but all he saw was an honest appreciation. "Yes, it is."

A side road cut through a grove of trees and emerged next to a hangar and an airstrip. Jumping down from the truck, Antonio opened the hangar's doors to reveal the Cessna Skyhawk residing inside. He walked around the plane, examining it closely for any visible problems, and running his hand along the wings and the rudder.

After peering under the fuselage for any signs of leakage, he glanced over his shoulder. Ruby hadn't moved. Seemingly transfixed, she stared out at him from the truck's passenger seat. She looked from Antonio to the plane, then back to Antonio again.

"You coming?" he called.

A full ten seconds passed before she opened the door and climbed down from the truck. After taking a few seemingly reluctant steps, she stopped just outside the hangar's opening.

"Your friend has his own hangar?"

"And his own private runway."

He stood silently while her gaze roved over the hangar, the plane, the adjacent runway and the acres of green rolling hills that seemed to stretch out to forever. Behind them the massive house was hidden from view by the grove of trees.

"He must be awfully rich," she finally said.

"Like King Midas, everything Jack touches turns to money in the bank."

"That makes him a lot richer than Joseph."

"A whole lot." Antonio waited a beat before adding, "He's also married with children. Two of his own and five adopted."

Ruby shot him an inquiring look.

He spread his arms. "I just thought I'd mention it, in case you were…considering."

"I see." She nodded her head. "That's very thoughtful of you, Michael. But I'm not. Considering, that is."

He got the distinct impression she was trying to tell him

something. But what could that be? That she actually cared enough for Joseph not to ditch him for someone richer? The thought gave him little comfort.

A gentle breeze blew her hair into her face, and she raised a hand to brush it back. The sun outlined her figure in a blaze of gold, and he found himself blinking against the sudden brightness. She was a vision. But a vision of what? A glorious future? Or his ignominious downfall?

Antonio felt a wave of self-disgust wash over him. What was he doing here? God, he was pathetic. There was no other creature on earth more pitiable than a man who lusted after a woman he could never have. Especially when he should never have wanted to have her in the first place.

"How did you and Jack meet?" Ruby asked as she entered the hangar and began walking the length of the plane.

"We were college roommates."

"Where did you go to school?"

"Penn State."

At the plane's nose she turned to face him. "Forgive me if this sounds pretentious, but I would have expected someone with your friend's background to go to, shall we say, a more prestigious university?"

"You mean like Harvard or Yale?"

She nodded. "Exactly."

"Jack's family was as middle class as mine. He made his money after college."

"Legally?" she asked.

"Every penny," he confirmed.

"That's good to hear."

Again, Antonio got the impression she was trying to tell him something. An objective bystander might conclude that she preferred honestly earned gains over ill-gotten ones. He, however, knew better. To Ruby money was money. She certainly had never seemed to care how Joseph came by the funds that paid for her creature comforts.

He looked into the fuel tanks and satisfied himself they were full.

"What are you doing?" she asked.

"Checking the fuel level."

"Isn't there a gauge on the inside of the plane for that?"

"There is. But the first thing a pilot learns is to never trust a fuel gauge." He nodded toward the sky. "Running out of gas up there is a lot...trickier...than running out down here."

Her lips twisted into a wry smile. "I see your point."

"Ready?" he asked.

She gave the plane another once-over, then bit her lip and nodded hesitantly.

"You look like you're having second thoughts," he said.

He almost hoped she was. Then they could both go home, and he could forget he'd done something this stupid.

"It's smaller than I thought it would be."

"You drive a two-seater sports car, Ruby. Compared to my truck, that's pretty small, too. Still, it gets you where you want to go. You're not afraid to ride in it."

"I suppose you're right."

She didn't sound convinced. Antonio's desire that no one experience fear at the prospect of air travel exceeded his need to put distance between them.

"I'm an excellent pilot, Ruby. For what it's worth, you have my word on that."

She visibly relaxed, the stiffness leaving her shoulders and her arms hanging loosely at her sides. "Of course you are," she said softly. "I trust you, Michael. I know you won't do anything to hurt me."

This time there was no mistaking it. She was definitely trying to tell him something. The possibilities made his heart race.

"Thank you," he replied. "I know you don't give your trust easily. I promise you, it's not misplaced."

He helped her up into the cabin, walked around the front of the plane and climbed in next to her.

"Buckle up," he ordered as he sank into the leather seat and continued his preflight check.

"Don't you have to file a flight plan?" she asked.

He didn't want to explain that the purpose of filing a flight plan was so that someone would come looking for you if you didn't arrive at your destination within a prescribed period of time. She was jittery enough as it was.

"There's no air traffic control tower here to file one with. Besides, we're not going far. I just want to show you a little of the countryside."

She reached out a hand and clutched at his arm. "Promise me one thing?"

The warmth of her hand distracted him, and he found himself studying the slender fingers curled around his wrist. "What?" he managed to say.

"No spins or acrobatic loops, please." She gave a tentative smile. "I have a weak stomach."

She really was scared. Because if there was one thing Antonio knew with absolute certainty, it was that her stomach was as weak as cast iron.

Placing one hand atop hers, he gave it a reassuring squeeze. "I promise, Ruby. No spins or loops. It'll be smooth sailing all the way."

Her hand dropped to her side. "Thank you."

"You're sure you want to do this?"

"I'm sure."

He wondered why she had so readily agreed to come, if she was so nervous. Could it be she also sensed their time together was fast coming to an end, and that she was as reluctant as he for it to end? Or was he just clutching at straws?

"You don't sound sure," he said.

She thrust out her chin. "I'm sure, Michael."

"Let's go, then."

He positioned the throttle and started the engine. A minute later he backed the Cessna out of the hangar and began taxiing to the runway. At the head of the narrow strip, he lined up with the centerline and brought the plane to a stop.

"You might want to hold your ears," he told Ruby. "I have to perform one final check. It's going to get noisy in here."

Holding the wheel full back and keeping his foot on the

brakes, Antonio powered the engine up to the prescribed RPM to make sure it would accept the demands of takeoff and flight. Satisfied, he released the brakes.

"Here we go."

He felt the plane come alive beneath his hands as it began speeding down the runway. The liftoff was so smooth, he was almost surprised to find that he was airborne. After banking, he climbed to an altitude of two thousand feet before leveling off.

There wasn't a cloud in the sky. Spread out before them was a panoramic vista of rolling hills, trees and lush green land. Tiny cars traveled on roads that twisted and turned like a thin, narrow gray river. Even Jack's house, when he turned and flew over it, looked small from up in the air. The entire view reminded Antonio of a picture on a jigsaw puzzle box.

He gave Ruby a chance to gather her bearings and look around before asking, "Well, what do you think?"

Her face, when she turned to him, was alight with pleasure, her eyes wide with wonder. "It's incredible, Michael. I've flown dozens of times before, but always in a jet. It's never felt like this. This is like...like..." She trailed off, obviously searching for the right words. "Like I stretched my arms out and suddenly I was soaring. No wonder you love it so much."

Antonio smiled his understanding. Even after hundreds of hours in the air, the feeling he got while at the controls of a plane never changed, never grew old.

"It's a feeling like no other, isn't it?" he said. "Up here, things just naturally seem to fall into perspective. No matter what my worries are on the ground, when I'm flying they're no longer important. For some reason, no problem seems that insurmountable up here."

Except for his problem of what to do about her. That wasn't strictly true, he acknowledged. He knew what he had to do to solve his problem with Ruby. He had to forget her. He just wasn't ready to. Not yet.

"How long can we stay up?" There was a wistfulness in her voice that tugged at his emotions.

"For a while."

"I wish I had my sketch pad."

"There's a pocket in the seat back. I know Jack keeps paper and crayons and such in there for the kids. It's not charcoal, but it should do in a pinch."

While Ruby poised a black crayon over a colored sheet of paper, Antonio pointed out local landmarks. He also studied her out of the corner of one eye. She was like a kid on her first visit to a candy store, exclaiming in delight over this sight and that. Her hand seemed to race across the paper. No sooner had she captured one image than she set the sheet aside and reached for another.

She was the most beautiful woman Antonio had ever seen, but it wasn't her beauty that captivated him so. The world was full of beautiful women. What set Ruby apart were her joy and her enthusiasm. When she looked at him as she did now, with her eyes aglow and her face all lit up at the prospect of portraying one small bush on a piece of paper, Antonio felt his chest grow tight. A primitive urge to possess her in the only way that mattered to a man took hold of him.

The way she looked now was one of hundreds of visions of Ruby that he carried around with him in his brain. Visions of her with two puppies scrambling across her lap. Visions of her sitting, barefoot, on a park bench. Visions of her reading Serena Bickham's old love letters with tears in her eyes. Visions of those same eyes darkening and her lips parting when he bent his head to kiss her.

The one aspect of her personality that he hadn't seen since that first Saturday was the incorrigible flirt. He was beginning to believe she used that persona as a defense mechanism to keep men at a distance.

It sure hadn't kept him away.

Despite her need to attach herself to a wealthy man—a need, given her background, he understood even if he didn't approve of it—the woman sitting next to him was someone he could really like.

She was someone he could spend endless hours with and never be bored.

She was someone he could…what? Love? His mind balked at the thought.

When it was time to head back—to the real world, to Joseph and to the police work that would ultimately end any positive feelings she had for him—Antonio had to fight the impulse to fly away with her into the blue, where no one could ever touch them, and never return.

For long seconds after he'd pulled the Cessna into the hangar and shut off the engine, he sat staring out the windshield at the back wall.

"Michael."

He turned his head. As she had been all day, she was smiling at him.

"Thank you so much. I can't recall when I've had such a wonderful time. I will *never* forget this day."

The pleasure he saw in Ruby's eyes was an honest pleasure. He saw something else, too, an emotion that made his heart pound and stole the breath from his lungs. In the depths of Ruby's beautiful green eyes was a feeling she didn't bother to hide. Desire. Desire for him.

He felt the sudden, urgent need to explain. "After this week…well, things are going to be happening. From here on in, Ruby, no matter what, I want you to know…" He broke off and looked away.

"What is it you want me to know, Michael?" she asked softly.

What could he say? That he never meant to hurt her? That he hoped her only involvement with Joseph was a romantic one? That he prayed with every fiber of his being that she wouldn't wind up in jail?

He gave an impatient shake of his head. He'd already said too much. Way too much. He wouldn't be crossing any more lines this day.

"Nothing."

"Look at me, Michael."

When he complied, she reached out a hand and placed it on his shoulder. ''What would you say if I told you I understand perfectly? That you don't need to explain any further.''

He swallowed convulsively. Taking her hand from his shoulder, he turned it palm up and kissed her life line. His voice husky, he told her, ''I'd say it was a nice thought, but that it was impossible.''

She seemed to peer straight through his eyes and into his soul. ''Is it, Michael? Is it really?''

It was getting harder and harder for him to breathe. He wished she would tell him whatever it was that she really wanted to say, instead of giving him all these cryptic messages.

''What do you want from me, Ruby?''

Her smile was so gentle it nearly broke his heart.

''So many things, I can't put them all into words. But right now, Michael, what I really want is for you to kiss me.''

Chapter 13

Blood roared into his ears, and heat washed over him. His heart thundered. He had no power, and no will, to resist. This, Antonio admitted, was what he'd really wanted when he'd asked Ruby to go for a plane ride. Incredibly, it seemed to be what she had wanted, too.

He reached out for her, and something jerked him back into his seat. Looking down, he saw that his seat belt was still fastened. With an impatient growl, he clawed at the buckle. Out of the corner of one eye, he saw Ruby struggling with her own seat belt. A minute later he had hauled her sideways into his lap, her arms were around his neck, and that glorious, wondrous, miraculous mouth of hers was pressed to his.

Nothing in his life had ever felt so good.

Nothing had ever tasted so delicious.

Nothing had ever seemed so right.

With a soft sigh Ruby curled her fingers into his hair and opened her mouth to him. In that instant the kiss bypassed friendly exploration and zoomed straight to mind-blowing passion. All Antonio could do was clutch at her arms and try to hold on.

His tongue tangled with hers, and he felt himself trembling. Every time she touched him, his entire body threatened to shake apart like a plane approaching Mach five. One thing was certain, he wasn't at the controls here.

Ruby proved she was, when, after removing her mouth from his, she managed in their cramped quarters to turn and face him, and to plant her knees on either side of him on the seat. With their gazes locked together, she slowly lowered her body so that her thighs rested atop his. From that position she slid forward until her breasts pressed into his chest and the warmth of her sex met the ridge of his arousal. Even clothed as they both were, the sensation was incredible.

Then she began moving against him.

Antonio gave a low groan. "Keep that up, sweetheart, and I won't be responsible for myself."

"Touch me, Michael," she murmured. "I want to feel your hands on me."

"Just try and stop me."

He cupped her bottom and pulled her even tighter against him. Moaning her pleasure, Ruby dropped her head back, and he took advantage of the opportunity to kiss and nip at her jaw and exposed neck. He grabbed her shirttail in his fists and shoved his hands up underneath. The skin of her back was hot, almost feverish. His mouth moved to the hollow of her throat as he slid his hands over her.

He had just unclasped the hook of her bra, when she reached back and took hold of his wrists. With a pressure that wouldn't be denied, she pulled his hands from her skin and leaned back far enough so that he couldn't reach that tantalizing mouth of hers. Heaven help him, she wasn't going to stop now, was she?

"Don't," he protested, his chest heaving.

Breathing heavily, her eyes still dark with passion, Ruby held his hands firmly to his sides. "Before we go any further,

Michael, I need you to answer a question. Can you do that for me?"

He was so aroused he could barely think. The smell of her was in his nostrils, the taste of her on his mouth, the feel of her on his fingertips, and she was choosing now, of all times, for a question and answer session?

"Do I have a choice?"

Her smile was understanding. "You do want to make love to me, don't you?"

She might have control of his arms, but he still was in charge of the rest of his body. In answer he raised his hips and pressed his arousal up against her. She rewarded the motion by giving a soft gasp.

"What do you think?" he said.

"I think," she announced, her voice not quite steady, "that before we go any further I should tell you something."

She scrambled off his lap and moved to the passenger seat. "And I think the only way I'll be able to get the words out is if I sit over here. I need to clear the air, Michael. I want total honesty between us before we make love."

Antonio felt like she'd tossed a bucket of cold water on him. While his arousal still throbbed painfully, the overwhelming urge to sink his flesh into hers died. He didn't want Ruby unburdening her soul to him. He didn't want her dragging reality into this precious, fleeting, vanishing time.

But it was already too late. Reality had reared its ugly head. He knew, no matter how badly he wanted to, that he couldn't make love to her. There was Joseph, not to mention Ruby's as yet unknown involvement in his illegal activities. Both were significant factors that, in the strength of his desire for her, Antonio had conveniently forgotten.

Lacing his hands in his lap, he stared out the windshield and fought for control.

"You don't have to tell me anything," he said in a low voice. "I don't want you to tell me anything. There will be no lovemaking, Ruby. I'm sorry I lost my head. Again. You're a beautiful woman, but you belong to another man. I won't cross that barrier."

"I'm not Joseph's woman."

The words were said so softly that at first he imagined he'd heard them. Whirling in his seat, he faced her.

"What did you say?"

Eyes gleaming like emeralds, she repeated, "I'm not Joseph's woman."

His heart slammed so hard in his chest, Antonio thought it might actually break free of his rib cage. "I...I don't understand."

"My relationship with Joseph is a sham, part of my job description. He's gay, Michael, and he doesn't want anyone to know. I am not now, nor have I ever been, his lover."

Relief coursed through him, along with a purely male satisfaction. She had never been intimate with Joseph. That she'd actually told him about Joseph being gay, thereby risking her job, said a lot. It said she trusted him.

His relief and his satisfaction were short-lived. Unfortunately, he still had no idea whether or not she knew about the drugs or how heavily involved she was in their distribution. She'd said she wanted to clear the air. If she confessed her involvement, what would he do?

Antonio drew a deep breath. He'd do what he had to do. There was no other choice. Too many innocent lives were at risk. Gazing at Ruby now, and seeing how earnestly she stared at him, it seemed a lifetime ago that she had been in his arms.

"I assume, since you're still sitting over there, that there's more you want to tell me?" It cost him dearly to utter the words.

"Yes, Michael," she said, nodding, "there's more." She drew a deep breath. "I'm a cop. I'm working undercover on this case, the same way you are."

For one endless moment, his mind went blank. She knew he was a cop. She said she herself was one. Everything suddenly fell into place. All the contradictions about her that had driven him crazy from the beginning suddenly made sense. How had he never seen it?

"You should see your face," she said.

"That comical, huh?"

"No." Her smile was understanding. "That wonderful."

"You really are a cop?"

A glimmer of amusement lit her eyes. "I really am. You can phone my contact officer if you want confirmation. Better yet, why don't you call your own contact officer? He'll tell you the same thing."

"What do you know about Joseph's drug dealings?"

"Just what you know. That he's using the vans to receive and distribute them. I spoke to my contact officer before you picked me up. One of the vans made an unscheduled stop on the way back to Pittsburgh."

"Drugs?"

She nodded. "They'll pick up the supplier when the rest of the arrests are made."

Meaning as soon as they figured out who was going to receive them. Things were starting to wrap up.

"What's your name?" he demanded. "Your real name."

"Laura. Laura Langley."

Laura. It suited her so much better than Ruby.

"Have you known the whole time?" he asked. "About me being a cop, I mean."

She shook her head. "I just found out last night."

That explained her unexpected change in attitude toward him. "Why didn't you say anything before now?"

"Because I was ordered not to tell you. For both of our safety."

"But you did tell me."

"I had to."

"Why?"

She bit her lip. "I had to let you know you were making love to Laura, not Ruby."

He stared at her for the space of a heartbeat. "Are you trying to get me to change my mind?"

"No. Just warning you that you don't know anything about Laura."

He saw the uncertainty in her eyes and understood. She was wondering who he was really attracted to.

"When you kissed me, Laura, who were you kissing? Me? Or Michael?"

"You, of course," she replied without hesitation.

He spread his arms. "But you don't know me. Not really."

She thrust her chin out in the now-familiar gesture that he found so endearing. "Yes, I do."

"Then tell me, Laura. Who am I?"

"You're a man who worried himself so sick over a couple of abandoned puppies, you called the shelter every day until you learned they were adopted."

He blinked his surprise. "How do you know that?"

"Because I called them, too."

"What else do you know?"

She smiled. "That you love puzzles. That you love to laugh even more. That, no matter how hard you try to hide it, you're just a sentimental softy. That you'll go tearing all over town after a woman you're not even sure you like when she appears to be missing. I don't think any of those things were make-believe. I *know* none of them were Michael."

Antonio let out a long breath. Until that moment he hadn't realized he'd been feeling his own doubts about Laura's attraction to him.

"And I know you, Laura. You're everything Ruby is not. First of all, you're incredibly intelligent. And you're a total failure at being an incorrigible flirt. Your enjoyment of food, from a McDonald's hamburger to filet mignon, is downright hedonistic. You love anything old, to the point where you will jump out of a still-moving truck and ruin your clothes just to examine it. You're much more comfortable wearing jeans and going barefoot than you are wearing a suit and heels. You're moved to tears by old love letters."

He paused to draw breath. "Most important, and I want you to listen closely to this, I could turn down Ruby O'Toole's advances without a second thought. But I could never say no to Laura Langley.''

Her lower lip quivered, and he thought he glimpsed a hint of tears in the corners of her eyes.

''You're not going to cry on me, are you?''

She burst out laughing.

''What's so funny?''

''You are. Who'd believe that an undercover cop would be so horrified over a couple of tears?''

''That's because they're your tears, Laura.''

She sobered immediately. The look on her face had his heartbeat accelerating.

''You keep talking to me like that, and I'm going to be in a puddle at your feet.''

''I'd rather have you in my arms.'' He reached out for her, and she came willingly.

''This is much better,'' he said with satisfaction when she was back in his lap and her arms were around his neck.

''Hmm,'' she murmured. ''There's only one problem.''

''What's that?''

''I still don't know your name.'' Her grin was pure impudence as she ran a finger down his cheek. ''I mean, if I'm going to make love with a man, the least I should know is his name. Don't you agree?''

He tightened his arms around her as his chest grew thick with need. ''Didn't your contact officer tell you?''

She shook her head. ''Like I said, he was concerned about our safety. He figured the less we both knew, the better off we'd be. The only reason he told me you were a cop was because I bullied him into it.''

''Laura Langley, bully,'' he teased. ''I bet you were a terror on the school playground.''

''You better believe it.''

He leaned forward and kissed her pert nose. ''My name is Antonio Garibaldi.''

''Antonio,'' she said slowly, as if savoring the taste of it on her tongue. ''That's much better than Michael. Do you know how hard you made this job for me, Antonio? How was I supposed to concentrate, when this very attractive, exceedingly annoying ex-con kept distracting me?''

A thousand questions revolved around in his brain. How? What? Who? Why? Ignoring them—the answers could come later, much later—he pressed a kiss to her forehead, than trailed his lips down the side of her face.

''No harder than you made it for me.'' He bit her earlobe and felt her tremble. ''I have never wanted a woman the way I want you, Laura. You feel so good in my arms.''

''I want you, too, Antonio. Desperately.''

''Say it again,'' he demanded.

''What?''

''My name. Say it again.''

''Antonio.''

He closed his eyes. ''You don't know how good it feels to hear my name on your lips.''

''Antonio,'' she repeated. ''Antonio, Antonio, Antonio—''

He smothered the words with his mouth.

''You want to go somewhere a little more comfortable?'' he asked between kisses.

Her fingers tangled in the hair at the nape of his neck. ''Where's the closest hotel?''

''About five miles down the road.''

''I don't think I can wait that long.''

He groaned. ''Neither can I.''

She glanced over the seat. ''Looks like there's room back there.''

Antonio followed her gaze. Apparently Jack had hauled something recently, because the two rear seats had been removed. It would be a tight squeeze, but then he wanted to get as close to Laura as was humanly possible.

By mutual, unspoken consent, they tumbled into the back in a tangle of arms and legs. He ended up on his side, propped up on one elbow, looking down at Laura, who lay flat on her back. He thought he could easily just look at her like this forever.

"You're so beautiful."

She swallowed and looked as if she might cry again. "You really think so?"

Reaching out a hand, he brushed the hair off her forehead. "I really think so," he said seriously.

"Know what I think?"

"What?"

Her arms circled around his neck and pulled his head down. "I think you talk too much. I think it's time you showed me some action."

He chuckled. "You do, huh?"

"Oh, yes," she breathed, tilting her head so that her mouth was just millimeters from his. "I do."

"In that case..."

Silence reigned as their mouths clung together. Fevered fingers tore at buttons and zippers, then caressed the skin they had revealed. Clothing was removed and tossed carelessly aside. Soft sighs, low gasps and murmured words of encouragement floated on the air.

When they were both naked, Antonio lowered his mouth to her breasts. Using his tongue and his teeth, he teased her nipples to turgid arousal. Arching beneath him, Laura cried out and clutched at his shoulders.

"Please," she said.

He gazed down into green eyes that were glazed with passion and felt an answering need. At that moment he wanted nothing more than to slide his length inside her tightness and lose himself to the passion she made him feel.

"Not yet, sweetheart. Not yet."

Needing to make sure she was ready for him, he ran one hand up the inside of her thigh and watched her eyes glaze over. She opened her legs for him, and his fingers sought and found the soft folds of skin that were the core of her femininity. She was so wet. Wet for him. It was all he could do to control himself.

Moving his fingers against her, he watched as her passion built. To his surprise it gave him immense pleasure just to pleasure her. Eyes closed, body tensed, she strained against his touch. Without warning she reached out a hand to grasp his arm.

"Wait," she cried, opening her eyes and struggling up onto her elbows. "I'm not ready."

He thought she was feeling shy about losing control in front of him. "Let it go, sweetheart," he encouraged, his fingers still moving. "Let it go."

"I will." Biting her lip, she stilled his hand against her. "Trust me, Antonio, I will. But first I have something to say. It's important."

He knew that with a few practiced movements of his fingers, he could make her forget what she wanted to say. With any other woman, that is exactly what he would have done. But this was Laura, and the expression on her face made him acquiesce. She wasn't teasing. She wasn't trying to draw the moment out as long as possible, thus tormenting him beyond all human endurance. In the midst of her highly aroused state, she was deadly serious.

"I hope what you have to say won't take too long," he teased. "I'm feeling rather…impatient at the moment."

She didn't smile as he'd hoped she would. Instead, body still tense, she regarded him with a soberness that held him captive.

"It's been a long time for me, Antonio. I want you to know that."

He felt the breath rush out of him. "How long?"

"Four years."

"Four years?" His brow furrowed. "But how? Why?"

She pressed a finger to his lips. "Not now. We'll get to explanations later. I just want you to know that I'm not entering into this lightly. And I never do this for the job."

"I know," he told her. His fingers worked on her again, and it wasn't long before she went over the top, her cries of pleasure echoing in the tiny confines of the plane.

With a groan he dropped his head into his hands. "Oh, no,"

he moaned, his jaw clenched in frustration. "I don't believe it."

"It's okay." Sympathy laced Laura's voice, and she gave his arm a reassuring squeeze. "I can wait."

Realizing she thought he had reached his peak at the same time she did, he took her hand and folded it around his hardness. "It's not that, Ruby."

"I can tell. What is it, then?"

Her fingers stroked him softly, and his desire and frustration grew in equal measure. "I don't have a condom."

"I do."

His body jerked in surprise. "You do?"

She met his gaze without embarrassment. "I was hoping today would end this way."

"You are an amazing woman," he told her.

She smiled. "It's about time you realized that."

Antonio took the condom Laura retrieved from her purse and sheathed himself. Placing both hands on either side of her, he poised himself over her body. Reaching out, she guided him home, and he slid into her molten heat with a groan of ecstasy.

He moved slowly at first, not wishing to cause her any discomfort. But when she wrapped her legs around his waist and surged against him, he lost all control. The pressure built up incredibly fast. He wanted to prolong it, to make it last as long as possible. He knew he was fighting a losing battle when, beneath him, Laura cried out and her body convulsed.

His release was tumultuous. "Laura!" he groaned as he rode the crest.

Pulling her to him, he rolled over onto his side. It seemed to take forever for his heartbeat to return to normal and his breathing to slow. With his arms tightly around her and her head nestled beneath his chin, Antonio had a revelation.

In the past when he'd been with a woman he had always held a part of himself back. With Laura, he had held nothing back. For the first time in his life he had made love with a woman.

* * *

The rising sun sent exploratory fingers of light into the room. One of them chased across Antonio's face, and he opened his eyes. Blinking, he stared in confusion at his surroundings. Nothing seemed familiar. Not the oak dresser, not the braided oval rug on the hardwood floor and definitely not the freshly painted white walls that were bare of any hangings that might personalize the room and give it character. Even the bed beneath his back felt strange. Where was he?

His left arm tingled uncomfortably, but when he tried to move it, an unfamiliar weight held it in place. Looking down, he saw Laura's head nestled against his bicep. Her upturned face was pressed to his chest. In a rush, his memory returned.

For long minutes he lay there unmoving, gazing at her. She was still fast asleep, her naked body pressed trustingly to his, her hair a wild tangle around a face that looked incredibly young and beautiful. His arm tightened around her as the intensity of the emotion that swept through him shook him to the core. With the exception of his family, Antonio had never felt this close to another human being.

He had never felt this vulnerable.

He had never felt this terrified.

After leaving the hangar they had come here, to the furnished apartment Laura was renting. They had spent the night in this bed, talking, laughing, eating take-out Chinese food and making love.

The first thing they had done was sift fact from fiction in their cover stories. Laura had told him about losing her husband and son. In return, Antonio had spoken about his family, their unusual closeness and the hardships they had faced when his mother had died. He had told her things he had never confided to anyone else. There had been so much they'd needed to know about each other, and so little time in which to find it all out.

Now it was morning, the dawning of a new day, and the time had run out. Their brief idyll was over. Everything was different. And this new…whatever it was…between them was a complication neither one of them needed right now.

Too bad they hadn't considered that before they let their hormones run amok.

The job had to come first. Antonio knew that. He knew Laura knew it, too. Joseph was expecting them both at the auction gallery within the next couple of hours. In addition, he and Laura were going to have to inform their contact officers that they knew the truth about each other, so that the final showdown with Joseph could be coordinated as safely and efficiently as possible. This was one collar both New York and Pittsburgh would have to share.

Things were winding up fast. Antonio could feel it in his gut. It would soon be all over but the shouting.

Then what?

In all likelihood Laura would return to New York, and he would remain here. Unless, that is, she was expecting him to ask her to stay.

While Antonio couldn't regret the hours they had spent together, or the confidences they had shared, a distinct uneasiness waged war inside him. One part of him wanted to run from Laura, as fast and as far as he could, while the other wanted to hold on tight and never let her go. She made him feel things he had never felt before, emotions he wasn't sure he wanted to feel. In the past he had always retreated before a relationship could threaten to reach this point. But, like a good undercover cop, she had sneaked up on him, climbed under his defenses and taken him unaware. Things had moved far faster and much further than Antonio had ever expected they would.

What now? he wondered again. What would she expect from him? What, if anything, would he be able to give?

Yesterday, and last night, in the euphoria of actually having her in his arms, he hadn't thought beyond the lovemaking. In the cold light of day, he heard again her saying that she wasn't entering into their lovemaking lightly. What she'd really been telling him was that, unlike the character she was playing, she didn't do casual affairs. Unfortunately, casual affairs were his speciality. Though, in a moment of challenge, he had told her he could sustain a relationship with her, he wasn't all too certain he could.

She'd been hurt enough in the past. Not only had she lost both parents but also her husband and son. Antonio didn't want to be the cause of any more pain in her life.

He needed time, he realized. Time to think. Time to analyze exactly what it was that had happened between them. Time to figure out what he wanted to do. Because this was no game. The rules that had applied to his previous relationships didn't apply here. He couldn't play with Laura's emotions. It wouldn't be fair. Nor could he make promises he wasn't sure he would be able to keep.

In a couple of hours they would have to put the previous night behind them and focus solely on the job they were sent in to do. They would have to ignore the intimacy they had shared. Until Joseph Merrill was in custody, they would have to relegate whatever was between them to the shadows, where no one could see. That should give him the time he needed.

As gently as he could, Antonio slid his arm out from under her. Laura moved restlessly and mumbled something, and he held his breath while, eyes still closed, she nestled into the pillow he had abandoned. Pulling the sheet up around her shoulders, he slid his feet to the floor and sat up.

The bed creaked when he stood, and he winced. Thankfully she didn't stir. Gathering up his clothes, and feeling like a heel and the worst kind of coward for sneaking out this way, he cast one last, longing look at the woman in the bed.

The ringing of the telephone woke her. Rolling onto her side, Laura reached out a hand and fumbled around on the bedside table until her fingers encountered the receiver.

"H'lo?" she said in a voice still thick with sleep.

"Ruby?" she heard Joseph ask. "Where are you?"

Still half-asleep, she couldn't understand why he was calling her. "At home. In bed. Why?"

"It's ten o'clock. The auction's been going on for an hour. Why aren't you here?"

Sitting upright and clutching the sheet to her breasts, she looked at the clock. Merciful heavens, it *was* ten o'clock.

"Oh, no," she cried. "I overslept. I'm sorry, Joseph. I'll be right in."

As she clicked the off button, memories of exactly why she had overslept replayed themselves in her mind. Warmth suffused her even as she groaned her dismay. If she was late, that meant Antonio was, too, and that one of the assistant auctioneers had had to start things off. How were they both to explain their tardiness without arousing Joseph's suspicion? Still, if he guessed what had happened between them, it was what he had wanted. She would just have to hope that the change in her relationship with Antonio didn't undermine Joseph's trust in her.

Or put Antonio at risk.

After replacing the receiver in its holder, she turned and reached for Antonio's shoulder. The only thing her hand met was the air. She was alone in the bed.

"Antonio?"

There was no answer.

She looked down at the floor. Her clothes were where she had left them, scattered at the foot of her bed. Antonio's clothes were gone.

Climbing out of bed, she reached into her closet for her bathrobe and belted it around her waist.

"Antonio?" she called again as she walked out into the hallway, peered into the empty bathroom and padded in her bare feet toward the living room.

He wasn't there, nor was he in the kitchen. There was no trace of him, not even a coffee cup in the sink. She felt the first stirring of unease. Why hadn't he wakened her? Why hadn't he said goodbye? Why had he—she didn't want to think the thought—sneaked away like a thief in the night?

Then she saw the folded piece of notebook paper on the kitchen table. Her name was scrawled across it in familiar handwriting. She stared at it for a long minute before crossing the room and picking it up. It took her another fifteen seconds to summon the nerve to unfold it and read the message Antonio had written inside.

Laura,
You were sleeping so soundly I didn't want to wake you. As we both know, these next few weeks are going to be important ones as far as the job is concerned. I understand now why our contact officers wanted to keep our true identities secret from us. Any indication to Joseph, or any other employee at the gallery, could put our lives in danger. Because of that, we need to stay as far away from each other as possible and keep all contact to a minimum until the job is concluded. When it is all over, then we can talk.

Antonio

The letter fluttered from her suddenly nerveless fingers to the floor. Well, at least now she wouldn't have to worry that Joseph would find out about the two of them. Because there was no two of them.

Nowhere in that brief, impersonal note, had Antonio mentioned his feelings about last night, other than that he didn't want anyone else to find out they'd spent it together. What had she expected? A declaration of undying love? A marriage proposal?

We're not Vincent and Serena, and we never will be. That's what he'd said to her after their first kiss. Upon reflection, she had thought the words to be Michael's alone. Obviously Antonio felt the same sentiment. If only she had listened.

So he wanted to talk when the job was all over. She smiled grimly. About what? Why he had left without saying goodbye? That would do her ego and her pride no good whatsoever.

The simple truth was that she was the one who had come on to him—thrown herself at him, if she was to be brutally honest. She was the one who had admitted that sleeping with him was not something she approached lightly. The only thing

Antonio had admitted was that he wanted her. Hardly the foundation for a lasting, meaningful relationship.

The real irony was how, back in West Virginia, he had insisted he could sustain a relationship with her. Yes, he'd been trying to get a rise out of her, and yes, he hadn't been serious. The proof was the fact that their relationship had lasted all of, what, twelve hours?

He'd also told her he could never say no to her. The letter lying on the floor made a mockery of those words. Because if he wasn't about to say a resounding no to her hopes and dreams, he wouldn't have written that they needed to talk.

She had no one to blame but herself for the way she was feeling. In her delirious joy over discovering that he was a cop and that it was okay to want him, she had neglected to ask a few crucial questions. Number one: Was it just sex for him? Number two: Did he, unlike Michael, believe in commitment? And, most important, number three: Was there even a remote chance that, at some later date, he might be able to commit to her?

Laura reached down and picked up the letter from the floor. To her right, in one of the counter drawers, she found a box of matches. Grabbing the box, she moved to the sink and set the letter aflame, crinkling her nose at the acrid smell of cordite and watching the paper shrivel and blacken, then turn to ash.

When her task was completed, she braced her hands against the cool porcelain of the sink, lowered her head and fought back tears. Control returned slowly. She looked at the ashes in the sink and shook her head in wonder. For the second time in her life her entire world was falling apart, and what was the only thing she could think about? That she had to destroy that letter. If, for some reason, Joseph or one of his cohorts was ever to search this place, she couldn't take the chance one of them would find it.

A twist of the cold water tap sent the ashes circling down the drain. Laura drew a deep, shaky breath. Joseph was expecting her. She couldn't fall apart now. She didn't have the luxury. What she did have was a job to do, and she would do it to the best of her ability.

She was glad Antonio had left without saying goodbye, she told herself. That way, temporarily anyway, they had both avoided any awkwardness. At least she hadn't told him she loved him. She still had her pride.

It was small consolation.

Chapter 14

The wire itched. Specifically, the tape holding the wire in place across Antonio's stomach itched. Like the devil.

He hated wearing a wire, avoided it whenever possible, and was only wearing one now because his contact officer had insisted. The case had reached critical mass. Since he and Laura had no way of safely contacting anyone while inside the auction gallery's walls, with Antonio wired he could raise the alarm if he saw or heard anything suspicious, or if he and Laura found themselves in danger.

While he understood the necessity, he still hated wearing it. It made him jumpy. Whenever anyone came near, his paranoia kicked into high gear, and all he could think about was the wire and hope it wouldn't be detected. Besides, it itched. He'd been wearing this wire for the past six workdays, and it was driving him crazy.

Resisting the urge to scratch, and thus risk dislodging it, Antonio moved through the warehouse storage room. It was a massive cavern whose concrete floor was criss-crossed with floor-to-ceiling shelving. Beeps signaling the nearby presence of a forklift pierced the air. Every now and then one would pass him on its way to the loading dock.

It really was too bad Joseph hadn't confined his efforts to the auction business, he thought, as his gaze traveled over the shelves. By intent, or by sheer dumb luck, he really had built himself a highly profitable operation. An operation that would likely go on the auction block itself when Joseph was arrested.

Moving through the aisles, Antonio studied the items that would be up for bid at this coming Saturday's auction. For each item, after comparing its tag number to the number on his listing, he tried to jot down at least one notation that would aid him in presenting it to bidders in an appealing manner. Most of the time it wasn't difficult. Occasionally, though, certain items, like the moth-eaten mounted moose head he was gazing at now, posed a real challenge.

Though he had every reason to expect that the auction wouldn't take place as scheduled, this exercise, as well as the physical movement, took his mind off his discomfort. It also put to use his nervous energy.

If all went according to plan, today would be the culmination of his and Laura's hard work. Today was D-Day. Everything was in place. The van had returned eleven days ago, filled with drugs that had an estimated street value of twenty million dollars. It had sat in the garage since then and was finally in line at the loading dock, waiting to be filled with items Antonio had auctioned off the previous Saturday. Surveillance of the van had revealed that its hidden contents hadn't been disturbed.

When the van left the gallery to make its deliveries, it would be followed. And when it made its most important delivery—if it made that delivery—the person who accepted the cargo would be arrested, along with the truck drivers, and the contents would be confiscated.

Somewhere outside the mammoth building that was the Merrill Auction Gallery, Antonio's backup team was staked out, listening to everything that went on around him. When the team received word that the drug delivery had been completed, and that the necessary arrests had been made, they would descend on the gallery. Joseph Merrill and his supplier would be only two of many to be taken into custody.

Ideally, to protect their identities as undercover cops, he and Laura would be included in the roundup. They would then be released because, rightly, there was no evidence of their complicity with Joseph. No one, not even Joseph himself, would be aware of their true roles, unless it became necessary for them to testify at trial.

The first thing Antonio saw when he rounded the end of the aisle was Laura. She was studying a group of paintings that had recently been delivered and looked beautiful as always in a black linen skirt and bright-pink blouse. She also looked coolly remote and utterly unapproachable.

Coward that he was, his first impulse was to continue on past to another aisle. He would have, too, if he hadn't seen Joseph standing at the other end, and if Joseph hadn't waved a hand, beckoning him.

Laura looked up as he neared. When she saw him, she immediately turned back to the paintings.

"Good morning," he said as he passed. The wide aisles allowed for easy movement of both forklifts and large furniture items. Though he hadn't come close to brushing against her, the scent of Laura's perfume filled his nostrils, and the heat from her body seared him. He could hear how her breathing had picked up tempo, or maybe it was his own respiration he was listening to. His heartbeat had certainly kicked up several notches.

He wanted to touch her. He ached to reach out and haul her into his arms. But most of all he wanted to kick himself for botching the whole thing so badly. What was wrong with him? He'd seen the promise of heaven in her eyes, felt it in her arms, and instead of reaching out for it with both hands, he had pushed her away from him.

In essence, he had frozen her out.

"'Morning," she replied in a chilly tone that confirmed his thoughts.

In the eleven days that had passed since they had made love—though he tried, he still couldn't think of it as merely sex—Antonio had made it a point to stay out of her way. He hadn't phoned her. He hadn't tried to catch her eye when no one was looking. He hadn't tried to engage her in idle conversation.

He told himself his behavior was for her protection, but he knew that wasn't the entire truth. He was also protecting himself—from what, exactly, he couldn't say. All he knew was that somewhere inside him he felt an immobilizing fear. It was buried so deep he had no words to articulate it. He was going to have to do some digging, but that required time spent in quiet reflection, something that was in rather short supply at the moment.

Thankfully, Joseph hadn't sent him and Laura out of town together. At least he hadn't had to contend with the prospect of working side by side with her.

The first couple of days after their night together, whenever their gazes had chanced to meet, Antonio had seen the questions in Laura's eyes. He had also seen her obvious hurt and bewilderment. Lately, though, whenever she looked at him, if she looked at him at all, the only thing he saw was her disdain.

He deserved it.

Though he'd longed to go to her, to try to explain, he'd held himself back. After all, what could he say that would make any sense? What could he say that would make either of them feel better?

Despite endless hours spent staring at the ceiling every night, unable to sleep, he didn't know yet what he wanted to do about the two of them. Of course, that assumed she still wanted to have something to do with him. Antonio knew very well what making that assumption might turn him into.

The only time they had actually spoken was at the joint meeting with their contact officers, and that conversation had centered around the details of the final showdown. During that time, Laura had remained coolly polite toward him, her manner totally professional. Her indifference had cut him deeper than if she had actually shouted at him.

"How's everything look?" Joseph asked, forcing Antonio back to the present.

"It's a decent haul. You should get a good price this Saturday." He nodded toward a truly hideous lamp, the shade of which was draped with a black fringe. "Of course, I'm not exactly sure how I'm going to describe that. And there's a moose head in another aisle that only a mother could love."

Joseph chuckled. "You'll figure something out."

"That's what you hired me to do."

"It is indeed. I have to tell you, I've been quite pleased with that decision so far."

"Thank you."

From this vantage point, Antonio could see the open doorway leading out to the loading dock. A forklift passed them and went through the door. Joseph also watched the forklift's progress.

He seemed antsy today, his foot tapping impatiently against the concrete floor. His hands were in constant motion, his eyes were overly bright, and there was an air of suppressed excitement about him. Something was definitely going on. Antonio could only hope Joseph's behavior indicated that the deal was finally going down, because as yet Joseph hadn't had the talk with him that he'd promised.

"Keep up the good work." Joseph clapped him on the back, and Antonio sent up a silent prayer of thanks that he'd been wired from the front. "Whenever you're up at that podium, all eyes are on you. That's the way I like it."

Antonio shot a hooded glance at Laura. Not every eye was on him. Not anymore.

"Thanks."

Forcing himself to breathe deeply, he cleared his mind of all thoughts but the job he had to do. If everything went according to plan, Joseph would be in custody by the end of the day. It would all be over.

And he and Laura would have their chance to talk.

* * *

By chance, the van left just as Laura happened to be passing the loading dock doorway. She watched its departure with mixed emotions. On the one hand it meant this job was coming to an end, and that was a good thing. On the other, it meant the job was coming to an end, and she and Antonio were going to have to have the talk he'd promised her in his note. When it was over, in all probability she would find herself back in Queens, alone, in a house so empty it echoed whenever she walked across the floor.

While the past eleven days had been torture, at least she had gotten to see him, if only from a distance. But when she went home, she wouldn't even have that painful pleasure anymore. Earlier, when he'd passed her in the aisle, it was all she could do not to throw herself at him. Only Joseph's presence and some tiny remnant of her pride had held her back.

And people said sadomasochists had problems.

With a heartfelt sigh she turned away from the doorway. She had only taken a step or two, when the hairs on the nape of her neck went up. Glancing to her left, she found that Joseph had fallen into step beside her.

It took all her self-control not to jump. She hoped he hadn't seen her preoccupation with the van. Thankfully he seemed as preoccupied as she was herself.

He came to a sudden halt, and she stopped, too. He looked off in the distance for a long minute before turning his attention to her.

"How was that new group of paintings that came in yesterday?" One hand jingled the change in his pocket.

Relief coursed through her. This was a question she could definitely answer. "I hate to be the bearer of bad news, but they're not very good."

"How much do you think they'll bring?"

"If anyone else but Michael were selling them, I'd say two, three hundred at the most. But with Michael at the podium, your guess is as good as mine."

"He does seem to be a genius at getting people to part with their money," Joseph said.

"Yes," she agreed, "he does." He was equally good at getting them to part with their hearts, too, she amended silently.

The jingling change in Joseph's pocket went silent. "Speaking of Michael. What exactly is going on between you two?"

Laura caught her breath. "What do you mean?"

"You don't seem your normal cheerful self around him. In fact, it looks to me like you two are avoiding each other. Something happen last time you were out on the road?"

The last thing she wanted at this crucial juncture was for Joseph to waste time speculating about them. Trying to look rueful she said, "If you want to know the truth, I did what you asked me to. I came on to him."

Interest sparked in Joseph's eyes. "And?"

She shrugged. "He turned me down flat." The words were harder to say than she'd expected them to be.

"He turned you down?" Joseph arched an eyebrow. "That must be a new experience for you."

Laura felt her throat thicken with emotion. Why did it have to hurt so much?

"He did, and it was."

"Did he tell you why he turned you down?"

No, and he didn't have to. She knew exactly why.

"Yes, Joseph, he did. He said that I belonged to you, and that he valued his job too much to ever put it in jeopardy."

"He said that, did he?"

Joseph seemed pleased. At least someone was happy with the way things were between her and Antonio.

"To the best of my recollection, those were his exact words. If I've been avoiding him recently, I guess it's because my pride is hurt." Her pride, her heart and her very soul, to be precise.

"Did you come on to him because I asked you to, or because you really are attracted to him?"

Laura went still. What should she say? She decided the safest route was to stick as close to the truth as possible.

"A little of both, I suppose." She gave what she hoped was a nonchalant shrug and flashed him a smile. "Else why would my pride be so injured?"

"Why indeed?" The change started jingling again. "This was the first time you've been interested in a man since your fiancé's death, isn't it?"

At first she didn't know what he was talking about, thought he might actually be referring to Jacob. The implications of that had her heart racing with panic before she recalled the cover story she'd given him what seemed like so long ago, when she'd started the job.

She nodded.

"It must hurt doubly, then, when you've finally worked up the courage to get back into the dating game, only to have him turn you down."

Joseph did delight in pouring salt on an open wound, she acknowledged wryly. "You can say that again."

"There are other fish in the sea, Ruby."

Maybe she'd been wrong about him. Maybe Joseph really was, in his own way, trying to be supportive. It didn't matter, though. No matter how many fish in the sea there really were, there was only one Antonio.

Her gaze slipped to the aisle where he stood, his back to them as he studied a silk brocade footstool. Her throat closed with emotion. He looked so blasted wonderful. And so out of her reach.

It didn't help that she could still feel the play of his muscles under her fingertips, could still taste him on her tongue. His masculine scent clogged her nostrils like hay fever.

Did he wish their night together had never happened? Was that regret she saw in his eyes whenever their gazes did chance to meet? She taunted herself with those questions and dozens of others every time her head hit the pillow at night.

She would have her answers soon enough. Today was D-Day. If all went well this afternoon, the case would be wrapped up in a neat little box and tied with a bright-red ribbon. Joseph and his partners in crime would be behind bars.

And then she and Antonio would get their chance to talk.

If only she weren't so certain she knew exactly what he was going to say.

"Would you come to my office in fifteen minutes?" Joseph asked. "There's something I want to talk to you about.

Her thoughts still on Antonio, Laura's answer was absent-minded. "Of course."

It was only after Joseph had turned on his heel and headed out to the loading dock, that she thought to wonder what he wanted from her.

Fifteen minutes later, as requested, Laura took a seat in front of Joseph's desk. Like the devoted right-hand man that he was, Matthew Rogers stood at Joseph's shoulder, gazing at her with his impassive brown eyes. She never could tell what the huge man was thinking, or if he thought at all beyond the job Joseph had hired him to do. She did know, though, that he lived and breathed to serve his employer. Which meant he had to know how things really were between her and Joseph.

She knew one other thing. When the backup team swarmed down on them, in all likelihood Matthew Rogers was going to put up one hell of a fight.

Not for the first time Laura wondered if Matthew and Joseph were lovers. There was something a little too overprotective about the way Matthew always hovered over Joseph that seemed to pass beyond the bonds of the employer-employee relationship. Not that it mattered or changed anything. She supposed she was allowing her mind to entertain whatever thought popped into it, versus the alternative of dwelling on the subject that weighed so heavily on her heart. Or, should she say, the man.

"You wanted to see me?" she asked.

"Yes, my dear, I did. Thank you for being so prompt."

It didn't surprise her when Joseph nodded to Matthew, who immediately melted into the scenery in a far corner of the room. She knew he was there to gauge her reaction to whatever it was Joseph wanted to talk to her about, although how a man his size managed to blend in so totally with his surroundings still amazed her.

Looking at Matthew, Laura had a sudden premonition. Before Joseph said another word, she knew exactly what was coming. Finally, after weeks of proving her worth to him, he was going to invite her into his inner circle.

Not so long ago that invitation would have filled her with excitement and a thirst to learn as much as she could. Today, with the machinery in place to bring Joseph down without it, it seemed a hollow victory at best.

If only she had been wired the way Antonio was. Then the surveillance team would hear firsthand whatever proposition Joseph put forward to her. Instead, she had reluctantly agreed to forego wearing one when her contact officer had argued that her closeness to Joseph increased the risk of detection. Antonio, who spent more time out of Joseph's presence, would bear a far lesser risk. They had both been expressly forbidden to bring any weapons into the gallery.

Joseph's fingers drummed against the desktop, and he seemed to be gathering his thoughts. "I have been exceedingly pleased with your performance, Ruby. In light of that, I think it's time we expanded your duties. But before we do, I need to warn you that you might be called upon to perform tasks some people might not find strictly...shall we say, legal. How would you feel about that?"

What she felt was the heat of both Joseph's and Matthew's gazes upon her. This was it. Her premonition had been correct.

It was ironic, really, that now that things were almost over, Joseph was ready to take her into his confidence. If only he had done this weeks ago, Antonio never would have been sent in. She wouldn't have lost her heart to him. She wouldn't be sitting here, resisting an overpowering urge to cry.

Now was definitely not the time to think of Antonio, she reminded herself. Laura could well imagine Joseph's reaction if she suddenly burst into tears.

"Will I be paid well for my efforts?" she asked, knowing that would be Ruby's number-one priority.

"Top dollar."

"Could you be more specific?"

Joseph named a figure that, had she been more like her alter ego, would have had Laura salivating.

"Is that specific enough?" he added, the hint of a smile playing about his mouth.

"I'll say." Laura paused. "Will I be in any danger?"

"I'll see that you're protected."

"Will there be any…touching?"

This time Joseph did smile. "You might be called upon a time or two to exercise your feminine wiles, but in a flirtatious manner only. I wouldn't advise you to take it any further."

Spreading her arms, Laura smiled Ruby's patented smile. "Then all I can say is, what's a little illegality between friends? It's just another word, after all. Like payday…my favorite."

"Good girl." Looking satisfied, Joseph sat back in his chair. "I knew I could count on you. Now for the specifics—"

A loud pounding on his office door interrupted him. Scowling, Joseph nodded to Matthew.

"What is it?" the other man called.

"It's me. Jimmy Dixon. I need to talk to the boss."

"Come back later. The boss is busy."

"It's important, Matt. It's about that new auctioneer of his."

Laura caught her breath.

"Michael?" Joseph's brows furrowed. "Let him in," he instructed Matthew. To Laura he added, "I'm sorry, my dear. Hopefully, this will just take a minute."

When Jimmy Dixon entered the room, Laura recognized him as one of the truck drivers. He was a tall, wiry man who always seemed full of nervous energy. Even so, Laura had never seen him this agitated before. His color was high, and as he stood before Joseph he began wringing his hands.

"All right, Jimmy," Joseph said pleasantly. "You have two minutes. What was it you wanted to tell me about Michael?"

Jimmy rushed into speech. ''I came here as soon as I worked it out, boss. I figured you'd want to know as soon as possible.''

''I appreciate your loyalty.''

''Thanks.'' Still wringing his hands, Jimmy just stood there.

''What would I want to know, Jimmy?'' Joseph asked with exaggerated patience.

''Ever since he started working here, I kept getting the strangest feeling, like I knew the guy. I kept my eye on him, watching and waiting, the way I knew you'd want me to. Especially when he started sniffing around the vans.''

''Michael was interested in the vans?''

Joseph's voice had gone dangerously soft, and Laura's hands clenched reflexively in her lap. Deliberately she forced them to relax. Her cheek muscles ached from the effort of keeping the smile pasted on her face.

Jimmy nodded. ''He tried to pretend he wasn't, but he always had his eye on us when we were loading. The same way Pete did.''

Pete, Laura recalled was the auctioneer Michael had replaced. The man who had disappeared without a trace. According to Pete's wife, he had discovered something that appalled him. Unfortunately, he wouldn't tell her what that something was. Instead, also according to Pete's wife, he had gone to Joseph with his discovery. No one had seen him since.

''So he watched you guys the way Pete did,'' Joseph prompted.

''Uh-huh. Only, unlike Pete, since he was an ex-con I figured he wanted in on the action. Still, I thought I should keep an eye on him.''

''You said you thought he looked familiar,'' Joseph interrupted. ''Have you figured out where you might have seen him before?''

Again, Jimmy nodded. ''That's when I realized I was wrong about him wanting to be in on the action. Dead wrong. It finally hit me a couple of minutes ago. I couldn't believe it. I still can't believe it. I mean, what's he doing here?''

A cold dread squeezed Laura's heart. She didn't need to use her sixth sense to realize what was coming. It was every undercover cop's biggest fear. That someone would recognize him and blow his cover.

"Jimmy," Joseph warned. "I said two minutes. Remember?"

"Oh, yeah," Jimmy said. "Right. Sorry."

"You heard the boss," Matthew said. "Spit it out, Jimmy."

The command was made all the more fierce by the lack of expression in Matthew's voice. If he had given Laura that order, she would have sat up and taken notice, which was exactly what Jimmy did now.

It was coming. As surely as the sun was going to set this evening and rise tomorrow morning, it was coming. Laura wished she could think of something to stop it, but all she could do was sit there helplessly and wait for disaster to hit. Why, oh, why had she ever let her contact officer talk her out of wearing a wire? And why hadn't she smuggled in her gun? She had to find a way to warn the surveillance team before something happened to Antonio.

Jimmy swallowed hard. "He's a cop, boss. He arrested me two years ago for dealing crack. The reason I didn't recognize him at first was because, back then, he had long hair and a beard. On the streets, his name was Tony Caruso."

Laura kept her gaze fixed on Joseph. A dangerous light now gleamed in the older man's eyes, and she felt a shaft of terror.

"You're sure, Jimmy?" he said softly.

"I'm sure. I'm not too smart about a lot of things, but I never forget a face, boss."

"Thank you, Jimmy. You did good. I won't forget. You may go now."

After the man left, Joseph turned to Matthew. "I was going to have a chat with Michael after I was done talking to Ruby, but it looks like my plans have changed. Bring him to me. Now."

Her terror growing, Laura fought the urge to catapult out of the chair and run straight to Antonio.

"I'm sorry, my dear," Joseph said to her, "but it appears our talk will be postponed longer than I had anticipated."

"That's okay," she managed to say. All she could think of was Pete. Did Joseph have similar plans for Antonio?

"I see you're as distressed about this as I am," she heard him say.

Laura's gaze flew to Joseph. She had to be careful here. Extremely careful. And she had to find out what Joseph had in mind.

"I am. He lied to both of us."

"Yes, he did," Joseph mused, rubbing his chin between his thumb and forefinger. "I have to wonder why. Why do you think he lied to me, Ruby?"

"If he's a cop, the way Jimmy thinks, then I'd say he was here looking for something. Maybe the illegality thing you were just about to tell me about."

"That's what I'd say, too."

"Doesn't that mean his superiors are looking at you, too?"

"Yes. That's exactly what it means."

"Aren't you worried?"

"Not a bit. Never fear, my dear, I have everything in hand. I always do. The cops don't know a thing."

Laura wasn't surprised at Joseph's supreme show of confidence. Most sociopaths, of which he was a prime example, never wavered in their belief that they would come out of any situation on top. Their whole world could be crumbling around them, the very ground beneath their feet shaking uncontrollably, and they'd still believe.

"But what are you going to do?" She had little hope he would give her specifics, but she had to try.

"Take care of Michael and lay low awhile."

"Am I still going to get my raise?"

To her amazement Joseph chuckled. "Ruby, Ruby, Ruby. Always looking out for number one."

"If I don't, who will?"

"Point taken. Don't worry. You'll get your raise."

The echo of footsteps in the outer hall announced Matthew's return. Presumably Antonio was with him.

"Do you mind if I stand there, with you?" she asked.

"You want to stay?"

Laura nodded. "He did hurt my pride, remember? I sure would like to see him get his."

She was in place behind Joseph, her hand on his shoulder, when Matthew led an unsuspecting Antonio into the room. To Laura the sound of the door locking behind them was as loud as a gun shot. If Antonio heard it, he didn't give any sign. She tried to warn him with her eyes, but his attention was focused solely on Joseph.

Think, Laura, think. He was wired. There had to be something she could say that would send the backup team in here on the double, without putting Joseph and Matthew on the alert.

Her gaze fell to Joseph's desk drawer, and she froze. He'd slid it open far enough for her to see the gun nestled inside. The Browning 9 mm looked as deadly as Laura knew it to be. She had to assume it was loaded. She also had to assume that Matthew was also armed.

And here she and Antonio stood, unarmed by order of their superior officers, like ducks in a carnival booth, just waiting to be picked off.

Surely, despite his reputation for ruthlessness, Joseph wouldn't shoot Antonio in front of witnesses. But then, Matthew didn't count. His loyalty to Joseph was without question. He probably knew where all the bodies were buried. She wouldn't be surprised if he'd buried them there himself.

Which only left her as a potential witness. Laura didn't kid herself. What was there to stop Joseph from shooting her, too? When it came down to a question of his freedom as opposed to Ruby's life, the answer was a no-brainer.

Laura wasn't worried for herself. While she wasn't yet ready to die, Antonio's safety was more important to her than her own. It was up to her to find a way out of this mess.

For weeks everything—except her feelings for Antonio—

had seemed to move at a snail's pace. Finally they had arrived at the point where they thought they could put Joseph away for good. How could it have all gone so wrong so fast?

"Matthew said you wanted to see me?" Antonio said.

Look at me, look at me, look at me! Laura willed. But Antonio kept his gaze stubbornly on Joseph.

"Yes." Joseph's voice was cool, controlled. "Remember that talk I told you we were going to have?"

Antonio looked at her then. But his gaze only stayed on her for a second before it passed to Matthew.

"Forgive me, Joseph, but I got the impression our discussion would be of a private nature."

"No need. What I have to say doesn't require a private audience. You're fired, Michael. I've just learned of your previous record. I won't have any ex-cons in my employ. It's bad for business. Matthew will accompany you while you gather up your belongings, and then he will escort you to your car."

Since the statement was so patently false—Joseph employed quite a few ex-cons, and they all knew it—surely that would alert the backup team that something was off-kilter in here. But would it be enough to send them in on the run? Or would they wait outside for Michael to emerge, secure in the knowledge that the moving van with the drugs was being followed, and that Joseph would be in custody shortly?

Laura couldn't take the chance. If Antonio left with Matthew, she knew exactly what would happen. The look in Joseph's eyes told her he had no intention of allowing Antonio to leave the building alive.

Before he could respond to Joseph's announcement, she snatched the gun from its hiding place in the drawer and pointed it at Joseph. If they weren't already, she knew her next words would have the backup team racing on their way.

"Freeze!" she yelled. "Police. Hands up in the air where I can see them. You're both under arrest."

Slowly Joseph and Matthew complied. In answer to the obvious bewilderment in Antonio's eyes, she added for his benefit, and for the benefit of the backup team, "They know you're a cop."

And now they knew she was one, too.

"So this is your secret," Joseph said. "I'm disappointed in you, dear. Even more disappointed than I am in Michael. And myself, for trusting you."

"You'll just have to deal with it," she said. Where was the backup team? Surely they would be breaking down the door any minute.

"So you and Michael were in on it from the beginning." Joseph shook his head and made a tsking noise in the back of his throat. "I have to say, you were very good. You certainly had me fooled."

Laura didn't say a word. Not only was Joseph trying to figure out how much she and Antonio—and, by definition, the police—knew, he was also trying to distract her. Obviously, Matthew hoped that he had, because out of the corner of her eye she saw him reach for his gun.

"Don't move," she ordered.

Matthew ignored her, pulling his gun quickly and aiming. She'd known he would be trouble. The one thing she had never expected, and hadn't taken into account, was Antonio. Before she could squeeze off a shot, he threw himself between her and Matthew.

"No!" he cried.

"No!" she screamed as Matthew fired. To her horror, Antonio fell to the floor.

She went on autopilot then. She couldn't think about Antonio, or rush to him to see how badly he was injured. Not now. If she did, they'd both be dead.

A cold anger seizing her, she squeezed off a shot. This time Matthew fell, his second shot going wide and his gun sliding across the hardwood floor to land at her feet.

Heart in her throat, Laura kept one eye on Matthew, who wasn't moving, and the gun trained squarely on Joseph. She didn't dare look down at Antonio. His silence was ominous enough.

Suddenly her anguish over whether or not he would ever return her love seemed meaningless. The only thing that mattered was that he lived. So long as he lived, she would gladly return to Queens, where she belonged, without shedding a tear.

Please, God, she prayed, *let him live. That's all I ask.*

Voices sounded outside the locked door, and Laura hoped it was the backup team and not more of Joseph's goons running to the rescue. She heard a loud crack, and the door splintered. Seconds later Matthew and Joseph were surrounded by armed policemen.

Then, and only then, did Laura drop to her knees beside Antonio.

"The ambulance will be here in a minute," one of the cops told her.

His face was chalky, his eyes closed, his breathing shallow. He was lying in an ever-expanding pool of his own blood. From what she could see, he'd been shot in the left side of his chest, far, far too close to his heart and lungs.

Heedless of the blood, and the fact that she could be destroying a crime scene, Laura pulled Antonio's head into her lap and gently ran a hand through his hair.

"Don't you die on me," she ordered, tears flowing down her cheeks. "Don't you dare die on me."

Chapter 15

Laura awoke with a start from a fitful sleep. Disoriented, she rubbed the crick in her neck and stared down at the vinyl armchair she was curled up in. Her gaze roved from her blood-stained clothes to a white tile floor, pale green walls, an overhead television and a hospital bed. It zeroed in on the bed and the still figure lying there, and her heartbeat quickened.

Antonio.

Relief washing over her, she watched the slow rise and fall of his chest. He was going to be okay. Thank goodness.

Outside the closed door of the room, she heard the ping of a bell announcing the elevator's arrival. When the doors swooshed open, what sounded like a dozen or more shoes echoed loudly on the tile floor. The echoing stopped at what she presumed to be the nurses' station. Because Antonio's room was located directly across from it, Laura couldn't help but overhear every word of the conversation that followed.

''There's no one here,'' a woman said.

''It's after midnight,'' a man replied. ''There are probably only one or two nurses on duty. Be patient. Someone will be back in a minute."

"Ring the bell," a second man ordered.

"Are you crazy?" the first man said. "This is the intensive care unit. You don't go around ringing bells at this time of night."

"Then why's it sitting there?"

"Never mind," the woman said. "Here she comes."

Laura heard the soft squeak of rubber soles hurrying down the hallway.

"You do the talking, Marco," the second man said. "Since you're a doctor, she'll relate to you better than she would to the rest of us."

"If only they'd taken him to Bridgeton General," a third man said, "we wouldn't have to go through all this. Marco would have been able to cut straight through the red tape to get us the answers we need."

"Well, Bruno, they didn't take him to Bridgeton General," the woman replied, "so we'll just have to make do. It might help if you took that scowl off your face. The way you look now, small children would run screaming from you."

"May I help you?" the nurse asked, sounding out of breath.

"Are you the nurse on duty?" the man whom Laura presumed to be Marco said.

"Yes. I'm Donna Brewer."

"Well, Nurse Brewer, I'm Marco Garibaldi, and these are my brothers and my sister. We're here about our other brother, Antonio Garibaldi. He was brought in earlier with a gunshot wound. Can you tell us what room he's in?"

"Mr. Garibaldi is in room 314."

"Thank you."

"Sirs! Ma'am! You can't go in there." Obvious distress laced the nurse's voice.

"We're his family," Bruno said. "Of course we can go in there."

"This is the intensive care unit," Donna Brewer replied. "It's after visiting hours. I can tell you that your brother is resting comfortably. Why don't you come back later, during visiting hours?''

''Would it help if I told you that Marco, here, is a doctor?'' Bruno said.

Laura heard a low groan, presumably from Marco. ''Bruno, you're not helping.''

''Well, it's true, isn't it?''

''You're really a doctor?'' Donna Brewer asked.

Marco sounded embarrassed. ''I'm really a doctor.''

''Are you on staff here?''

''He works at Bridgeton General,'' Bruno supplied.

''Then, no,'' she said, ''it won't help. But good try.''

''Excuse me.'' This was a voice Laura hadn't heard before.

''Yes?'' Donna Brewer sounded cautiously polite.

''Hello. I'm Carlo Garibaldi.''

''Police Chief Carlo Garibaldi,'' Bruno interjected.

''Bruno,'' Marco warned.

''You'll have to forgive all of us,'' Carlo said. ''We're a close, not to mention, headstrong and excitable lot. You see, we just found out a couple of hours ago that our brother was shot. It's taken us this long to find him. As you can imagine, our emotions are a little on edge right now.''

''I'm sorry, Mr. Garibaldi, for your upset.'' Donna Brewer sounded genuinely sympathetic. ''For all of your upset. But rules are rules. I don't make them, but it is my duty to enforce them.''

''As Bruno told you, I'm a cop,'' Carlo said. ''Believe me when I say I understand how important rules and regulations are. I only wish we had more determined citizens like yourself out there on the streets, upholding our laws the way you uphold the rules of this unit. It would certainly make my job a lot easier.''

From her seat just inside Antonio's room, Laura had to smile. Apparently Antonio wasn't the only Garibaldi with the ability to charm. If Carlo was even half as handsome as his younger brother, Nurse Brewer was probably preening like a peacock.

"Thank you," Donna Brewer said. Her pleasure was obvious.

"Believe me, also," Carlo continued, "that none of us wants to make your job more difficult than it already is. Still, given the circumstances, couldn't we bend the rules this once? Couldn't we just take a peek at him? So we can call our father in Florida and tell him we saw, with our own eyes, that Antonio is okay?"

"Even if visiting hours weren't over, hospital rules allow only two visitors at a time."

Donna Brewer was definitely wavering, Laura decided.

"Then we'll go in two at a time," Carlo said.

"That won't work."

"Why not?"

"There's already someone in there with him."

Laura sat up straight.

"Who?" Bruno asked. "We're the only family he has."

"The woman who came in the ambulance with him."

"It's after visiting hours," Marco gently pointed out. "Yet you allowed her to stay."

"She fell asleep. I didn't have the heart to wake her."

"We definitely need to speak to her," Carlo said. "Can't you see that? She'll know what happened to him."

They were silent while Donna Brewer mulled things over. "Very well," she finally said. "I'll let you go in, one at a time."

"Thank you," Carlo replied. "That's very generous of you. I hope you don't mind, though, if I ask one more favor."

Donna Brewer gave a long sigh. "What is it, Mr. Garibaldi?"

"You want to keep things nice and quiet out here, right?"

"Right."

"Well, if we go in one at a time, the rest of us will be out here, waiting. We'll try to be quiet, really we will, but whenever five people are gathered in one place...well, you know."

"Yes," Donna Brewer said wryly, "I know."

"But if we all go in together, we promise to be quiet as

mice. We won't stay long. We won't touch anything we're not supposed to touch. The plus is that it will be quiet out here, and you'll have us out of your hair faster."

Laura wondered if Carlo Garibaldi would run out of charm before Donna Brewer ran out of patience.

"Okay," the nurse said. "You can all go in. But five minutes only. After that, I call security."

"Nurse Brewer, you are a princess among nurses."

"Thank you. You now have four minutes and fifty-five seconds."

Charm and patience had both just expired, Laura thought. Apparently Carlo Garibaldi realized it, also, because he didn't try to bargain for any more time.

Her gaze was fixed on the door when it swung inward. Six people, five of them men, barreled inside. The group came to an abrupt halt, almost running into each other, when they saw Laura.

So this was Antonio's family. She would have known it, even if she hadn't overheard the conversation with Donna Brewer, just by looking at them. The resemblance to Antonio was unmistakable.

She was thankful for the unexpected glimpse into Antonio's family life. It was obvious that the Garibaldis were a boisterous, impetuous, emotional group. Equally obvious was their love for, and loyalty to, each other. No matter what happened, Antonio would be okay. He wouldn't be alone.

"Hello," the man in front said. "I'm Carlo Garibaldi, and this is my sister, Kate, and my brothers, Roberto, Marco, Bruno and Franco. You are?"

Laura climbed out of the chair. She knew she looked a mess, that her outfit was destroyed and her hair in wild disarray, but she didn't care. After everything that had happened today, the way she looked, or even what Antonio's family thought of her, seemed unimportant. The only good thing was that she had put Ruby behind her. She didn't have to pretend to care. Besides, after tonight, it was highly unlikely she would see any of Antonio's siblings again. It was highly unlikely she would see Antonio again.

Choking back sudden emotion, she said, "I'm Laura Langley. I worked undercover with Antonio on the Merrill case."

Bruno eyed her up and down suspiciously. "I know most of the cops Antonio has worked undercover with. He's never mentioned you."

"That's because this is the first time we've worked together. I'm with the NYPD. They brought me in special on this case."

Marco separated himself from the back of the group and moved to the foot of the bed, where he began flipping through the chart hanging there.

"He's not hooked up to any machines, just an IV," Roberto observed. "Surely that's a good sign."

"How is he?" Kate asked.

Laura thought she was directing her question to Marco, but when she looked at the woman, Kate's gaze was squarely on her.

"He's going to be fine," she said. "The surgery went well. Miraculously there was no damage to any internal organs. Right now he's sedated. He should awaken by morning."

"How did it happen?" Franco asked.

Laura bit her lip. "Our cover was blown. Antonio took a bullet that was meant for me."

Bruno nodded. "That sounds like Antonio. Always sticking his neck out."

"You've got blood on your clothes," Kate said, going a little pale. "Is that...Antonio's blood?"

Memories surged over her, and Laura experienced anew her feelings of horror, shock and helplessness, and her dreadful fear that Antonio might actually die. Unable to speak, she nodded.

"So you're the one," Carlo said.

As one, six pairs of eyes centered on her.

She was the one? The one what?

"I'm not sure I understand."

"You're the one he told me about," Carlo explained. "The one he asked my advice about."

"He asked your advice about a woman and you didn't tell us?" Bruno demanded.

"He's never done that before," Franco said. "This must be serious."

"I didn't tell you," Carlo replied, "because he told me that she—Laura—was the opposite of everything he found admirable in a woman." He turned to Laura. "He never said you were a cop."

"He didn't know until recently. Our contact officers thought it safer to keep us in the dark."

"So you were playing a role the way he was."

"Yes."

Carlo nodded his head in understanding. "I'm glad I was right."

Laura had to ask. "About what?"

"That you weren't who you appeared to be. I told him that, you know. That he wouldn't be so attracted to you if you were really the kind of woman he thought you were."

Laura turned her attention back to the figure in the bed. So he'd told his brother he was attracted to her. Unfortunately, no matter how hard she wished it could be otherwise, he wouldn't let it go any deeper than that.

The door opened and Donna Brewer marched in. "Time's up," she said crisply. "Everyone out. Quietly."

When Laura fell into step behind them, Carlo turned back. "Stay here with him. He needs you."

Donna Brewer nodded her assent, and Laura sank back down in the chair, her gaze going to the man in the bed.

The sun was just beginning its climb over the horizon when she made her decision. Moving to the side of the bed, she looked down at Antonio for a long minute before leaning over and kissing him tenderly on the lips.

It was time.

"I love you," she said, a tear rolling down her cheek. "I know I promised myself to leave without complaint if you would only be okay. But that's not the reason I can't stay. I know you're not ready to commit to me. Another woman might stay and fight, hoping to wear you down. The problem is, I've already had enough pain to last two lifetimes. I don't want to delude myself that you might someday change. It's best if I leave now and go back to Queens where I belong, while I at least have my dignity. While I still have the strength."

At the door she paused. Turning, she gave him one long, last look. "Thank you for teaching me that I still have a life. It's time I went and lived it."

Feeling more nervous than he had on the morning of his first auction with Joseph, Antonio stood on the porch of a two-story brick house located in the heart of Queens. His finger was poised just above the doorbell.

Four weeks had passed since he had taken the bullet meant for Laura. Four weeks during which his body had slowly healed, while the ache in his heart had continued to worsen. Four weeks during which the investigation into Joseph's activities had wound to a satisfactory close—it would be a long time before he tasted freedom again. Four long, endless weeks, during which Antonio hadn't heard so much as a peep from Laura and during which he had tried to get his head screwed on straight.

Doubts assailed him as he stared at a front door that had been painted a bright red. Maybe she wouldn't want to see him. She'd left without saying goodbye, after all. Maybe she didn't care anymore. Maybe his actions had served to kill her fledgling feelings for him.

There was only one way to find out. He'd never been one to back away from a challenge, and he wasn't about to start now. After drawing a bracing breath, Antonio pressed his finger to the doorbell.

This was the real Laura, was his first thought when she opened the door. His Laura.

She stood there, staring at him, wearing a pair of faded jeans and a loose-fitting blouse. Her feet were bare, and her hair had been pulled back into a ponytail. She wore no makeup. Nothing in his life had ever looked so wonderful. The only thing that kept him from sweeping her into his arms was her total lack of reaction at the sight of him.

He thought he saw a flicker of surprise cross her face and a flare of emotion deepen the green of her eyes. Then there was nothing. Absolutely nothing.

"Hello," he said.

"Hello. You're looking well."

She was acting as if they were complete strangers. Of all the possible scenarios Antonio had imagined, the one thing he had never expected was her indifference. He couldn't help wondering, in the midst of the despair that seized him, if this was how she'd felt the morning after they made love, when she woke to find him gone.

"Can I come in?" he asked.

"Of course."

He followed her into a sparsely furnished living room. Her sketches lined the walls.

"You left without saying goodbye," he said when she turned to face him.

Laura perched on the edge of an armchair. "I did say goodbye. You just happened to be unconscious at the time."

"Why were you in such a hurry to go?"

She shrugged. "The job was over. You were out of danger. I saw no reason to stay."

With a wry twist to his mouth, Antonio conceded that he deserved that. He had, after all, acted like a first-class heel. He only wished she would betray by some word or action whether she was actually glad to see him.

For the first time he noticed the boxes piled around the room. "Are you moving?"

"No. These are some of my husband's and son's belongings. I'm donating them to charity."

Antonio didn't know what to think. "They told me you quit the police force. Why?"

"Because," she replied, "the reason for my joining is no longer relevant. I became a cop to use the rage I felt over Jacob's and Jason's deaths in a positive manner. The rage is gone now. I'm ready to move on with my life."

"What does moving on mean?"

She plucked at a piece of lint on the arm of the chair. "It means I'm going to return to my first love, which is art history. I'm going to take a year off to sketch and relax. After that I'll probably return to teaching."

Antonio drew a fortifying breath. Obviously, donating her husband's and son's belongings and quitting her job was Laura's way of breaking with the past and starting anew. The only question remaining was how much of the past she was putting behind her. Was the time they'd spent together included on the list?

"Did you come all this way just to say goodbye?" she asked. Rising, she walked to the window, parted the curtains and stared outside. "If so, you could have saved yourself a lot of time and trouble by picking up the phone."

It was hardly the sign he was waiting for, but Antonio forged ahead.

"No. I didn't come to say goodbye. I came to tell you that I quit the police force, too."

Laura whirled to face him, her shock at his announcement written clearly across her face. At last, a reaction from her.

"Why?"

"I've been feeling restless and dissatisfied with my work for some time now. I didn't understand why until I started working for Joseph. That was when I realized how much I love that world. Standing at the auction block, working the crowd, I felt a sense of purpose and satisfaction I never did in police work. I've decided to become an auctioneer full-time."

"That's wonderful, Antonio. I wish you all the luck in the world." Her sincerity was unmistakable.

"Thank you." He took a step toward her. "Why did you

blow your cover?'' He took another step. ''Why did you put your life on the line the way you did?''

He saw emotion in her eyes and felt a flare of hope. She wasn't as indifferent to him as she seemed.

''I was just doing what any cop would in the same situation. I was standing up for a comrade who was about to walk into an ambush. After all, didn't you do the same thing for me? Didn't you take a bullet that was meant for me?''

''That's all it was? You were just doing your duty?''

''What else could it be?''

Her chin jutted out, and he knew what she was thinking. Why should she be the one to admit anything? Especially after the way he had acted. At least, he hoped that was what she was thinking.

''You know,'' he replied, musing, ''learning that I want to be an auctioneer was only one of the things I've discovered about myself this past month. Like you once suggested, I finally examined my life. It took a long time, and it wasn't very pretty, but I did it. Know what I found?''

''No, Antonio,'' she replied softly, ''I don't. What did you find?''

''That the Merrill job introduced me to three of the most courageous people I've ever met. The first two were Vincent and Serena. They were both orphans, yet they had the courage to love each other. Then there was you. You lost your husband and your son, yet somehow you opened your heart to me. And I trampled on it.''

He waited for her to say something, anything, but she just stood there, staring at him.

''Do you realize that for years, ever since my mother died, I've been daring the Fates to come and take me, the way they took her? That's why I took so many risks. That's why I became a cop. That's why I went undercover. And that's why the only relationships I would allow myself were of a temporary nature. I was doing whatever I could to avoid facing the magnitude of my loss.''

His last step brought him directly in front of her. ''I'm not running anymore,'' he announced. ''I don't want the Fates to take me. I want to live. Oh, how I want to live. What's more important, I am ready and willing to take the one risk I would never allow myself to take—the only risk in life worth taking. Can you guess what that is?''

Wordlessly, her eyes wide, Laura shook her head.

''I want to experience the love my parents shared, the love you and I read about in Vincent's and Serena's letters. And I want to experience it with you, if you will let me. Because I love you, Laura. I will always love you. That's why I took that bullet.''

Tears welled up in her eyes and spilled over her cheeks.

''Don't cry,'' he pleaded. ''Please, Laura, don't cry. I can't bear it.''

She fell into him then, and his arms closed around her in a vise.

''Am I dreaming?'' she asked, her head against his chest.

''If you are, then we both are.'' His voice lowered. Once again he asked, ''Why did you blow your cover like that? Why did you put your life on the line for me?''

Pulling back as far as his arms would allow, she looked up at him with a gentle smile. With one hand she cradled his cheek.

''Silly man. Don't you know by now that I'm madly in love with you?''

''Enough to marry me?''

''Yes. Oh, yes!''

It was the answer he'd prayed to hear. This time, when he saw the love shining in her eyes, there was no hesitation, no pulling back. His only thought was that he hoped she would always look at him that way. His arms tightened around her again, and they tumbled together onto the sofa.

Much later, cradled in his arms, Laura asked, ''Where will we live?''

''I don't care.'' His heart full, Antonio traced a finger over her swollen lips. ''I can be an auctioneer anywhere.''

''And I can sketch and teach anywhere. I was really impressed with how friendly and helpful the people are in Pittsburgh. Plus, that's where your family is. Why don't we live there?"

"If that's what you want."

"It's what I want," she said.

He grew serious. "I'm sorry I ran out on you, Laura. You have my solemn vow that I'll never run from you again."

"And you have my solemn vow that, if you do, I'll go after you. With my gun."

He gave a mock shiver. "Thanks for the warning."

"It's not a warning. It's a promise."

"There is one thing I haven't told you," he said.

"What's that?"

"I think it's only fair to let you know that I come as a package deal."

Her eyebrows went up. "A package deal?"

He nodded. "I have five brothers and one sister who will meddle endlessly in our lives. And I have dogs. Two of them. Puppies, really."

Understanding dawned in her eyes. "The puppies we picked up in West Virginia. You're the one who adopted them?"

"Actually, I sent Carlo to get them. He and his wife kept them for me until I got out of the hospital. So, what do you think?"

"I've met your family. I like them."

"They like you, too. And the puppies?"

"Who wouldn't love a puppy?"

"So you're going to accept the package deal?"

"Try and stop me," she replied with a broad smile. "In fact, I can't wait to unwrap it."

"Neither can I."

He unfastened the buttons of her blouse with fingers that weren't quite steady. His heartbeat kicked into high gear when her smile changed to a gasp and her eyes went slumbrous. His hand closed around her breast, and he paused.

"Laura?"

"Hmm?" She sounded breathless, and impatient for him to continue.

"Just like Vincent Bickham, I knew the first minute I saw you that you were meant for me. You think their love was special? I promise you, you ain't seen nothing yet."

In answer she raised her arms to him, and Antonio went home.

* * * * *

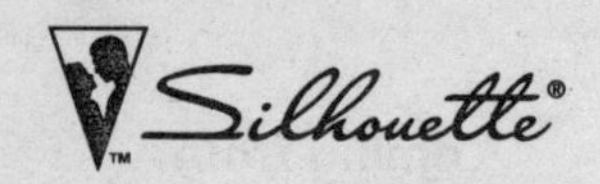

INTIMATE MOMENTS®

COMING NEXT MONTH

#1177 THE PRINCESS'S BODYGUARD—Beverly Barton
The Protectors
Rather than be forced to marry, Princess Adele of Orlantha ran away, determined to prove that her betrothed was a traitor. With her life in danger, she sought the help of Matt O'Brien, the security specialist sent to bring her home. To save her country, Adele proposed a marriage of convenience to Matt—fueled by a very inconvenient attraction....

#1178 SARAH'S KNIGHT—Mary McBride
Romancing the Crown
Sir Dominic Chiara, M.D., couldn't cure his only son, Leo. Without explanation, Leo quit speaking, and child psychologist Sarah Hunter was called to help. Dominic couldn't keep from falling for the spirited beauty, as together they found the root of Leo's problem and learned that he held the key to a royal murder—and their romance.

#1179 CROSSING THE LINE—Candace Irvin
When their chopper went down behind enemy lines, U.S. Army pilot Eve Paris and Special Forces captain Rick Bishop worked together to escape. Their attraction was intense, but back home, their relationship crashed. Then, to save her career, Eve and Rick had to return to the crash site, but would they be able to salvage their love?

#1180 ALL A MAN CAN DO—Virginia Kantra
Trouble in Eden
Straitlaced detective Jarek Denko gave up the rough Chicago streets to be a small-town police chief and make a home for his daughter. Falling for wild reporter Tess DeLucca wasn't part of the plan. But the attraction was immediate—and then a criminal made Tess his next target. Now she and Jarek needed each other more than ever....

#1181 THE COP NEXT DOOR—Jenna Mills
After her father's death, Victoria Blake learned he had changed their identities and fled their original home. Seeking the truth, she traveled to steamy Bon Terre, Louisiana. What she found was sexy sheriff Ian Montague. Victoria wasn't sure what she feared most: losing her life to her father's enemies, or losing her heart to the secretive sheriff.

#1182 HER GALAHAD—Melissa James
When Tessa Earldon married David Oliveri, the love of her life, she knew her family disapproved, but she never imagined they would falsify charges to have him imprisoned. After years of forced separation, Tessa found David again. But before they could start their new life, they had to clear David's name and find the baby they thought they had lost.

SIMCNM0902